Praise for

LAURAINE SNELLING AND HER BOOKS

"Reminding us that love can spring forth from ashes, that life can emerge from death, Lauraine Snelling writes a gripping and powerful novel that will inspire and uplift you."
—Lynne Hinton, author of *The Last Odd Day*

"Snelling writes about the foibles of human nature with keen insight and sweet honesty."
—National Church Library Association

"Snelling is good at creating suspenseful twists and turns."
—Bookbrowse.com

"Lauraine's writing is both humorous and convincing."
—Leslie Gould, author of *Beyond the Blue* and *Garden of Dreams*

"The emotional takeaway of [*The Way of Women*] is reminiscent of Karen Kingsbury at her best. The characters' issues are neither surface nor easily solved. A challenging, fulfilling read."
—*Romantic Times*

"*Ruby* leaves you feeling uplifted and is a treasure readers should mine from the choices available."
—Bookloons.com

One Perfect Day

~ A Novel ~

LAURAINE SNELLING

NEW YORK BOSTON NASHVILLE

Scripture taken from the NEW AMERICAN STANDARD BIBLE®, Copyright © 1960, 1962, 1963, 1968, 1971, 1972, 1973, 1975, 1977, 1995 by The Lockman Foundation. Used by permission.

FaithWords
Hachette Book Group USA
237 Park Avenue
New York, NY 10017
Visit our Web site at www.faithwords.com.

Printed in the United States of America

First Edition: October 2008

10   9   8   7

FaithWords is a division of Hachette Book Group USA, Inc. The FaithWords name and logo are trademarks of Hachette Book Group USA, Inc.

Library of Congress Cataloging-in-Publication Data

Snelling, Lauraine.
One perfect day : a novel / Lauraine Snelling. — 1st ed.
p. cm.
Summary: "CBA bestselling author Lauraine Snelling delivers an emotional punch in a captivating contemporary novel about two women whose faith and families are tested by an event that is both devastating and miraculous"—Provided by the publisher.
ISBN-13: 978-0-446-58210-0 (trade pbk.)
ISBN-10: 0-446-58210-7 (trade pbk.)
1. Donation of organs, tissues, etc.—Fiction.   2. Family—Fiction.   I. Title.
PS3569.N39O54 2008
813'.54—dc22
2008003279

Dedicated to all those who have been willing to donate the organs of their loved ones that others may live. The waiting lists are long. Mark the donor dot on your driver's license. Others will be glad you did.

Acknowledgments

$\mathcal{T}$he idea for this book began one night when I was speaking at a reading group in New Hampshire, thanks to my almost-daughter, Julie. Kris Frank, who worked for the New England Organ Bank, and I got to talking about her job as donor coordinator, and the basis for this novel arose from one of her stories. You never know where a story will come from. Thanks Julie and Kris.

My gratitude also goes to all those I've come in contact with who tell me their stories of organ donation, both donors and receivers, some of them close friends and family whom I've watched and prayed with through the process. What an amazing miracle this can be.

I always owe a debt of thanks to agent Deidre Knight, the entire staff at FaithWords, along with my personal team who gives me tremendous support, critique, and encouragement. I am most blessed.

Always, to God be the glory and may He use this book to bless others far beyond our knowledge.

Blessings,

Lauraine

One Perfect Day

Chapter One

Nora

Gordon, where are you?

Betsy, a middle-aged yellow Lab, looked up as if she had heard Nora speaking. The two—owner and pet—had been best friends for so long that the twins frequently teased their mother about mental telepathy—with a dog. Betsy thumped her tail and gazed up from her self-assigned spot at Nora's feet.

Leaving the bay-window seat, where she'd been staring out at the moon lighting fire to the frost-encrusted winter lawn, which sloped down to the lakeshore, Nora crossed the kitchen to set the teakettle to boiling. Tea always helped in times of distress. She brought out the rose-sprinkled china teapot and filled it with hot water. Tonight was not a mug night but a "stoke up the reserves" night. If there had been snow on the ground, this was the kind of night, with the moon so bright every blade of grass glinted, when she would have hit the ski trails. An hour of cross-country skiing and she'd have been relaxed enough to fall asleep whether Gordon called or not.

So, instead, she drank tea. As if copious cups would make her sleep deeply rather than toss and turn. Perhaps she would work on the business plan if she got enough caffeine into her system.

Betsy's ears perked up and she went and stood in front of the door to the garage.

Nora's heart leaped. Gordon must be home after all. But why hadn't he called to say he was at the airport? His business trip to Stuttgart, Germany, had already been prolonged and here they were trying to get ready—with just four days until Christmas. The last one for which she could guarantee the twins would still be home. Her last chance for perfection. When he'd told her a week ago he had to fly to Stuttgart again, the word "again" had echoed in her head.

Betsy's tail increased the wag speed and she backed up as the door opened.

"Mom, I'm home." Charlie, the older twin by two minutes, and named after his father, Charles Gordon Peterson, came through the door in his usual rush. "Oh, there you are." Grinning up at his mother, he paused to pet the waiting dog. "Good girl, Bets, did you take good care of Mom?" Betsy wagged her tail and caught the tip of his nose with her black-spotted tongue. "Smells good in here." He glanced around the kitchen, zeroing in on the plate of powdered-sugar–dusted brownies. "Heard from Dad?"

"No." Nora cupped her elbows with her hands and leaned against the counter. At five-seven, she found that the raised counter fit right into the small of her back. When they'd built the house, she and Gordon had chosen cabinets two inches higher than normal, since they were both tall. Made for easier work surfaces. "Go ahead, quit drooling and eat. There's a plate in the fridge for you to pop in the microwave."

"Where's Christi?" Charlie asked around a mouthful of walnut-laced brownie.

"Upstairs. I think she's finishing a Christmas present."

"Are we going to decorate the tree tonight?"

"We were waiting on you." *And your father, but somehow he always manages to not be here at tree-decorating time.* While Gordon was not a "bah, humbug" kind of guy, his idea of a perfect Christmas was skiing in Colorado. They'd done his last year, with his promise to help make hers perfect this year. *Right. Big help from across the Atlantic.* While Nora knew he'd not deliberately chosen to be gone this week before Christmas, it still rankled, irritating under her skin like a fine cactus spine, hard to see and harder to dig out.

Charlie retrieved his plate from the fridge and slid it into the microwave, all the while filling his mother in on the antics of the children standing in line to visit Santa. Charlie excelled as one of Santa's elves, a big elf at six feet, with dark curly hair and hazel eyes, which sparkled with delight. Charlie loved little kids; so when this perfect job came up, he took it and entertained them all in his green-and-red elf suit. He could turn the saddest tears into laughter. Santa told him not to grow up, he'd need elves forever.

"One little girl had the bluest round eyes you ever saw." Charlie took his warmed plate out and pulled a stool up to the counter so he could eat. "She had this one great big tear trickling down her cheek, but I hid behind my hands"—he demonstrated peekaboo with his fingers—"and she sniffed, ducked into Santa, caught herself and peeked back at me. When he did his 'ho ho ho,' she looked up at him with the cutest grin." He deepened his voice. "'And what do you want for Christmas, little girl?'"

Charlie shifted into shy little girl: "'I—I want a kitty. My mommy's kitty died and she needs a new one.'" He paused. "'And make sure it has a good motor. My mommy likes to hold one that purrs.'" Charlie came back to himself. "Can you believe that, Mom? That's all she wanted. She reached up and kissed his cheek, slid off his lap and waved good-bye."

"What a little sweetheart."

"I checked with Annie, who was taking the pictures, and got their address. You think we could find a kitten that has a good motor at the Humane Society?"

"Ask Christi, she'd know." Christi volunteered one afternoon a week at the Riverbend Humane Society and would bring home every condemned animal if they let her. She'd fostered more dogs and cats in the last year than most people did in a lifetime. She'd found homes for them too, except for Bushy, an older white fluffy cat, with one black ear and one black paw. His green eyes captivated her, or at least that was the excuse for his taking up permanent residence.

"I will. Be nice if there was a half-grown one with a loud motor."

"Loud motor for what?" Christi, Bushy draped across her arm, wandered into the kitchen, a smear of Sap Green oil paint on her right cheek, matching the blob on the back of her right forefinger. Tall at five-nine, with an oval face and haunting grayish blue eyes, she looked every bit the traditional blond Norwegian. As much as Charlie entertained the world, she observed and translated what she saw onto canvases that burst with color and yet drew the eye into the shadows, where peace and serenity lurked. Christi would rather paint than eat or even breathe at times.

"A little girl asked Santa for a kitty for her mother"—he shifted into mimic—"''Cause Mommy's kitty died and she is sad.'"

"That's all she wanted?"

"Gee, that's what I thought too." Nora motioned toward the teapot and Christi nodded. While her mother poured the tea, Christi absently rubbed the paint spot on her cheek.

"There are three cats for adoption right now. I like the gold one, she loves to be held. The other two would rather roughhouse."

"You think it would still be there until after school?"

"I'll call Shawna and tell her to hold it for you. Are you sure you want to do this? What happens if she doesn't really want it?"

"Can anyone turn down one of Santa's elves?"

"You'd go in costume?"

"Why not?"

"I could paint you a card."

"Would you?"

"Sure, have one started. All I need to do is change the color of the cat. Luckily, I made it white, like Bushy here." She rubbed her cheek on the cat's fluffy head. "How long until we decorate the tree?"

"Give me five minutes."

"Okay, you two start on the lights and I'll finish the card. You want me to sign it for you?" Christi had taken classes in calligraphy and had taught her mother how to sign all the Christmas cards in perfect script.

"You know, you're all right for a girl." Charlie bounded up the stairs to his room, where all his herpetological friends lived. Arnold, a three-foot rosy boa that should have been named Houdini, was his favorite.

Nora handed Christi her mug of tea. "Take a brownie with you."

"Thanks, Mom. You heard from Dad yet?"

"No." Nora knew her answer was a bit clipped.

"Something must be wrong." Christi's eyes darkened in concern. "Did you call him?"

"I tried, cell went right to voice mail."

"So, he was on it?"

"Or he let the battery run out." As efficient as Gordon was, you'd think he could remember to plug his phone into the charger. The two women of the family shared an eye rolling.

"He'll call."

"Unless he's broken down someplace."

"You always tell me not to worry."

"Well, advising and doing are two different things." Nora set her cup and saucer in the dishwasher. "Want to help me unroll the lights?"

"I was going up to finish that card."

Nora checked her watch. "Ten minutes?"

"Done." Christi scooped Bushy up off the counter, where he'd flopped, and headed up the stairs, not leaping like her brother, but lithe and regal, the residuals of her years of ballet and modern dance.

Nora and Betsy headed for the living room, but when the phone rang, she did an about-face and a near dive for the wall phone in the desk alcove. "Hello."

"Nora, I'm sorry I didn't call sooner."

"There, you did it again." She tried to sound harsh, but relief turned her to quivering Jell-O.

"What?"

"Apologize. Now I can't be mad at you." His chuckle reminded her of how much she missed him when he was gone. "Where are you?"

"Still in Stuttgart. Art and I got to talking and I didn't realize the time passing. I had to get some sleep."

"You're up awfully early."

"I know. Trying to finish up. Is the tree up yet?"

"What, are you trying to outwait me?"

"What ever gave you that idea?" He coughed to clear his throat.

"You okay?"

"Just a tickle. Look, I should be on my way home this afternoon. I've got to wrap this thing up, but I told them the deadline is noon and I'm heading for the airport at three, come he-heaven or high water."

"Well, don't worry about the tree." She slipped into suffering servant to make him laugh again. "The kids and I'll get that done tonight." It worked. His chuckle always made her smile back, even when he couldn't see her.

"They have school tomorrow, right?"

"Right. Last day, so there'll be parties. I have goodie trays all ready to take."

"You made Julekaka for the teachers again?"

Nora chuckled. "Gotta keep my place as favorite mother of high-school students."

"Is that Dad?" Charlie called from the stairs. "Tell him to hurry home. I have to . . ." The rest of his words were lost in his rush.

"Charlie says to hurry home."

"I heard him. Give them both hugs from me."

"Do you need a ride from the airport?" She glanced at the clock. Nine P.M. here meant four A.M. in Germany. Good thing Gordon was a morning person.

"No, I'll take a cab. I love you."

"You better." She hung up on both their chuckles. How come just hearing his voice upped the wattage on the lights? And after twenty-two years of marriage. As people so often told them, they were indeed the lucky ones. "Please, Lord, take good care of him," she whispered as she blew him a silent kiss. She joined Charlie in the living room, where a blue spruce graced the bay window overlooking the front yard, where she and Gordon had festooned tiny white lights on the naked branches of the maple, which burst into fiery color in the fall, and the privet hedge, which bordered the drive. Lights in icicle mode graced the front eaves, while two tall white candles guarded the front steps. She'd filled pots with holly up the flagstone stairs and hung a swag of pine boughs, red balls and a huge gold mesh bow on the door.

"Here." Charlie handed her the reel of tiny white lights and pulled on the end to plug it in.

"I already checked them all this afternoon. Just start at the top of the tree."

They had a third of the lights on the eight-foot tree when Christi joined them, setting the finished card on the mantel to dry. "I didn't put it in the envelope yet, so don't forget this in the morning, or are you coming home before going over there? Shawna said she'll put your name on the golden cat. She's already been fixed, so she is ready for her new home." Christi picked up another reel of light strings. "You need to put them closer together."

"Yeah, right, Miss Queen Bee has spoken," Charlie mumbled from behind the tree.

"You don't have to get huffy."

"You don't have to be bossy."

"All right, let's just get the lights on." All they had to do was get through this drudgery part and then all would be well. Gordon always tried to skimp on the lights too. Like father, like son. Silence reigned as they wound the lights around the tree branches, punctuated only by a "hand me another reel, please" and "ouch" when a spruce needle dug into the tender spot under the nail. Nora sucked on her finger for a moment to ease the stinging. Inhaling the intoxicating spruce scent brought back memories of the last years and made her grateful again for all the joys they'd had. One more thing to miss tonight, the rehash she and Gordon always did post–tree trimming, when the children had gone to bed, like Monday-morning quarterbacking, only with more smiles and laughter. Much of the laughter came because of Charlie's clowning around.

"What if she doesn't like the cat?" Charlie asked.

"Then we'll take it back," Christi said matter-of-factly.

"By 'back,' I'm sure you mean to the Humane Society. Bushy would not like another cat around here." Nora's hands stilled. This she needed to clarify.

"Of course, Mom."

Nora looked up in time to catch a head shake from her daughter and one of the "I'm trying to be patient" looks Christi was so good at. Why was it so quiet? "Oh, I forgot to put the music on. *Messiah* all right?"

When both twins shrugged, she knew they'd rather have something else, but were giving her the choice. She crossed to the sound system, hit the number three button and waited a moment for Mariah Carey's voice to flow out. She'd play the *Messiah* after they went to bed. They'd all attended the "Sing-Along *Messiah*" concert the second weekend in December. At least Gordon had been home for that tradition.

A bit later they all three stepped back with matching sighs.

"All right, throw the switch." She looked at Charlie, who had taken over that job years earlier. This certainly was a night for memories. When the tree sprang to life, they swapped grins and nods. The ornaments were the easy part.

By unspoken agreement, they decided to hang the ornaments, which they'd bought one per year on their annual family shopping trip and dinner-out tradition, higher in the tree to keep away from batting cat's paws and a dog's wagging tail. While the twins snorted at her sentimentality, she hung the ornaments they'd made through the years, some like the Santa face with a cotton ball beard, beginning to look more than a bit scruffy, but dear nevertheless. The ornaments that their Tante Karen had given them through the years on their Christmas presents brought up memories and set the two to recalling each year and what their interest had been then.

Nora knew that her sister watched both the twins and the shops carefully through the year to find just the perfect ornament. When the twins had trees of their own, they would already have seventeen ornaments each to take with them. The thought made Nora pause. The home tree would look mighty bare. She hung the crocheted and stiffened snowflakes she had made one year and had given for gifts. Then three little folded-paper-and-waxed stars she'd made in Girl Scouts took their own places.

When they'd hung the final ornament, they stared at the box with the glorious angel that always smiled benignly from the top of the tree.

"Let's leave that for Dad." Christi turned toward her mother.

"I agree." Setting the angel just right with a light inside her to make her shimmer was always Gordon's job—for years because he was the only one tall enough and now because they wanted him to have a part, no matter how many miles separated them.

Charlie shrugged. "I am tall enough, you know."

"I know." Nora gathered her two chicks to her sides and they admired the tree together. "Thank you. I know it is late, with school tomorrow, but I really appreciate your helping the tradition continue." She tried not to sniff, but her body went on automatic pilot.

Charlie's arm around her back squeezed and Christi leaned her head against her mother's. Together they turned and surveyed all the decorations; the mantel was the only thing that Nora changed year after year, and all was done but hanging the Christmas stockings. The hooks waited. Charlie picked up the flat box that held the cross-stitched or quilted stockings and they each hung up their own. Nora hung hers and Gordon's, while the kids hung the ones for Bushy and Betsy.

"Now Santa can come." Christi smoothed the satin surfaces of her crazy-quilt stocking, with every satin or velvet piece decorated with intricate embroidery stitches, cross-stitch, daisy chain and feather. "When I get married, will you make my husband a sock to match?"

"I will." *Just please don't be in too big a hurry.* Not that Christi was dating anyone. She often said she left all the flirting up to her brother, since all the girls were after him all the time.

But Nora often wondered if Christi was a bit jealous, not that she would ask. Her daughter talked more with her father than she did with her mother. Unless, of course, it was a real female thing.

"Anyone for cocoa? The real kind? I can make it while you get ready for bed. I'll bring the tray up."

"And brownies?" Charlie asked.

"Fattigman?" Christi loved the traditional Norwegian goodies Nora made only at Christmastime.

"Of course, and since you'll be getting home early tomorrow, you can help me with the sandbakles."

Charlie groaned. Pressing the buttery dough into the small fluted tins was not his idea of fun.

"'He who eats must press.'" Christi sang out the line her mother had often repeated since the time they were little.

Nora watched her two swap shoulder punches as they climbed the stairs. No matter how much they teased each other or argued, the bond between them ran deeper than most siblings. Gordon called it spooky; she figured it was a gift from God.

Time to make cocoa, as her family had called it. In her mind, hot chocolate came in a packet or tin. Good thing she'd picked up the miniature marshmallows. Betsy padding beside her, she returned to the kitchen to fix the tray. If only Gordon were here. Carrying the tray up the stairs was his job.

Chapter Two

Nora

He didn't call.

Nora glared at the clock. How could six A.M. come so quickly? Taking into consideration the seven-hour time difference, Gordon should have called and left a message. No beeping on the phone equaled no message. He said he'd call. She scrubbed sleep from her eyes and stumbled into the bathroom. She stared into the mirror. Bags under the eyes—not a good sign. Her roots needed Honorio's careful attention. The highlights he so skillfully wove made her hair look nearly the dark blond color it had been when she was Christi's age. And she needed a haircut. Knowing his schedule, she knew the hair treatment would have to wait until after Christmas. This morning her grayish blue eyes, which so matched her daughter's, looked bleary, underwritten with lines of resentment.

The hot shower helped to revive her somewhat, and the coffee she knew was ready downstairs, thanks to modern technology, would take her the rest of the way. Her to-do list was already on the second page. That thought flared more resentment. Nearly half the list was Gordon's Christmas shopping, which he would arrive too late to accomplish. Again.

"You better get rolling," she announced with a tap at each twin's bedroom door, and continued on down the stairs, Betsy right in front of her. She let the yellow Lab out, an act of mercy, before pouring her coffee. Then she put down dog food and took her mug, Bible and journal to the drop-leaf table in the bay window. Instead of sitting on the built-in padded bench seat, she took her favorite captain's chair, only to jump up at the yip at the door to let Betsy back in. Barking this early would not be pleasing to the new neighbors, both of whom worked swing shift.

Nora had found her current page in the journal and started to write when a movement near the refrigerator caught her eye. Betsy looked up at the same instant and emitted a strangled yelp. Sure enough, Arnold was out again and slithering for his favorite warm spot on the top of the refrigerator. Not that there wasn't a heater on his terrarium, but the rosy boa loved to roam.

Nora had gotten over her squeamishness for all things creepy and crawly years ago. Even as a toddler, Charlie had carried in his pockets worms and crickets and whatever else moved slow enough for him to catch. Good thing they lived in Minnesota, where dangerous reptiles, spiders, and insects didn't.

She did, however, draw the line at returning Arnold to his lair. At least when Charlie was home. Striding to the bottom of the stairs, she shouted upward, "Charlie, Arnold is on the loose. You are going to have to put a lock on that creature's house." She headed back to the kitchen at her son's "Coming!" and sat down to her journal again. If she'd gotten up at her normal five thirty, she'd have had the peace she needed. Peace to replace the irritation at Gordon for not calling, for not carrying his organization skills over into his family life and for simply not being home. She re-read her verse for the day:

"Come to Me, all who are weary and heavy-laden, and I will give you rest." If that didn't fit her pre-Christmas marathon, nothing would.

She'd heard a story once about a woman who had laid her burden at the foot of the Cross, walked away, then, feeling something missing, returned and picked it up. Nora knew that might well be her story. Laying down the burden of being angry with Gordon was easy, but the snatching back? If Jesus was indeed the Prince of Peace, He could leave some on her doorstep. Sarcasm in her devotions, that's all she needed. She dropped her head into her hands. "Father, forgive me, but is it wrong to want this to be a perfect Christmas, this last Christmas the kids are sure to be home?" Hoping for a holy whisper, instead the pounding of male feet down the stairs heralded that her son was in a hurry.

Nora shook her head. "You know most mothers would freak out at having a snake slither up on their refrigerator."

"I know. You're the best." Charlie carefully coiled the snake in one arm and snagged a breakfast bar off the counter with the other. On his way back upstairs, she heard, "If you want a ride, be ready in ten," to what Nora knew was the closed bathroom door. His twin, Christi, was not a morning person, unlike her brother, whose eyes snapped open in concert with his mouth and his brain. Christi needed to process that morning had indeed arrived and she was expected to be part of the day prior to noon.

Betsy laid her head on Nora's knee and gazed up at her with adoring eyes. "Yes, I know you want to go for a walk. We'll go as soon as they are out the door, okay?" The dog brushed the tile floor with her tail and sighed in delight when Nora rubbed her ears.

A new set of feet stomped, one stair at a time, as though their owner were being dragged. Christi set her backpack on the counter with a sigh and retrieved a banana from the bowl of fruit.

"Good morning to you too," Nora said.

Christi nodded without looking at her, slowly reaching for the Honey Nut Cheerios, her favorite cereal. She fixed her bowl, slicing the banana on top with artistic perfection. After perching on the high stool at the counter to eat, words at last emerged. "Don't forget I need a ride to church to work on the sets." She was painting the moveable scenery to be used in the Christmas Eve pageant. "Thought for sure I'd get finished last night."

"Did anyone come and help you?"

"Nope, no-shows."

That—most likely—had not truly bothered Christi, who preferred her own company when creating. Next year's Christmas Eve pageant would have to get along without her daughter. What would Nora and Gordon do, once they were on their own for Christmas? She couldn't begin to imagine the empty nest so eagerly anticipated by some of her friends. Not yet; Christmas loomed too large, with too many things left unfinished. She was already behind, thanks to Gordon. She made another addition to her list. This afternoon she would move all the packages out of hiding to under the tree.

"How's your dad's present coming?"

"Finished it last night."

"After we decorated the tree? That was really late."

"Last time I had. It has to dry enough so I can wrap it."

"I know he'll love it."

"You haven't peeked, have you?" Christi looked up from

fishing the last cereal out of her bowl, her voice wearing an accusing cloak.

"No, I didn't peek. You didn't invite me to." *And I'd never invade that privacy you deem so important.* She often wondered where her daughter got that obsessive need to guard the things she created. Really, to guard herself. Was it just the obsessive tendency toward perfection, to which she surely was heir? According to the matrimonial surveys, Nora knew that Gordon should be a slob, the opposite of her neatness, but, instead, he was even more neat than she. Had she wanted, she could have eaten off the floor of his garage, to beg an old cliché. Not that she'd ever wanted to, of course.

"You ready?" Charlie paused at the refrigerator, took out the half-gallon milk jug and glugged several swallows. Unlike his sister, he would tell a perfect stranger his entire life story. An open book and friend to all was her Charlie. The twins couldn't be more different... nor more devoted to each other. They knew when the other was coming down with some bug; Christi professing her finger hurt when Charlie got as much as a sliver. Sympathetic... something or other, the pediatrician had called it.

Nora waited for Christi's response, and when it came, she cracked a smile.

"Eeeuw, Mom, make him stop that! Won't you ever grow up?"

"In a hurry." He wiped his mouth with the back of his hand, put the cap back on and set the milk back on the top shelf.

Nora had learned to keep her mouth shut. As to the germ problem that Christi moaned about? None of them had died yet.

He headed for the door to the garage, backpack slung

over one shoulder and stocking hat stuffed in his down parka pocket.

"Aren't you going to eat more than . . . ?"

He brushed his mother's cheek with a kiss. "No time. Come on, snail, or you'll have to ride the bus."

"I'm coming. Get the car out, I'll meet you in front." Christi set her cereal bowl in the sink.

"You want a mug of coffee with you?" Nora asked.

"No." She paused a moment as if thinking. "No thanks," she added politely, but in the vague tone that indicated she'd already tuned out her mother.

"Have a good day." Nora raised her voice so Charlie would hear her too. As the door slammed shut, Christi headed for the coat closet, her own door slam following Charlie's.

Nora felt silence descend. On to her list and the pursuit of the perfect Christmas. Then a quick look back at the kitchen revealed Christi's backpack on the counter. Another difference between the two. Charlie's life rode in his backpack; Christi rarely seemed to know where hers was. This morning was a case in point. Nora leaped to her feet and grabbed the pack, yelling "Wait" as she tore out the front door. "Here!" She hollered louder to be heard over the rumble of Charlie's Jeep and waved her arm to catch their attention. Charlie hit the brakes and Christi leaped from the car and ran back to her mother.

"Thanks. That was dumb." She took her backpack and half slipped on the icy walk before hustling back to the car.

"I love you!" Nora blew them kisses, ignoring what she knew to be their eye rolling and "Oh, Mother" looks. Too bad. She had rights and a mother's duty to remind them of the important things. And that included this year's perfect Christmas.

Once the absent and *uncommunicative*—her stomach tightened as she remembered—Gordon returned, she'd have the chance to remind them all to make this year the very best. She and Betsy turned back into the house, Nora shivering and the dog dancing her anticipation of the coming walk.

Twenty minutes later, Betsy was in her glory and Nora's nose was nearly frozen. Her mind, however, bubbled like boiling water as she reviewed her to-do list, uncharitable thoughts of Gordon periodically intruding.

Her normal speed-walking wasn't a good idea this morning, with all the ice patches on the road and sidewalks. All she needed was to slip on the ice and break something. Now, wouldn't that be a wonderful way to ruin Christmas? Betsy trotted along beside her, not bothering to stop and sniff all her usual haunts, so they covered two miles in good time. When speed-walking, she usually did four to five.

The pregnant gray clouds thickened on their way home. The weatherman's prediction for snow was looking more possible all the while. The wind had picked up too. By the time she and Betsy made the front door, the snow had begun in earnest. She'd hoped for a white Christmas.

Back in the house, she hung her down parka in the hall closet and tossed her gloves and hat into the basket attached to the inside of the door. Inhaling pine, cinnamon and vanilla, she paused long enough in the living room to give the tree a judicial going-over. No need to change anything anymore. During the early years, she had often moved ornaments around to cover any bare spots the children had left. No tinsel to redistribute. They'd given up using tinsel years earlier when their first cat had ingested several strands and had to have surgery to clean her out. Ah, the memories floating around the tree and throughout the house. What would it be like when the kids had their own lives? Grandchildren, she decided. But perhaps she was getting ahead of herself.

In the kitchen, she poured herself a cup of coffee, dug out a chew bone for Betsy and drew in a deep breath. She'd better speed up. First, finish the last of the Christmas baking. She set the supplies for frosting and wrapped the round loaves of Julekaka, the Norwegian form of Christmas bread, with cardamom, currants and bits of candied fruit inside. She dropped almond flavoring into the powdered sugar, butter and cream frosting, adding one more layer to the scented house. She frosted each loaf, made a circle of candied cherry halves in red and green, set the loaf on a plastic Christmas plate, wrapped the entire thing in clear sheets of plastic and added a bow and name tag.

After checking her watch, she crossed "Julekaka" off her list. She'd already decorated the boxes used for the three kinds of brownies and other cookies she was taking for the kids' parties. As mother-in-charge, she'd made sure there would be plenty of treats, including homemade popcorn balls, Christi's favorite. She knew she had a reputation to uphold. All the teachers commented on the nice things she did for them throughout the year. She figured she couldn't thank them enough for the fine jobs they were doing with her children.

In the next three hours, she crossed "sandbakles," a Norwegian cookie, or tart shell, off the list and packed it up. Next item: Charlie had requested hamburgers for supper, not the fast-food kind, her kind. She brought out the ground beef, added a packet of onion soup mix, a few glugs of barbeque sauce and Worcestershire sauce, then began forming patties, big ones, the kind her men liked. Betsy yipped at the back door and she crossed the room to let her out. The snow was already sticking to the ground, the wind tossing the powder on the covered patio furniture. She frowned. Big, fat flakes, the kind that covered the ground quickly and shut out the light early.

Clutching her list, Nora paused at the window and watched the bits of tissue float down, dancing and twirling in the puffs of wind. As always, her heart thrilled at the first snowfall of the season; they'd usually had several by now. Each year was different, but switching to cross-country skiing from speed-walking always gave her a leap of excitement. When the lake froze over, they skated too, and Gordon set his fish house out. While there had been ice around the shore, the middle was all open water. She let Betsy back in, gave her a treat and turned on the stereo for Christmas music to flood the house. There would be time for all those activities in the days to come, but now was the time to work. She finished the patties, wrapped them one more time and placed them in the fridge.

She chewed the inside of her cheek. To call Gordon's office or not to call to find out if he'd contacted them? A quick glance at the swollen to-do list solved the question.

"He did? On time. Okay, many thanks." Nora hung up the phone and acknowledged she was officially seething. Gordon had called the office to tell them his flight was on time and when he would be landing. *His office.*

At least she had information, she consoled herself. But it didn't make her feel any better. On to delivery, and…she gulped. Picking up Christi at three. She'd nearly forgotten. That meant she couldn't stop on the way home and do Gordon's shopping. She rather hoped he was sitting next to someone obnoxious on the plane. Someone who wanted to tell him all about widgets.

Ashamed, she decided she needed a boost in her Christmas spirit; so she hurried into a special red Christmas sweater, with snowmen knitted in white angora yarn and wearing black felt hats with a jingle bell on top. She'd bought it at the end of last year's season, like she did most Christmas decorations, including the special china she would use on Christmas Eve and Christmas Day. Her black velvet pants fit perfectly, in spite of the goodies she'd munched as she cooked, baked and wrapped.

Once she had the SUV loaded, she bade Betsy good-bye; then list in hand, she headed out to deliver all the treats, including some to a couple of shut-ins from church and to finish errands. Two blocks from home, she had to up the wiper blades to high to keep up with the dumping snow. It was quickly moving from beautiful to trouble and would do nothing to speed her along. Would Gordon's plane have difficulty landing? Mentally she reviewed the winter prep Gordon and Charlie had done on Charlie's Jeep: blanket, flares, winter antifreeze, snow scraper. He'd be okay. He was a good driver and had grown up in snow country. She double-checked to make sure her cell phone was charged and actually in her purse.

Right, leave the worry in God's hands. And fight the frissons of anger at having been ignored that kept blindsiding her. The other side of her kept whispering that there would be a good reason to stay calm; whatever was happening was out of Gordon's control.

That thought was not particularly calming either.

White swirled and danced, so she turned her lights on. She should have brought cookies with her, since she was late.

Something to soothe the savage beast, not that Christi would be savage, but Nora never appreciated the silent treatment either.

Christi ran from under the overhang as soon as she pulled up. "You're late, Mom. You know I've got a tight schedule."

"I know. Sorry." She glanced over her shoulder to pull back out into the traffic. "You want to stop at Burger Hut for something to eat?"

"No, let's just get to the church."

Nora's phone rang and she handed it to Christi. "Hope it's your dad."

"Hello? No, we're on our way to church." She covered the phone. "Charlie wants to know if it is all right for him to take a couple of guys home after the party."

"To our house?"

"No, their houses."

Nora regarded the snow caking along the bottom of her windshield. "This snow is looking worse than the weather gal predicted."

Christi listened, then turned to her mother. "He says it's supposed to lighten up. He says the guys aren't wearing hikers or winter coats and that you'd hate to have them walk home in this." She smiled.

Nora nodded agreement with a chuckle, then shook her head after Christi punched off. "Your brother could sell snow to Eskimos."

Nora swung the car into the church parking lot. She could see tire tracks through the accumulated snow.

"I'll see if I can get a ride home, okay?"

"That would be a help. Or maybe Charlie can swing by here and pick you up. Let me know." This was one of those times she was glad both her children had cell phones. While she often hated the intrusive things, keeping in touch was easier with them than without. So why had Gordon called the office and not her? They would have to have a conversation when he got home.

In what seemed like minutes instead of hours, it was time to head back out into what Nora would nearly call a storm, to pick up Christi. Charlie—in the middle of his charitable ride giving after the party—had called to say he'd be home late.

Christi leaned her head against the headrest. "Charlie call?" Those two were always checking on each other as though they shared one heart.

"Said he'd be home about ten. I'll fry us some burgers as soon as we get home."

"Good, what about Dad?"

Yes. What about Dad? As annoyed as she was, Nora felt concern creeping in with the snow. "I'm going to call and see what the flight is doing in this snow."

Christi nodded. "Okay. I'm starved."

"But you finished?"

"We did. Might have some touching up to do, but Mrs. Sorenson and Bruce came to help."

When they got inside, Christi bit into a buttery sandbakle before even removing her jacket. She devoured a second one and headed off to put her things away.

Nora checked on the number and dialed the phone, holding it between ear and shoulder as she dug out the frying pan. So much for grilling outside. She punched in the flight numbers and listened for the response. The last leg of Gordon's flight had been delayed out of New York and should arrive in Minneapolis between ten and eleven.

She and Christi were just finishing their burgers when she noticed Christi's frown.

"What's wrong?"

"Oh...a headache," Christi replied. She rubbed her temples and moved her head around to pull the tension out of her neck muscles.

Nora glanced at the clock. Charlie should be home by now. Gordon was out in the snow. Her Christmas felt scattered, as though already changing. She didn't like it. She stacked their plates and took them to the sink, then returned and rubbed her daughter's neck and shoulders.

"Um, thanks, Mom, that helps."

Betsy stood and looked toward the living room, her ears pricked. She woofed when the doorbell rang, then barked several sharp yelps as she headed for the front door, Nora right after her.

Chapter Three

Jenna

*O*ver here, stat!"

Jenna turned at the doctor's command. The emergency room at Jefferson Memorial had escalated beyond busy with the arrival of two ambulances from a pileup on the interstate. Although she wished no one to suffer, the controlled chaos forced her to operate as nurse Jenna Montgomery, not as Heather's mother. It helped her push down, with professional efficiency, the ever-present pain that nagged at her gut—that...perhaps this was their last Christmas together.

Grabbing the end of the gurney, so one of the EMTs could return to the ambulance, Jenna caught the words the woman threw over her shoulder as she left.

"We have two more."

Two more, how bad? The questions buzzed Jenna's mind as she automatically checked the saline bag hanging on a post above the patient. Obviously, they were heading for the OR, and from the look of the man on the gurney, it might not be soon enough. They pushed through the swinging door and handed their charge off to the green-garbed OR team.

Jenna headed back down the hall at a trot, adrenaline pumping energy into her legs and mind. This man must have been the most severely injured if they did triage at the door.

She dodged another gurney, this one bearing a small body, and raced down the hallway.

They had a knife wound in cubicle one, asthma in two and alcohol poisoning in three, plus all the chairs in the waiting room were full of people getting antsy with the wait. So much for Saturday night at the circus. While they were the closest hospital to the accident, they were not a major-trauma center, one of the reasons she agreed to work in the ER. She'd done her years at the University of Southern California Medical Center in Los Angeles and moved away to a small town, partly to get out of it. Here in North Platte, Nebraska, their main patients were those on welfare who used the ER as a doctor's office.

Another gurney trundled into the now-crowded ER and she motioned them to a long wall. While they'd practiced disaster procedures, this was their first execution. Bad choice of words.

"Mary Ann, call in some of the reserves." She gave the order in spite of the fact that she wasn't the charge nurse tonight, but Parker was up to her elbows with the knife wound on a man who was coming off a high. His growls could be heard clear to pediatrics.

"Get me an orderly, stat." The order came from the knife wound cubicle. Oh, oh, Parker was mad. The man she was working on had made a big mistake.

The teenager on the gurney by the wall had tears streaming down his face.

She stepped to his side. "Is the pain that bad?"

"No, it was my fault." He turned his head away, so she wiped his tears, since one of his arms was in a sling and the other taped to a firm board.

She checked the injury ticket tucked in beside him. Possible concussion, X-rays needed on left shoulder and right arm. The right side of his face was already swollen, looked like it needed an X-ray too. Painful, but not life-threatening. "Have your parents been notified you are here?"

"I think so. My dad's gonna kill me." He looked up from his less swollen eye. "He is."

"I seriously doubt that." In a rush, thoughts of life without Heather filled her mind, closing her throat. For a moment, she couldn't speak, then managed, "He's going to be grateful you are alive...." She heard her name being called. "I'll be right back." She patted his hand and turned away. "Coming."

"Can you go talk to those waiting, please?" Dr. Madison always took time to be polite with the nurses, one of the traits that made him so popular.

Jenna nodded and pushed her way through the door that locked from the outside. She stopped in front of the occupied chairs lined up around the room and relayed her message. Reaction was mixed, mostly unhappy, others trailing out to make new plans.

"Thank you for understanding," Jenna said, although she knew they hadn't. She turned back to punch in the numbers on the keypad and return to the ER. Someone shouting from behind the closed door sent her hurrying through. The man with the knife wound was now brandishing a hypodermic needle and screaming obscenities. Parker leaned against a wall, clutching her arm. Two familiar EMTs pushed through the door from the ambulances, one of them big enough to take out the screamer, and the other blond and cute, a cheerleader type known for her ability to talk someone down.

Jenna stepped into the cubicle to check the vitals of the

asthmatic. The middle-aged man was sitting on a stool, the pulse oximeter attached to his thumb. He raised his eyebrows.

"Quite a production out there," he said, his voice still raspy.

"You're telling me."

In the next cubicle, Jenna smiled at an older man and his wife. "Let's go for a ride," she said, motioning for one of the orderlies. Together they lifted the man from the examining table to a gurney and trundled him out the door.

Maybe they could start caring for those waiting now. It was proving to be quite the night. Soon she'd be crawling into her own bed, visions of a perfect Christmas...well, not exactly *dancing* in her head, but she'd do her darnedest to make it memorable for her and Heather. One just like the old days.

When Jenna had handed her charge off to the floor nurses, she paused long enough to get a drink of water before returning to the ER.

"You had a bad time, huh?" the nurse asked.

"You can say that again." The medical floor, with the lights dimmed in the hall and patients sleeping, seemed like a haven after the chaos below.

"How's Heather?"

It caught her off-guard, this mention of her daughter's name, spoken with caring and warmth. They'd been in and out of this hospital so many times that everyone knew her daughter—and loved her. The question made her shift from nurse to mother, and she rolled her bottom lip between her teeth. With a sigh, she answered, "Getting weaker."

"Any movement on the donor list?"

"Not much." They'd been on it for months. Should have been on the list for years, but with so many people needing heart transplants, the patient had to reach a near critical level of need before being added to the list. The fastest way off the list was dying. Jenna knew all the reasons for the rules, but it was different when the patient was her only child. Although at twenty, Heather wouldn't appreciate being called a child, even though due to her frailness, she seemed so young.

"I'll pour you a cup of coffee and you can drink it on the way down."

"Thanks, I take it black." While she waited, Jenna rubbed her forehead and leaned her rear against the counter, sighing out the adrenaline that had kept her hopping. Hopefully, the caffeine would restore some vitality.

She took the proffered cup. "Thanks." And headed for the elevator. Third floor was medical and orthopedic, while the ER took up a big part of the street-level floor. She pushed herself back to nurse mode.

Back down in the ER, the chaos created by the druggie had settled and patients were being moved through the examining rooms as efficiently as usual. Those from the accident were taken care of, a helicopter transporting the most severely injured man to another hospital, the small child still in surgery and the others treated and either released or moved to another floor.

By the time six forty-five A.M. rolled around, they'd even had some time to catch up on the charting. Jenna tapped the enter key on the screen to finish her shift as the blast of an ambulance siren split the early morning.

"You go home," said the nurse who came on in fifteen minutes.

Jenna hesitated, instinctively turning toward the doors when they slid open to admit the same two EMTs and a gurney with a slight form under the blanket. Her breath caught so quickly, she sagged a bit in the knees. The light hair spilling out from the still body—could it be an adult, so small?—looked familiar. Just like the strands on the daughter she'd left so reluctantly hours earlier. Heather. *Oh, Heather.*

~ Chapter Four ~

Jenna

The crisp bite of the weather on her nose belied the sun lifting itself above the horizon. Jenna quietly closed the car door and leaned against it, closing her eyes, forcing herself to take deep breaths and not whimper. The aftermath of realizing that the last patient on her shift wasn't her daughter had drained her of...of what? What had she had before? She'd already been running on empty. The few seconds when the child on the gurney had become Heather had been the manifestation of everything she'd prayed to God to be saved from.

What the sun did best at this time of year was set all the diamond snowflakes afire, although the icicles could begin dripping by midmorning, and black asphalt patches showed through the plowed streets and sidewalks. Six inches wasn't bad for a first real snowfall.

Taking both hands to wipe her wet cheeks, she straightened her shoulders. She needed to see Heather, hold her. She'd promised to make waffles. And a perfect Christmas. Would her daughter still be here when the strawberries ripened and they could enjoy their favorite breakfast of waffles with strawberries and whipped cream? Somehow frozen ones just didn't make the grade.

The house greeted her with silence. A note on the table said that Matilda next door had been in to check on Heather. She was sleeping now, but the neighbor had seen the kitchen lights on during the night. Sometimes when she couldn't sleep, Heather would heat milk in the microwave, add vanilla and sip it while checking e-mail and message boards. One of her favorites was a chat room for those on transplant lists.

Heather would get really quiet for a few days after a post announced that one of her online friends had passed away.

Jenna had nightmares about writing that post for her daughter. Leaving her jacket, gloves and ski band for her ears in a heap on a kitchen chair, she left her purse beside the computer and hurried down the hall. The oxygen machine hummed in Heather's bedroom and a meow announced that Elmer, Heather's half-Siamese cat, wanted out. Heather usually made sure the door was open a crack so Elmer could use a paw to drag it farther open and find his litter box in the bathroom. Elmer had a way with opening things.

After letting the cat out, Jenna peeked in to see her daughter's limp hair spread over the pillow, so like the little girl in the ER. The omnipresent oxygen prongs were in her nose and there was more color in the faded pink sheet than Heather's face. Even with the oxygen, there was a faint bluish tinge around her mouth and eyes. Her poor heart could hardly pump enough blood to get sufficient oxygen. Jenna resisted the urge to check her daughter's pulse — Heather always woke up — but instead left the door slightly open for Elmer and detoured to clean out the litter box before heading for her own room and a welcome shower.

Standing under the pulsating spray, she closed her eyes and lost herself in the steam, the water and the weariness. Even though she considered herself a woman of faith, the fear that

Heather's...leaving...was imminent could not be contained as it had been in other years. Four days before Christmas and they'd not even put up the tree yet. What kind of mother was she?

You didn't wake me up."

Eyes bleary from lack of sleep, Jenna looked up from her pillow to see Heather standing beside her bed, with Elmer draped over her arm. Her long flannel nightshirt looked so much like the long flannel gowns of younger years that it took Jenna a moment to orient to today. Her little girl with the wispy gilt hair was still there inside the emaciated body of her grown daughter. Jenna's mumble changed to real speech as she forced a smile. "You were really sleeping and I didn't want to disturb you. Besides, I desperately needed a few winks."

"You want me to make breakfast?"

"Wouldn't you rather have waffles like we planned?"

"Real ones that you make, not the freezer kind." Elmer squirmed in her arms, so she hefted him up to be held against her chest, where he licked her chin with a raspy tongue.

"I thought so." Jenna stretched her arms with balled fists over her head and yawned. Oh, for the chance to sleep twelve straight hours or until she woke up naturally, not with a cry for help or the phone with more bad news. *Please, Lord, let today be the day.* This had been her prayer for so long that it was automatic. The day for a heart transplant, the day their new life would begin. One look at Heather's pale face told her another transfusion would be needed soon.

"You taking a shower first? I could go start the bacon."

"No, let me wash my face and brush my teeth. I had a

shower last night." Last night, right. She glanced at the clock. Two point five hours ago, to be exact. She sat up and searched for her slippers with her feet.

"We'll go to church later?" Heather asked, a small smile pulling up the corners of thin lips.

Since Dr. Cranston had said no crowds, a televised church service had been their church, the living room their sanctuary and the lumpy couch their pew. This had become their normal worship for the last few months. Thank God for congregations that could afford to tape their services for the benefit of those housebound. Heather hadn't been a regular at youth group or choir for longer than Jenna cared to remember. And with her erratic hours at the hospital, she wasn't able to do much better.

Jenna staggered into her bathroom, turned on the water and stared at the face in the mirror. Dark shag-cut hair that hadn't been on the pillow long enough to become bed head, hazel eyes that looked sunken into dark circles and a wide mouth that needed a reminder on how to smile without encouragement. Worry and fear chased away any vestiges of fat on her petite five-foot frame. Arlen used to call her pleasantly rounded. She needed belts on all her pants nowadays. Once, she had been considered cute and attractive, now all she looked was worn. Would all this waiting and hoping have been any easier had her husband been there to hold her when she cried and share the care of their failing daughter? She'd never know; a sniper's bullet in some unpronounceable place in the Middle East had made sure of that.

She concentrated on brushing her teeth. You'd have thought she'd have learned to not look in the mirror by now. All it did was make her more depressed. After tousling her hair with damp fingers to give it some body, she dressed and, still slipper-clad, made her yawning way to the kitchen, where the smell of frying bacon perked up her taste buds.

"You'd better hurry, the bacon's near done." Heather, now catless, pointed to the waffle iron. "It's heating."

"Yes, Ms. Chef. I will indeed hurry. However, you might turn that frying pan on low to give me a bit of time."

Heather did as suggested and asked what she'd asked for the last week. "Do you think we can decorate the tree today?"

"Yes." Guilt shortened Jenna's reply. She brought the ingredients out of the pantry and set them on the counter. "You up to it?"

A nod accompanied the turning of bacon strips. Heather rolled her head around, stretching her neck. "I'll sit down for a bit."

Keeping one eye on her daughter, Jenna cracked an egg and poured the yolk from one half-shell to the other, the egg white slipping into the small bowl for the mixer. The yolk went into a second bowl for the batter. She set the two egg whites to beating on high and continued measuring the oil, milk and flour into the hand-beaten egg yolks. Using a mix would be easier, but these were the lightest and crispiest waffles anywhere. She'd bake them all and freeze the leftovers. Like father, like daughter—this had been his favorite breakfast too.

Strange, she would have thought that after eighteen years, the memories would be faded. But she could see him sitting in the chair at the table as if it were yesterday. Only he'd never grown facial lines or slashes of silver in his dark-blond hair.

"Mom?"

"What, sweetie?"

"Did you return Grammie's call?"

"I talked to her yesterday before work."

"She called last night and left a message."

Guilt cut like a scalpel. "No." Jenna's sigh came from deep within, where she tried to banish futile things like sighs and guilt. "I forgot to check the machine."

"We can call her after breakfast. The waffle maker is ready."

"No, she's not."

"I mean the machine." A chuckle actually brightened her eyes.

"Oh." Jenna folded the stiffly beaten egg whites into the batter and tossed the wire-whip into the sink. "Here goes." She poured the right amount of batter onto the grid and closed the lid. "Now we wait."

"Oh, the bacon."

"I'll get it." Jenna pushed the frying pan to the back of the stove, and taking a mug off the rack, she poured herself a cup of long overdue coffee. "You want some?"

"No thanks. I'd rather have hot chocolate."

It was the waffle-and-beverage ritual. Same questions, same answers. Only it wouldn't be the same much longer. *Oh, Lord, I cannot do this. I cannot watch my daughter die.* She forced energy into her voice. "Coming right up." Keeping her hands busy usually helped keep her mind at bay, but not anymore. She would have to try harder. She would not let Heather see her fear. Heather needed hope.

After setting a mug of water in the microwave, Jenna took a packet of mix out of the apple canister on the counter and a sip from her coffee. The light still glowed on the waffle maker.

She set the packet and the mug of hot water on the table in

front of Heather and grabbed two plates out of the cupboard. Lifting the lid on the machine with a darkened light, she frowned. Stuck. Why hadn't she sprayed it with Pam? Because it was supposed to be nonstick. Calling herself unprintable names, she grabbed a fork and dug the waffle off the grill. Half responded to her demands and half needed to be encouraged.

"It's just a waffle, Mom." A note of pleading made Jenna catch her breath. Her daughter was far too intuitive. They didn't talk about the end of Heather's life. They only talked about the transplant list, the others on the transplant list, Elmer, Jenna's job. Anything but their real issue.

"I know." Another sigh. "I know." She fetched the spray and doused the waffle maker before closing the lid to let it heat again. Even with all the oil in the batter, the blasted thing stuck. *You should have...* She ignored the inner voice and took a swig of her coffee, immediately regretting her action. Now her tongue burned along with her throat. Her nursing years helped her keep her stoic mask in place. "Darn" was not a strong enough word.

Pouring more batter into the machine gave her permission to keep her back to the table, where Heather was stirring her hot chocolate as if lumps on the top were a world-crashing event. After closing the lid with a silent admonition, which included something like "stick again and you'll see the insides of the trash can," she poured herself a glass of water and held the coolness in her mouth to cut the scalded sensation. So much for hurrying. As her mother always said, "The hurrieder I go, the behinder I get."

This time the waffle fell away from the lid as she stuck the fork into the crispy dough. "Perfect." She poured in more batter, closed the lid and carried her offering to the table. "Did you want a fried egg with this?"

Heather shook her head in the negative. "But thanks, Mom, you're the best."

The compliment nearly undid her. Jenna blinked and reached over to pat her daughter's hand. This was fast becoming a morning for way too much emotion.

With her own waffle on a plate and a reminder to herself to bake and freeze the remaining waffles for later, she pulled the plug on the machine. She sat back down at the table so she and Heather could eat together, something that didn't happen often enough. When she did take time for breakfast, a bowl of cereal or a bagel were a big deal. Often she came home from her shift too tired to eat and collapsed in bed like she had this morning, and usually noon had come and gone by the time she woke up.

But today was a special day. Tree time. It might be the last... *Do not go there.* She forced her mind to think on something else.

"So, did you ask Grammie?" Jenna asked.

"Uh-huh. She doesn't think she can come for Christmas."

Jenna laid her fork on her plate. "Why not?" Even though she knew better, she had to ask.

"Harold wants to go to Emily's house."

Harold was her mother's second husband. He had a hard time dealing with Heather's increasing frailness; so, like so many people, he opted to stay away. Harold was not one of her favorite people. Emily was *his* daughter, and with two small boys, she needed them to help open the mountain of presents.

Jenna had heard this excuse before. And her mother didn't have the gumption to put her foot down.

A few minutes later, Jenna's plate was scraped clean; Heather picked at hers. She'd fallen away from keeping up her side of the conversation. Jenna's instincts picked up. Was her face paler?

"But Uncle Randy is coming." Her daughter smiled weakly and then let her gaze fall back to her plate. Uncle Randy was Arlen's younger brother, still single at thirty-seven. Jenna sometimes wondered about his not having a girlfriend, but he always made up for the other missing relatives. That had been another loss this last year, her father-in-law succumbed to the big C. And since Heather had been in the hospital again, she'd not been able to attend or help out with the funeral. Randy and his sister, Jessica, had taken care of everything. Not that Denver was that far away, but she'd not dared to leave. Jessica still held a bit of a grudge, but Randy had reassured her that he understood and caring for a barely living daughter was far more important than a funeral.

"Mom?"

Jenna jerked her mind back from woolgathering, whatever that meant, and smiled at her daughter. "Sorry. How about we leave the cleanup until later and I'll bring in the tree?"

"Good. I'll put in a CD of carols."

"Please." Jenna stared at her daughter, her assessing inner nurse kicking back into control, the inner and outer mother trying not to think, *Here we go again.* "How about if you and Elmer stretch out on the couch while I get the boxes?"

"'Kay." Heather pushed back her plate with half a waffle not eaten. She glanced around the room. "You know where he is?"

"I'da thought right here for a handout, but if he's not snooz-
ing on the back of the chair, I'll go find him." Elmer's favorite place, other than on Heather, was the back of the recliner
when the morning sun warmed the dark blue fabric.

Jenna watched as her daughter pushed her chair back,
stood, paused for the world to stop spinning—like she always
had as her heart grew weaker—and after pushing her chair
back in, made her slow way to the living room. Listening to
the conversation between girl and cat, Jenna knew Elmer had
been found. She dumped the last of her coffee down the drain
and grabbed her jacket off the peg by the door. The garage
was not heated.

By the time she'd hauled the plastic-covered fake spruce
tree in from the garage, along with all the boxes of decorations, Heather was sound asleep on the sofa, covered by Elmer
and the red-white-and-green crocheted afghan that waited all
year in the interior of the leather ottoman for December 1
when Heather dragged it out. The afghan had definitely seen
better days. Carols floated through the house, offering at least
a semblance of Christmas cheer.

Why didn't she let Heather use the afghan all year long if it
gave her comfort? Shaking her head at another of those rules
for living that she'd grown into, Jenna set the tree in front of
the window that looked out onto the narrow front yard and
thence the street. The sun was indeed doing its work of melting away the first snow. The ridges left by the snowplow were
shrinking into ice lumps as the black asphalt overtook the van-
ishing white. Once the tree was in place, she pulled the plastic
bag off the top and folded it to be used again. Straightening all
the flattened branches and making sure the white lights were
still wrapped around the branches took more time.

Still Heather slept on. Jenna wrestled with timing: Should they leave now or give the child a few more minutes of building Christmas? When was panic and when was wisdom? *Oh, Father, You promised to give wisdom to those who ask. Well, it's me again.*

Jenna plugged in the lights to make sure all the strings were working. Sure enough, right in the middle, one was out. She dug in a box for the tester bulb and started in. Granted, leaving the lights on the tree made for ease in setting it up, still the testing was a pain in the rear. With Bing Crosby singing of a white Christmas, she headed back to the kitchen for another cup of fortifying coffee. On the return, cup in one hand, she laid the back of her other on Heather's forehead. Sure enough, just as she'd suspected, she was warm, not hot yet, but not normal either.

So, do we wait a bit, take some aspirin and see? Or go in now?

"I'm not going to the hospital." Heather's voice caught Jenna by surprise.

"I thought you were sleeping."

"I was, but I felt your hand. You said we could decorate the tree today." Heather pushed Elmer off to the side and scooted back against the arm of the sofa, where she could see the tree. "There's a string of lights in the middle that aren't working."

"Thank you, Ms. Supervisor. I was working on that, but I needed a coffee fix." Jenna held her cup up to prove it. "I will get right back on it." She knew she should have bought the new lights that didn't act this way, but restringing the entire tree was a monumental task.

"Sorry. Even with part of the lights out, it looks pretty."

Jenna put her cup down and picked up the tester again. "You watch, it'll be the one at the end."

"Then go from that end now."

"Good idea, why didn't I think of that?" Jenna did three bulbs and tossed her daughter a raised-eyebrow look. "So even the light wires work to make a liar out of me." She inserted one more. "Bingo." All the lights came on. She stepped back to view her handiwork. Lights made all the difference. "You feel up to this?"

Heather nodded. "I'll choose and you put them on the tree?"

"No fair." Another indication that Heather was not telling her how cruddy she really felt. Heather loved hanging each ornament on the tree and talking about the story behind it. Jenna pushed the two boxes over to the couch, setting them on the coffee table so Heather could reach them without having to bend over. Bending over made her puff.

A five-foot tree didn't hold an awful lot of decorations. Jenna set the angel in place and stepped back to sit on the sofa, where Heather sat cross-legged, the cat in her lap. The next Christmas ritual and then they were out the door for another trip to the hospital for Heather.

"I love Christmas trees." Heather laid her head on her mother's shoulder.

"You love Christmas period."

"I know. My dad really loved Christmas too, didn't he?"

Jenna began the recitation she did each year. "He did, especially after you were born. He said Christmas is for children and he planned on having lots of Christmases with you and whomever else God brought to us."

This memory time had become a ritual with them. Since

Heather had been only a little over two when her father was killed, she didn't really remember him, but she remembered all the stories they'd shared and Christmas was a good time to bring them up.

Especially if this was to be their last Christmas.

Chapter Five

Nora

*W*ho could it be?

Nora leaned down to calm the dog, which was now barking with authority. "Easy, girl. That's a good dog." Keeping her hand on the normally affable dog's collar, Nora flicked the switch for the front-porch light and turned the dead bolt. They never used the front door unless company was coming. She could hear Gordon scolding her in her head: *"Check the peephole, always check the peephole. You never know who could be out there anymore."*

She pulled open the door, saw them and stepped back in shock. A man and a woman, both in black police uniforms, down to the guns, badges and spray cans. *Is it Gordon?* The thought wiped all sense from her brain. She stared at them for what seemed like an hour.

"Are you Mrs. Gordon Peterson?" the man in front asked, his eyes speaking sadness and compassion.

A wild thought zipped through her mind. If she said she wasn't, could she hold bad news at bay? "Yes," she said.

He identified himself and the silent woman as from the Riverbend Police Department. "I'm sorry to inform you, ma'am, but your son, Charles, has been in an accident."

"Ch-Charlie?" It didn't register. "But he's on his way home . . . he called me and said so."

The woman spoke. "Please, could you get your coat and we'll take you to the hospital?" Even as she asked the question, she extended her hand. Instinctively, Nora backed away.

"What is it, Mom?" Christi's voice. "It's Charlie, isn't it?"

"Yes." The woman's gaze left Nora and focused on Christi, who'd emerged from deeper in the house. "Would you like to come with your mother? We'll take you to the hospital."

Nora turned slowly toward her daughter as if learning a new language of the body. "How did you know?"

"My head, remember my head." Christi didn't look at her mother. Only at the two police officers. Her voice didn't sound like hers. It was breathy, hesitant.

"Miss, could you help your mother here?"

"My coat, yes, my purse." *Think, think. Next step.* "Leave a note for Gordon."

"Ma'am, it is important you come right now."

"I'll get our things." Christi spun away and pulled open the door to the coat closet. Nora watched her daughter grab two coats, dash to the desk, where her mother's purse sat, and rejoin them. "Here, Mom." She handed her a jacket and pushed her out the front door, ordering the whimpering dog to back up and stay. In an instant, Christi had taken *her* role—that of the organized one, the one who made everything work. Nora swallowed. Why couldn't she think? She made her feet step toward the threshold. *Get to Charlie.*

As Christi slammed the door behind them, Nora thought she heard the phone ringing. *Call my cell.* She sent the thought through the air as she was hustled out to the police car waiting in the driveway.

The officer held the door for her. "Watch your head."

They say that on all the shows, Nora thought, her mind revving from its frozen state to race off to inconsequential things, because it could not deal with what might be. As they backed into the turnaround, she leaned forward. Information. She needed information, like she needed better air than what was closed up in this car. "Can you give me any more information?" Her voice came out higher than normal and she swallowed to overcome the dry flakes cascading down her throat.

The female officer turned and spoke over her shoulder, while her partner drove rapidly down the silent street. "Your son was involved in a head-on collision." The words sounded professional, dry. Then her voice cracked. "The driver of the other car swerved into the right-hand lane. I'm so sorry."

"Head-on. Oh, my God, is Charlie dead?"

Christi gripped her mother's hand. "No, no, he's not dead. I can feel him. Hang on, Mom. He's waiting for us."

"He's been severely injured, Mrs. Peterson."

"And the others in his car?"

"One other boy was in the car. He's at the hospital too."

A sheet of ice encased Nora's heart. Head-on. "Was... was...the driver of the other car drunk?" She waited for an answer.

The woman shook her head. "I'm sorry. We can't give you that information, Mrs. Peterson."

Nora's hands ached from being clenched so tightly. "I always told my family not to drink and drive."

"Charlie didn't drink, Mom, you know that. He wouldn't drive drunk even if he did drink. He's not stupid."

"Gordon, you should be here," she murmured under her breath. Christi squeezed her hand harder.

"That's my dad," she told the woman in the front seat. "He's supposed to be coming in on a flight from New York."

"What time?"

"Ten, I think."

"Do you know for sure he is on that flight?"

"No." Nora forced herself to join the conversation. "He didn't call."

The ensuing silence sounded like an indictment against Gordon. Maybe it should be. *He should be here,* she thought numbly.

"Do you have his flight number?"

"No, but he's on United. He always flies United, even though this is a hub for Northwest. He just prefers United." Now she was babbling, but she couldn't seem to stop herself. "They were delayed in New York. He's returning from Germany, a business trip."

"Mom."

Nora turned to her daughter. Christi's face seemed to go in and out in the shadows, like she was moving a spyglass around. Just like the one her father had that she'd played with as a little girl.

The male officer finished talking to his shoulder radio as they pulled to a stop in front of Riverbend General Hospital. "Officer Dennison will take you to your son. He's already in ICU. I'll check on your husband's ETA."

"Thank you." Nora tried to open the rear door, but there was no handle. The panic she'd been swallowing burst up from her lungs. She banged on the door convulsively, until Officer Dennison swung it open and extended her hand.

Nora reached out with her left hand and the strength of the

young woman flowed between them. She managed to get out of the car, Christi right behind her.

"Come with me." Officer Dennison took Nora's arm and guided them through the door and past the information desk to the elevator.

All the times I've been here as a volunteer and now it is my son. My only son. Lord God, what is going on here?

It was all a mistake anyway. She watched the numbers change above the door as the elevator rose to the sixth floor. This was all a bad dream, something newspaper articles were made of. It couldn't be happening to them. After all, they went to church every Sunday and believed they were children of God. He promised to protect and care for them.

The door slid open and they stepped into another hall. Officer Dennison guided them to a waiting room, where several groups of people huddled. One woman was crying. They kept on walking through the room and down another hall to a door that said NO ADMITTANCE. Nora knew the routine. You had to push the button or pick up the phone and tell them you were there and whom you wanted to see.

The door swung open and the officer ushered them through.

A nurse, wearing burgundy pants and a white top that had stick-figure medical people drawn with crayon in greens and burgundies, waited as they moved into the ICU. "Come with me." Her voice was soft, but she enunciated clearly, her eyes warm with compassion.

Nora looked swiftly around. Which room? Where was Charlie? "My son?"

"I need to mention a couple of things. Then we'll see Charlie. I promise." She motioned to a quiet space by the raised counter. "We have your son on a ventilator and IV, oxygen and a catheter. He seems to be resting comfortably."

"Good, let me see him."

"In a moment. But you have to know, he is unresponsive."

"You mean he is in a coma?"

The woman nodded. "He has had a severe head injury."

Surgery. They would do surgery. Oh, where is Gordon?
"When will he go into surgery?"

"The doctor will be along soon, Mrs. Peterson. Right now, you do need to know that Charlie looks terrible."

"All that matters is that he is alive." Nora swung her gaze around the circular room. Which one was Charlie?

The nurse looked from Nora to Christi, who had been silent, her right hand locked in her mother's left. "You are his sister?"

"Twin sister." Christi gave her a level stare. "And I know he is alive."

"I see." With a brief nod, she said, "Come with me."

Nora stared at the nurse's back in front of her. She didn't want to see the forms in the beds, plugged into all manner of machines. The room was dimly lit, which made her tunnel vision easier to maintain. She stopped and blinked when the nurse stopped, sucking in a deep breath to prepare herself.

The boy who lay in the middle of the bed did not look like Charlie. His head was bandaged down to his eyebrows, one side of his face so swollen that his eye was only a line dusted with eyelashes. How could he have shrunk so from the time he left this morning until now?

"Charlie?"

No response, not even a flicker. She glanced around at the monitors. She recognized the jagging line for the heart, the

numbers for the blood pressure and oxygen levels. His chest
rose and fell, his left hand was taped to a board with the IV
line in the back of his hand. Nora curled her fingers around his
right hand, which lay open on the sheet. "Charlie, it's Mom.
Can you hear me?" She shot a look at Christi, who had tears
running down her cheeks. "They say that even in a coma, the
patient can hear." She squeezed his hand, but when there was
no response, she rubbed the back of it with her thumb. The
patient. This was Charlie, her firstborn, the joy of her days.
Surely, he would be waking any minute and tell her he would
be fine. And what was for supper?

The nurse returned with another chair. "You can talk to
him, tell him about your day and getting ready for Christmas.
Talk about the things he likes."

Nora nodded. As if she didn't know how to talk with her
own son. "Thank you." She knew she sounded stiff, but if she
relaxed even the smallest bit, she might collapse on the floor
and then they'd have two people in the hospital.

She sat down in the chair by the bed, still clinging to Charlie's hand. Staring at his poor beat-up face, she remembered a
time he'd fallen off his bicycle; he must have been five or six.
One side of his face raked the gravel, leaving him looking like
tenderized meat. Even though she had iced his face immediately, it swelled up then too. Nothing like this, but... and he'd
been crying, the salty tears stinging in the open scrapes. She
glanced up to see a doctor standing in the doorway. Had he
said something?

"Yes?" The word came out in a croak. She tried again.
"Yes."

"I'm Dr. Crawford." He kept his clipboard in front of him, a
barrier between them. "I admitted your son."

What does one say in a situation like this? Being polite was always necessary. "Thank you." She waited for him to continue, but he kept studying his clipboard as though all answers were contained there. *If you can't help, just go away.* "Have you heard anything about my husband?" Her yearning for and anger at Gordon warred within her. Part of her wanted his arms around her. The other part wanted to strike at him and scream that once again he wasn't around for the important things.

The doctor checked his clipboard. "No, was he in the accident too?"

"No. No, the police officer said he'd see if he could bring Gordon here from the airport."

"No, I know nothing about that." He cleared his throat and his shoulders rose and fell in a sigh. "I have to ask you some difficult questions. I'd prefer if you came with me. Perhaps..." He looked toward Christi.

"My daughter."

"I see. Your daughter could stay here with your son. This won't take long."

"Can't it wait until later? Surely, we could talk while he's in surgery."

Another glance at the clipboard. Then, slowly, in a gentle voice, "I think we've done all that we can."

"You think he's going to die, don't you." Christi didn't ask a question. Her voice was flat like the statement.

Nora turned back to Charlie. She heard a voice rasp out, "Lord, please, I beg of You." It was her own. "Heal my son. Spread Your healing hands over this room and reduce the swelling, knit the bones back together and restore my son. In Jesus's precious name." Where was the peace the Bible promised? The assurance that God would do as she asked? No, this was beyond asking, this was pleading.

"I wish Daddy was here."

"Me too." Interesting that Christi had reverted to the childhood name. She'd not heard her call her father "Daddy" for a long time. It was "Dad" now. Nora reached up and stroked her son's face. All his curls were hidden by the turban of white gauze.

Christi leaned over the bed and whispered into her brother's ear.

Nora heard only the sounds, but not the words. The two of them had always whispered to each other, sometimes not even needing to do that. Somehow they had a method of communication all their own, perhaps from their time in the womb. She'd read that about twins.

The monitors continued their duty, blinking sentinels in a sea of despair.

The litany in her head continued. *Please, God, please. Heal my son. Help him open his eyes and see us. Even the slightest squeeze from his fingers. Bring Gordon here.* How long had they been here? It felt like days or hours stretched like the Silly Putty that the children used to play with.

She heard a throat clearing behind her. "Please, Mrs. Peterson, come with me for only a few minutes. We won't be far away."

Nora heaved a sigh. "All right." But when she tried to stand, her legs and feet refused to hold her and she sat back down. "Sorry."

"Take your time."

She wiggled her feet and endured the pins and needles of returning circulation. When she felt more normal, she tried again and waited for the pain to cease. "Call me if—when—there is any change," she said to her daughter.

"I will."

"I'll be right back, Charlie." She followed the doctor to a small room that looked to be for conferences. When the doctor motioned for her to sit in one of the orange plastic chairs with metal legs, which made stacking easy, she shook her head. "If it is all right, I'll stand."

"Please." He motioned to the chair again.

Nora heaved a sigh and did as asked. She locked her hands in her lap, then unlocked them and flexed her fingers. Staring at the table, she waited, but when he only cleared his throat, she looked up at him. He was young, looked hardly older than her own children. Maybe he wasn't a doctor after all, but then he'd said he admitted Charlie.

"Mrs. Peterson, has anyone mentioned organ donation to you?"

It was a brutal slap from nowhere. "No, why would they? Charlie is strong, he'll make it through this."

"Your son has the organ donor dot on his driver's license." He pulled something from his clipboard and pushed it across the small round table toward her.

Charlie's driver's license. His picture. His signature. Leave it to Charlie to get a good picture taken for his license, not a mug shot like the rest of them.

"How old is he?"

"Seventeen. He'll be eighteen in January." Couldn't he figure that out by looking at his birth date? His questions were beginning to irritate her. *Let's get this over with so I can return to my son.*

He was still regarding her as though he were waiting for her to give the right answer. Well, he'd have to keep waiting. She had no clue what he wanted her to say.

"Mrs. Peterson, when your son came into—"

"His name is Charlie."

"Yes, ma'am. When Charlie was admitted to our hospital, he was already comatose. The brain function is minimal. We thought at first he was gone."

"But he is breathing and his heart is beating."

"Yes, because he is on the ventilator. If we turn that off, he will not last long."

"Then don't turn it off. Give him a chance to recover."

"Nora!"

"Gordon!" She flew out of the chair and across the small space to throw herself into his arms. "Oh, thank God you are finally here. He's telling me Charlie is already dead." With that, the tears broke loose and she sobbed into his chest.

Chapter Six

Jenna

*J*enna watched the color returning to her daughter's face. She had referred to hospital rooms as their second home more than once in the years since her daughter was born. That she was a nurse meant she spent more time at their second home than their real home. This particular room with the beach scene painted in tans and greens on the medical floor had been theirs more times than she wanted to count.

"An amazing thing, platelets." The male voice from behind her made her look over her shoulder.

"Hi, Doc."

"Each time gets shorter, doesn't it?" Dr. Avery Cranston, called Dr. Avery by his long-time patients and friends, walked around the bed to check Heather's vitals. He noted something on his pad and looked over the top of his half-glasses. "You look like you could use some rest, young lady."

"Yeah, right. *Young.* Somehow I feel about a hundred or so tonight."

"Won't help her any if you get sick."

"I know that, but, well, you know what the ER was like last night. And today I had promised Heather we would decorate the tree. I figured early this afternoon that we needed to run in here, but she wanted to finish decorating first. And so we did."

"An hour or two wouldn't make much difference. Her temp is down again."

"It didn't get very high. I'd have been in here sooner if it had."

"So, let's see, you worked a twelve-hour ER shift with major casualties, went home, made breakfast—"

"No, I slept a couple of hours in there."

"I see. And then you made breakfast—"

"Homemade waffles, no mix. They're really very good. You should come over sometime and join us."

"Sounds good to me. And then you decorated the tree and some other things and strolled in here."

"Well, not strolled. The carolers were doing that. I put her in a wheelchair and zoomed her in. Helps when you know who's in charge."

"Remind me where you are on the list, Jenna," he said.

"Who knows? It all depends on the matches at this point." Jenna paused. "I feel so guilty praying for a donor, when I know someone else is going to lose someone they love." She chewed on the knuckle of the index finger on her right hand. She'd had a nick there and the skin had grown tough. She needed to use some Bag Balm on it. Too bad there wasn't Bag Balm for her heart to ease the constant underlying ache.

He nodded. "I understand that. If only more people would register as donors. Accidents happen and . . ." He stopped. "But you know all that." He turned to smile at Heather when her eyes opened. "Hey there."

"Hi, Doc."

"Feeling better?"

"I think so."

"I hear you got your tree up."

"And the presents under it. Elmer found the one for him. You think he could smell the catnip?" Heather yawned and glanced up at the hanging bag. "Still some to go, huh?"

"Yeah, you'll be here about another hour. Unless you want to stay the night?"

She rolled her eyes. "Like really."

"Like I hope you have a good Christmas and I don't want to see you back in here for a while."

"Like I'll do my best."

"I know." He patted Jenna's shoulder as he passed by. "And you get some rest."

"I will. Thanks." She knew he hadn't needed to stop by, but he'd been one of her main cheerleaders ever since they had moved to North Platte. Her mother had been upset that they were leaving the better hospitals of the Los Angeles area, but Omaha wasn't that far away and they had a good heart center there. And Dr. Avery Cranston practiced here. He'd been a major heart surgeon until a heart attack of his own forced him to leave the stress of a big practice, and here he could work part-time and fish when he wanted. He and his wife had taken Heather under their wings and had become more like grandparents than her own were.

She and Heather along with Uncle Randy were invited to their house on Christmas Day, if Heather was strong enough. He'd promised no crowds, a delicious dinner and Rummikub until they dropped. Heather loved the game as much as her mother did. Two could play as easily as three or four.

"Did you sleep?" Heather asked.

"Sort of." Jenna leaned back in her pseudorecliner, which

made into a bed when necessary. She'd spent many nights on that kind of bed at Heather's bedside. She knew that she'd passed the need of sleep and now it would take a sledgehammer to put her out. Or sleeping pills, which she refused to take in case she wouldn't hear Heather call, or a glass of port. The last was the easiest, but she hesitated. Last time...

"Is Uncle Randy still coming for Christmas?" Heather's voice was foggy.

"Far as I know."

"Good."

When no more was forthcoming, Jenna watched as her daughter slipped back into sleep. Was her breathing easier too?

What if this was the year God decided to do a miracle and heal this child of his? What if this Christmas was the miracle Christmas and not the last? He didn't need another heart; He could fix the one she had. Jenna knew that she couldn't count the number of times she'd prayed for that answer. It wasn't that she didn't believe in miracles, because she did. She'd seen them happen. One time a group of women surrounded the bed of a sick friend, and when they finished praying, the cancer was gone. The docs had a hard time believing it, but Jenna grew up on the song about the blind seeing and the lame walking. He'd brought Lazarus back to life—what about an easy thing like fixing a heart?

Sometimes faith was hard to hang on to.

Especially when it was your only child. Wasn't one death in her family enough? She leaned her head back and closed her eyes. In the dark of the night like this, maudlin came easy.

But when she got home again, and Heather and Elmer were tucked into bed, Jenna climbed into her own and prepared to lay awake. Perhaps she should just go clean the bathroom or something. But the next thing she knew, sun was sparkling on the snow. She got up, checked on Heather, who was sleeping peacefully, and crawled back into bed. Since today was her second day off, she'd take the good doc's advice and grab some extra shut-eye.

She woke hours later, with Heather sitting cross-legged on her bed, stroking the purring fur muff in her lap and staring at her mother. "You used to do this when you were little."

"I know. And it still works. You didn't call Grammie."

Jenna groaned. "Is she mad?"

"Working at it."

Jenna moved her head around to pull out the kinks. "What time is it?"

Heather leaned forward to see the digital clock on the nightstand. "Noon."

"Have you eaten?"

"Yes. I was hungry."

For a change. Thanks to the life-giving blood. So her mother was ticked off that she hadn't called back. Well, Jenna was ticked off too. Her mother could have managed to be here for Christmas if she'd put her foot down. Now, that would be a miracle indeed. "What did you have?"

"A waffle in the toaster."

"Good thing I froze the rest, huh?" While Heather had been sleeping yesterday, she'd baked and frozen the remaining waffles. "That sounds good. Put one in for me, will you, please?"

"Are we making fudge and divinity today?"

"Fudge for sure. You feel up to making Rice Krispies cookies?"

Heather snorted and laid the back of her hand against her

forehead, drama-style, mimicking a television ad. "I think I can, like, manage. Divinity?"

Making divinity always made Jenna think of Arlen. It was his favorite. She'd mailed a tin of divinity to more than one far-flung base those early years. "I guess so."

When Jenna finished her waffle, Heather handed her the phone. "Call your mother."

Jenna hit three on the speed dial and waited for her mother to pick up. Four rings and the answering machine clicked on. Relieved and feeling guilty about feeling relieved, she left a message, including "Now it's your turn." After clearing off the breakfast things, she wandered into the living room, where Christmas music played softly. Heather and Elmer had taken over the couch again, both sound asleep. He had the grace to open one eye.

Jenna left the room and went back to the kitchen to toss a load in the washing machine. She eyed her to-do list. Heather's handwriting made her smile. "Number one: grocery shopping. Number two: pay the bills. Number three: take a nap." Maybe that wasn't such a bad idea. An afghan and the recliner?

She made the marshmallow crème fudge recipe, easy since she'd bought walnut pieces, put the square pan of fudge in the fridge to set up and took the mixing bowl and a spoon into the living room. There was something extra good about licking the utensils.

"You brought that for me?" Heather was awake again.

Jenna handed her the bowl. "I'll be right back." She returned with another spoon and the two of them scraped the bowl clean. Watching Heather lick the last smidgeon off her spoon struck Jenna a blow to the solar plexus. She'd better file this memory away with all the others. A possible last-time event. Such a silly thing, making fudge. Would it help in the years ahead to beat off the loneliness? Would she work all the holidays so that those who had families could be home with theirs? Hard work was a fairly effective antidote for painful memories. *Faith, sister. You got to have faith,* she ordered herself. But she had to turn away so Heather wouldn't see the tears.

"Mom, it's okay." Heather leaned against her mother's back. "I know you are thinking 'last-time, build a memory' thing because I do that so often too. But you are so strong and I don't want to bring you down."

"So neither of us say what we really want to—need to—say to each other, huh?" Jenna turned and wrapped her arms around her daughter. "Okay, here goes. Ah, Heather, I can't bear the thought of you leaving me. But I can't stand to see you suffer like this either. I pray and pray for God to heal you and He hasn't."

Heather wiped her tears on her mother's shirt. "Now, it's my turn. Don't freak, Mom, but sometimes I lay in bed and think of heaven. It has to be a wonderful place. And when I can't get enough air, I think about running through meadows there, singing and twirling. I can breathe."

"But I want you healed this side of heaven. I want to see you run and laugh and twirl myself, here on earth. I want you to fall in love and get married and have children. At least one daughter, because I want you to have the same joys I've had." Jenna reached for the box of tissues on the end table.

Her daughter's gaze was shy. "I've wanted to talk about these things with you. Here's more. Sometimes I think I see Jesus standing at the foot of my bed. But He hasn't said 'Come with Me' and so I know it isn't time yet."

Oh, God, I can't endure this. Jenna blew her nose and

mopped her eyes. "I think I'm drowning." She blew again. "Do you think of dying a lot?"

"No, but when it comes, I am ready."

Jenna clutched her daughter more tightly. *Lord, take me instead. Let her have a life.* Quiet stole around them, until Elmer inserted himself into their tangle of arms, his purring bringing even more peace. "Heather, I want you to know that I will fight for your life to the very end, but if you can communicate, even if only a squeeze of the hand, I'll know you know and you don't have to wait around to take care of me."

"And you won't stay mad at God?"

"Not forever."

"I get mad at Him once in a while." Snuggled in her mother's arms as if she were three instead of twenty, Heather's voice took on a dreamy quality. "Not as much now as I used to. I wanted to get out there and play with the other kids, but I couldn't. It just wasn't fair."

"No, that's one thing I've learned, life is not fair."

"But you and I do things, you know, like cooking and making cards. I love making cards, and if I had all the other stuff, we might not have had that." She glanced over at the wall cabinet, which housed all their supplies. "We almost need a separate room for our stuff."

"I know."

"I just wish you didn't have to work so hard."

Was there gentle judgment in that comment? Jenna's ever-present guilt sniffed for it. As she watched Heather gather her long hair into her hands and then let the gold cascade, she recalled the other small form with gilded hair. Had the child made it to surgery? Made it through surgery? She hadn't even opened the paper, not that there had been much time.

She stroked Heather's hair, hair soft and fine, like when she'd been little. A few years earlier, they'd tried a perm on it, since Heather had always wanted thicker hair. What a disaster, but it hadn't held. Most likely due to all the meds she was on. "But you do know that I love my job."

"I know." Silence again.

Jenna leaned her cheek on Heather's head. They sniffed in unison.

"Okay, as long as we're sharing, you know what I want for you?" Heather asked.

"No, what?" Jenna stared at the lighted tree. If she didn't get up, she'd fall asleep. Yet she couldn't move.

"I want you to get married again. I've been praying for a man for you to love and who loves you as much as Daddy did."

"Well, don't go trying to set me up, okay? I've had enough of that through the years." One blind date after another. Too many.

"I won't. But keep in mind that I'm praying for that."

The way God answered prayers for them, she wasn't going to hold her breath. Jenna sighed. "How about a piece of fudge?"

Chapter Seven

Nora

We have to talk with them." Gordon had just returned to the ICU from filling out and signing all the forms. He brought some back up with him. They stood sentinel around Charlie's bed. He looked no different than the first time she had seen him. *Wake up, Charlie. You've got to fight.* Nora's eyes were scratchy. If she closed them, they would flood with tears. Gordon, on the other hand, was a mess. Bags under his eyes and the sides of his face seemed to have slipped down around his jawbone. He, who was so vital, looked faded like a photo left in the sun too long.

"Not right now, all right?"

"But, Nora, if there is a chance the transplant team could harvest some of the organs and help others, surely—"

"Dad," Christi interrupted. "Charlie is still alive. I know. I can feel him. And if he can hear us, what would he think—*harvesting*?" Christi's voice shook.

Nora turned her back on her husband. "That we gave up, that's what he'd think and then maybe he'd give up." Hot, flicking flames of rage assailed her stomach. She couldn't stand to look at him. Always the realist, that's what Gordon was. How could he accept Charlie's death so easily, when the monitors indicated otherwise? She stared at the monitors. Heartbeat was slow, within range, but Nora knew it was the ventilator working for him. And yet, if they took him off the ventilator and he died right away, they wouldn't be able to use any of his organs. And Charlie had said he wanted to be an organ donor. No parent should have to make this choice. *Lord God, what am I—what are we—to do?*

Gordon cleared his throat. "I called Pastor Luke."

"Thank you." Nora stared at her son's face on the white pillow, hoping, praying for any sign that he heard them. Was he paralyzed? She'd not thought to ask them that. But, surely, one needed a spinal cord injury to be paralyzed. They would have mentioned that if...If only she could shut off her mind. The Bible said, "Be still and know that I am God." She was still as could be, but He didn't seem any nearer, if present at all. And there was no way she could keep her mind from chasing rabbit trails faster than Betsy did.

She looked over at Christi, who had her eyes closed. Hopefully, she was getting through to the heavenly throne room better than she was. *Lord, please, I'll do anything, give up anything, just restore my son.* What could she possibly give up that neared the value of Charlie's life? At the moment, nothing else held any meaning whatsoever.

Gordon brought in another chair and set it just behind hers. Why were they letting the family stay all the time like this? Wasn't the ICU run on a strict "five-minute visit per hour" routine? Somewhere in all her volunteer information she thought she remembered reading that.

The need to use the restroom drove her from her chair. "I'll be right back."

"Can I get you anything?" Gordon asked.

"No. Restroom." She hurried from the room, only stopping on the way to tell the nurse where she was going.

"I'll watch for you to beep you back in," the nurse behind the counter assured her.

"Thanks." Why was it that even the most minuscule act of kindness triggered the tears?

She hurried through her business, then wet a paper towel and laid the cool surface against her cheeks. With a sigh, she turned away and tossed it in the trash. Cold water could not drive the heat away.

Back in her chair, she avoided Gordon's gaze and laid her hand over Charlie's again. Christi remained in her chair, unmoving, eyes closed. "Sorry to have to leave, but nature called, you know? Son, if you can hear me, I'm just reminding you that I love you. We all love you and we're praying God will give you back to us." Was that right? Technically, God hadn't taken him away yet. Charlie was still here. Christi had laid her head on the cotton blanket near Charlie's hand. Was she sleeping? Would be good if someone could. This might be a long vigil.

A nurse came in, checked the lines, asked if there was anything she could get them, and when they said no, she left. Hours, or was it minutes, beeped by as the monitors marked time. Her mind played tricks on her, flipping back to happier days, to the time Christi had been in the hospital with dehydration from the flu. Living in her head was easier than living in an ICU room.

She turned at the sound of street shoes. Gordon rose to greet their pastor and friend of ten years or more. Tall like her husband, Luke's shoulders were beginning to curve in, as if to protect his heart, which held the grief and cares of so many. His usually merry eyes held shadows.

"Thank you for coming." The two men shook hands and then Luke drew Gordon into his arms. When they drew apart, Gordon was blinking and fighting the tears.

Luke laid a hand on Nora's shoulder. "Any word?"

She shook her head. "I think they've all given up." She laid her cheek against his strong hand. "Just tell me that God is going to pull this one off."

"I wish I could."

"That's not the right answer."

"I know. At times like this, I have no right answers, other than God is in control and He never changes. He loves us all, all the time."

Nora straightened. "This doesn't feel much like love." She tried swallowing the tears, but they overwhelmed her. She sat rigid in the chair, letting them fall, only sniffing when she had to. Gordon handed her his handkerchief and she strangled it before mopping her eyes and cheeks. "They want us to sign the organ donor papers."

"Charlie can live on that way."

She kept her voice even with superwoman effort. "I want Charlie with us, not pieces of him scattered all over." She wanted to scream at him, scream at everyone. How dare they speak like that in front of Charlie?

"I know you do."

His voice was so gentle, she could feel her face crumble again. *Someone yell at me, hit me, do something so I can fight back.*

"Would you like me to pray?"

"I hope you have been, like we all have been." That was

rude. What ever happened to grace under pressure? "Forgive me. Of course we want you to pray." She knew the promise: "Where two or three are gathered in My name, there I will be in the midst of them." *Okay, God, You promised, now it's time to live up to that promise.*

Luke took one of her hands and Gordon the other. Christi rose, blinking, and came around the bed to join them. Nora clutched Charlie's hand, like plugging in a lifeline.

"Father God, we come to You so broken and hurting that we can hardly speak. We thank You that Your Holy Spirit is praying with and for us with words beyond what we know. You and You alone have the power to restore Charlie to his family, to our greater family. He is a son to be proud of and we rejoice for all the years we have known him. We know that he is Your child, that You are his Lord. We are asking, pleading, that You will show us mercy and restore this young man to us. Heal his injuries, heal his body, soul and mind. We ask also for Your grace to get us through this horrendous trial. You said You would never leave us and we cling to that promise. In Your son's precious name. Amen." He squeezed Nora's hand, but he didn't let go.

She glanced up to see tears streaming down Gordon's face as he stared at his son. She handed him back his handkerchief and glanced around to locate a box of tissues, always brought with the bag of supplies. In this room, however, no nightstand stood next to the bed. No plastic bag with a basin, tissues, toothpaste, toothbrush. Her brain froze on the meaning.

Even though Charlie was in the ICU, where patients came to get well, neither the doctors nor the nurses had expected that to happen here. They had decided Charlie was already dead.

She half rose from her chair, then sat back down again. "Pardon me, I'll be right back." She strode out to the nurses' command center and stood. A man in blue scrubs tapping on a computer keyboard looked up.

"How may I help you?"

Nora regarded him silently, her heart beginning to seize, its beating in her ears turning to a rush. She did not know how he could help her. She did not know why she was standing there. *Think, think. Oh, yes.* She'd fled the room to...to...find someone who would say that her beautiful Charlie was not dead.

"Um." She began to rock forward and backward, arms clutched around herself. *Somebody tell me Charlie is not dead.*

"Perhaps some water? Which patient are you here to see?"

"Charlie Peterson. I'm with Charlie Peterson. Charlie Peterson." If she kept saying his name, she could change this terrible mistake.

"I just came on shift." He came around the counter, smiling at her. "I'll check his chart." He rose and went to a hanging-file form.

The last shift. Shifts changed at seven. Was it morning already? She looked around to find a clock, then remembered her watch. Seven fifteen. The police had come to the house at, what, ten thirty or so? They'd been here over eight hours. Not possible. Nora turned on her heel and returned to Charlie.

A woman in a white coat over khaki pants and a red polo shirt, wearing running shoes, greeted her from Charlie's bedside. Gordon stepped over to Nora and put his arm around her. She grabbed his hand. Luke tried to smile at her, but it failed.

"I'm Dr. Lennings," the woman said to Nora. She shook their hands as each of them introduced themselves.

"I'll be leaving now, if that is all right?" Luke looked from Gordon to Nora. "Or I can wait for you in the waiting room?"

"Or you can stay," Gordon said simply.

"If you want."

"I do."

The two men looked at Nora. She shrugged. Luke stayed.

The doctor studied the monitors, checked Charlie's eye responses with her flashlight, touched the bottom of his feet with another instrument and listened to his heart and lungs. She turned to them with a slight sigh. "Charlie's condition remains unchanged." Another two thumps of Nora's heart; then the doctor continued. "It's time to go to another room and talk about our options."

Charlie's whole life had been options. "You want to come, Christi?" Nora asked her daughter.

"No, I'll stay with Charlie."

The others filed out and followed the doctor to the same room Nora had been in before. When they were seated around the table, the doctor laid her clipboard on the surface and looked each one of them in the face before beginning. "I wish I could be giving you good news, but"—she shook her head—"I can't." She laid her hands on the table, palms down, fingers spread. "I'm confirming what you've already been told. Charlie has no brain activity. He is continuing to breathe because of the ventilator. That keeps his heart pumping. But, technically, he is dead. The body cannot live for any length of time without the brain, once the machines are turned off. Now we can keep him on the machines, and if there were any hope, I would gladly tell you to do that." She again searched their eyes. "Do you want that for your son?"

No, of course not! Screaming seemed an appropriate response, and since she didn't want to do that, Nora kept her mouth locked.

"The next question we have to decide is, are you willing to let Charlie's organs help save other people? His driver's license is marked as a donor, but since he is not of age, you will have to make the final decision. The longer he remains on the machines, the fewer organs we can use."

"Use," "harvest." Disgusting words when applied to her Charlie.

"Mrs. Peterson, Mr. Peterson, your son can give the gift of life to someone else with his heart, lungs, liver, kidneys. His corneas will help someone see and his skin will heal burns. Medical science has learned of ways to use so much healthy tissue, but you have to allow us to do that."

"By turning off the machines," Gordon said.

"But Christi said she knows he is still here," Nora argued. "She can sense him."

"I've heard of that with twins, but medically, that is not what I see."

The door opened partway. "Dr. Lennings?"

"I asked to not be disturbed."

"I know, this is an emergency."

"I'll be back as soon as I can. You can use this room to talk in as long as you need."

Nora watched the woman stride from the room.

"I think we should do what Charlie wanted." Gordon reached for her hand.

Nora drew back. "I can't decide now." She looked to Luke. "What do you say?"

"This isn't my decision, and if I were in your shoes, I'd be in the same struggle. But I do know of people who are living today because someone else was compassionate enough to do this."

"So, you're saying I'm being selfish?"

"No. But—"

"Have we given up that God is going to heal my son?" She stared from one man to the other, her gaze drilling into their souls. She saw Gordon flinch. What had she said? She replayed the words. *Ah, "my son." Not "our son," but "my son." That's right. My son.* She felt like a lone lioness protecting her cub. *Come near and I'll claw you to death.* She stood and, without a word, headed for the door.

Back in the room with the beepers, the lines of tubing and the dim light at the head of the bed lay Charlie, exactly the same. She studied his face and his arms and hands. Wouldn't she know if he was really dead? Would Christi know? She swung her attention to her daughter, who was now staring at her brother. Staring like she did when trying to memorize, to see inside and understand something she was going to paint.

"What is it?"

Christi shook her head, a minuscule movement, as if she couldn't afford anything that might break her concentration. Her shallow breathing matched the rhythm of the monitor. Leaning closer, she turned her head slightly, then rolled her lips together and her shoulders dropped. With tear-filled eyes, she turned to her mother. "I can't find him anymore."

Chapter Eight

Jenna

How fast can you get to Omaha?"

Jenna stared at the phone, then put the receiver back to her ear. "Dr. Avery?"

"Yes. Compatible donor. Heart can be at the Nebraska Medical Center in Omaha in two hours." His sentences were short, staccato. "Friend of mine will be at the airport warming up his plane by the time you can get there. You're all packed, right?"

Jenna nodded, unable to speak.

"Jenna?"

"I-I'm here. Yes, always." She glanced at the round clock on the wall above the table. Nine fifteen, mountain time. "We'll be there in fifteen minutes."

"We're all praying for you. Oh, and make sure you have your cell phone on. Merry Christmas."

Merry Christmas! Merry Christmas. God had answered her prayer. She turned off the teakettle and headed for the bedroom. At least she was already dressed. "Heather, oh, my God, dear God, thank you, God. Heather, wake up. We have a heart!"

Heather sat up in bed, blinking and rubbing her eyes. "You mean it?"

"Get your clothes on and I'll start the car."

"What about Elmer?"

"Matilda will take care of him. It's all set. I've got the bags with me. Dress warm." Jenna grabbed the two bags out of the closet and jerked her coat off the hanger. After stuffing her arms in the sleeves, she hauled the bags out to the garage. She threw them in the rear of the SUV and ran back for her purse. "How you doing?"

"Fine, um . . . good."

Jenna jerked the plug on the Christmas-tree lights and headed for Heather's room. Elmer slipped out the door as she went in. She grabbed Heather's shoes from the floor. "You can put these on in the car. I'll get your coat." On the way past, she snagged the afghan from the sofa. All the while, *please, God, get us there* ran over and over in her mind. Hearing Heather padding down the hall, Jenna hooked her purse over her arm and held out the ski jacket so Heather could shove her arms in. "Go, go, go!" She glanced around the kitchen one more time and pulled the door closed behind them, her hands shaking.

In the car, she checked for car keys. Where were her car keys? She dug in her purse, muttering to herself. She always put them in the same place—why weren't they there? Panic swelled.

"Try the front." Heather had one shoe on and leaned back against the seat to catch her breath.

"Bingo." Jenna held up the car keys. "Thanks." She inserted the key in the slot and the car turned over immediately. She kept it tuned and in perfect shape for such a time as this. She checked one more thing. Yes, the oxygen tank was in the rear also. Her cell phone—where was her cell phone? Back to digging in the bottomless pit. "I can't find my cell phone."

She threw open the car door and charged back in the house. Where had she left it? *Lord, I need my cell phone.* In the charger, on the kitchen counter. Time. What time? Five minutes left. They'd not make it in fifteen. She grabbed both phone and charger and flew out the door again, ignoring Elmer's pleas for attention. His cry turned into a yowl, part of his Siamese heritage. It even pierced the door to the garage, so he had followed her into the laundry room. She leaped into the car and hit the garage door opener.

"I heard Elmer." Heather clutched the Christmas afghan around her shoulders.

"I know." Jenna checked the mirror to make sure the garage door was high enough and shifted into reverse. As they backed out, she hit the button again, but didn't bother to wait and make sure the door closed. What was the fastest way to the airport and the least likely sighting of cops?

She stopped at the stop sign and looked to her right. A cop car with flashing lights. *Not today, Lord. What is going on?* He pulled in front of her and rolled down his window.

"Are you Jenna Montgomery?"

"Yes, sir."

"I'm your escort. Follow me." He hit the siren and peeled out.

Jenna swung in behind him, hardly believing her eyes. She glanced at Heather, who wore a face-splitting grin. "You okay, baby?"

"Mom, watch the road."

They sailed through a stoplight and picked up speed. Good thing the road was straight. Traffic pulled off and they zoomed by. At the airport, a man swung open a gate to the field and the car in front of her drove on through, Jenna following. They screeched to a halt in front of a four-seater Learjet, the engine already roaring.

The police officer whipped open her door. "Hand me your keys. I'll take care of your car. You grab the bags. I've got your daughter."

Another man ran up and hoisted the oxygen tank on one shoulder. "Come on, he's ready to roll."

Jenna fumbled with the bags and a different man took them from her. "Anything else you need?"

Jenna checked her shoulder, purse in place. "I guess not." She ran after the man who got to the stairs as the policeman ducked in the plane with Heather in his arms. The other three climbed in and the officer finished snapping Heather's seat belt.

"We'll be praying, sweetheart. You hang on for the ride." He motioned Jenna into the seat next to her. "The oxygen tank is right behind you. Your bags are stowed and you've got the best pilot around. The cabin is pressurized, so you should be okay." He touched his forehead as he backed away. "Go with God."

"Thank you, thank you." Jenna fought around the tears. The door slammed and she saw the steps rolling away at the same time as the plane started to move. They were airborne in what seemed seconds.

"Did all this really happen?" Heather stared at her mother.

"It did. I have no idea how, but it did." Jenna leaned her head against the seat.

Heather clung to her mother's hand. "He carried me right up the steps."

"Who? Oh, the police officer? Probably a good thing you're such a lightweight."

"Do you know his name?"

"I've seen him at the ER. Jason, James, something like that." She closed her eyes to think better. "Jamison. No, Jamiston. Wendell Jamiston. They call him 'Dell.'"

"He was one good-looking guy."

"Heather, he's old enough to be your father."

"I know."

A click and the intercom came on. "Welcome to our own friendly skies, ladies. This is your captain speaking, John Wayne, and my sidekick, Kirk Douglas. We'll be cruising at thirty-four thousand feet and should arrive in Omaha in forty-seven minutes, where an ambulance will be waiting to transport you to the hospital."

Jenna looked at Heather and they both broke out in giggles.

How am I ever going to afford all this? The thought managed to sneak in around Jenna's mix of euphoria and apprehension. Whoever all these good angels were, they'd have to take payments. Probably for the rest of her life, but who was counting? She stared out the window as another thought snuck through. Dear God, Heather's miracle had been someone else's grief. *Oh, Lord, help the family. Comfort them, bring them peace. Thank them for their sacrifice.*

Chapter Nine

Nora

Did we do the right thing?

Nora stared out the car window. Snowflakes danced, but instead of beautiful and bringing joy, all she could think was sliding vehicles and the scream and crash of metal on metal. With both arms wrapped around herself, she huddled into the door.

Couldn't he turn the heater up?

You can't blame Gordon. She knew the thought made sense, but right now she wanted to blame everyone, scream at everyone and do over the last twenty-four hours. How could Charlie be gone like that and the world keep on turning? How could her lungs pull in air and her hands feel cold when her heart was leaking from the gigantic hole where Charlie had been ripped out?

She heard Gordon say something to Christi and heard her daughter answer, but the words didn't compute. Leaning forward, she increased the heat to MAX.

Where was God when you needed Him? That was the question of all questions. If this was what walking with the Lord was like, she wanted no part of it. Tears stung her eyes again. Where did they all come from? Surely, the well would dry up soon. They turned into the driveway, the grass blanketed in white. The sun hurt her eyes, so she closed them, sensing when the garage enveloped the car. Gordon turned off the ignition. They sat there, all three of them, as if turned to clay.

But clay didn't sniff. Christi did again and again.

The noise screeched on Nora's nerves. Charlie was dead and the whole world should be silent.

Finally Gordon got out and came around to open her door. He'd not done that for a long time. Somehow the common niceties had disappeared, and who knew when or why? She turned and set her feet on the garage floor, ignoring the hand he extended to help her. Had her leg muscles atrophied in the last few hours so that she could hardly stand? When she swayed, he took her arm and this time she let him. She could hear Betsy barking a greeting. Had someone come and let her out?

"Come on, sweetheart." He opened the door for Christi too. "I will."

Together Nora and Gordon mounted the steps to the house and she walked through the door ahead of him. Betsy greeted her with high yips and frantic tail wagging. She ran ahead of them, sliding on the floor and ran back to sit in front and quiver, tongue lolling, eyes pleading.

Nora leaned down to ruffle her dog's ears and received a quick swipe across her chin. "Good girl. Yes, we're home." *But not all of us, Charlie will never come through this door again and say, "Hi, Mom. What's for supper?"* The tears took over and she left the dog to greet the others. Shedding her jacket, she dropped it on a chair, along with her purse and gloves. Snatching a tissue from the box, she made her way to the bedroom. Here she could hide and block out the light, the sounds, everything that spoke of life. She jerked the drapes closed, went to the bathroom without turning on the light, flushed and grabbed a cloth on her way out. Without taking off her clothes, she crawled into bed and pulled the down comforter over her head. Somehow she had to get warm.

Perhaps if she slept, she would wake and this would all be a bad dream. Shivers attacked her again.

She sensed Gordon before he spoke.

"Can I bring you a cup of coffee?"

"No."

"Another blanket?"

"Yes." If only the chills would leave. Maybe she was coming down with something. What if she did? Something fatal; then she could join Charlie and she wouldn't have to endure all this pain. No one ever said grief was a physical pain, that her whole body would ache like she'd been beaten with a huge stick. That her mind screamed in pain and her soul had vaporized.

Childbirth, even with twins, was nothing like this. That pain had been for life, for a time that seemed long then, but looking back, it was only a blip on the screen. Birthing pangs came in waves that ebbed and flowed. Death pain filled her universe.

The added weight made it impossible to breathe. She threw back the covers and rushed to the bathroom, hand clamped over her mouth. But no matter how hard and often she heaved, nothing came up but bile that burned all the way. Sinking down on the floor, she laid her cheek on the edge of the bathtub. Perhaps if she took a hot bath, she could get warmed up. The wrenching shivers attacked again from the cold tile floor.

After turning on the hot water, she watched the steam rising, still too tired, too weak to stand up. She heard the click of toenails on the tile and the rasp of a warm tongue on her cheek. Betsy whimpered and snuggled up under Nora's chin, clearing away the tears as fast as they fell. Nora buried her face in the dog's warm fur and sobbed.

At some point, she reached over and turned off the faucet. The steam in the room ran rivulets down the tile surround. She lifted her head and stared through bleary eyes. Undressing seemed like scaling Mount Everest, but she finally left off hugging the dog, stood and shucked her clothes. She stared at the water; she should have put in bath salts. Dipping in her fingers, she realized the hot water had run out earlier, so the water in the tub was hot, but not enough to burn. As she sank down into the warmth, she opened the stopper on lavender bath salts and shook some into the tub. Not that she could smell anything, as plugged up as her nose was.

Nora leaned back against the foam neck form she kept for long soaks. Usually she lit candles and played soft music; the tub was a place to relax and soak away the cares of the day. How long since she'd taken a bath rather than a shower?

Who cared?

With her eyes closed, the scene in the hospital room came back. The silence when the ventilator stopped clicking, the monitors ceased beeping, Charlie quit breathing. His heart ceased beating within minutes. The doctors had been right. He was dead, his spirit had left—and she'd not known when.

Her face scrunched up again and the tears resumed. The quiet, the terrible, life-sucking quiet. She clenched her teeth to hold back a scream. The doctors had said to take their time in saying good-bye, but she kissed his cheek, whispered "I love you" and hurried from the room. Gordon joined her in a few minutes, and Christi finally left the room and let her father take her arm to lead both his wife and daughter away from the stillness. Back to where nurses cared for patients who were trying to get well, other families visited their loved ones, machines hummed and clicked and an old man moaned.

Luke had been waiting, embraced each of them, said something Nora couldn't remember, and then said he'd call tomorrow to talk about "arrangements." She recalled *that* with sharp clarity. Arrangements.

She swirled the now-tepid water with wrinkled hands. The shivers were starting again. With the water draining, she stood and pulled a bath sheet from the towel bar, drying her arms and wrapping the rose-colored towel around her.

Betsy looked up as Nora stepped out on the rug. Tail swishing the floor, the dog sat up, never taking her eyes from Nora, who sat down on the closed toilet with a thump. Her legs just wouldn't hold her up. Would she have to crawl to the bed, because there was nowhere else she could bear to go? She heaved a deep breath and tried again, keeping one hand on the counter, then the wall as she opened the door. The cold from the bedroom clashed with the heat from the bathroom, making her shiver again.

Retrieving sweatpants and a sweatshirt from her drawer, she sat down on the bed, pulled them on and rolled herself back up in the comforter. Her feet. Furry slippers from under the bed took care of that. This time she dropped into a deep black hole and slept.

Sometime during the night, she woke to find her pillow wet with tears. Gordon slept on, his gentle snores proof of that. She stole from the bed to use the facilities and found the bathroom all put back in order. Betsy padded in from her bed at the foot of Nora's bed and sat in front of Nora, waiting for her usual pats. She put a paw up on Nora's knee and whimpered, deep in her throat. Nora could feel the dark eyes pleading for attention, for understanding to know what was wrong.

"She spent the evening in Charlie's room," Gordon said, watching her from the doorway. "After searching the house for him. Then she came back and jumped up on the bed and lay beside you."

"Do you think she knows?"

"I'm sure of it." Gordon grabbed a tissue from the holder on the counter and blew his nose.

"She never gets up on the bed." Nora put her arms around the dog's neck and rubbed her ears. "Do you suppose dogs cry?"

"I don't know, but they feel pain and—" Gordon turned away, his weeping contagious.

Back in bed, they held each other until the tears dried up again. With her head on his shoulder, Nora's eyes burned. She could hear the steady thump of his heart and a sob catch in his throat. "If only I had—"

"Had what? Kept him locked in his room for the rest of his life?"

The desolation in his voice matched the void in her.

"Accidents just happen," he added.

"True, but if that other driver was drunk, I swear I'll..." *You'll what?* That voice again, the one that drove her crazy at times.

"I'd want to kill him myself, but what good would that do?" His words sounded lost in the stillness. "It wouldn't bring Charlie back."

No, it wouldn't bring Charlie back. Nothing would. She turned over, and with her husband's arm around her, she cried herself back to sleep.

Chapter Ten

Jenna

*S*ometimes a minute lasted an hour.

Jenna checked her watch again, then looked closely at the second hand. Yes, it was moving. No, the battery had not died. Two hours gone by. What stage were they in now? Was the new heart in place? Had they hit any snags? *Lord, what is happening? This waiting is driving me crazy.*

She'd tried to read a magazine, but her mind refused to register words. The television played on a shelf high in the corner. The laugh tracks made her cringe. Nothing could be that funny. She watched an older woman, who sat by herself, knitting away. Would that help if her hands were busy? They were busy by the pile of tissue in her lap, shredded tissue, finely torn into tiny bits, which would melt in water or disappear on a puff of wind, a tiny snowbank that would match those growing outside. She'd gone to stand by the window a couple of times and, with dusk falling, had seen the flakes floating through the pools of light from the lampposts.

Her brain had been busy as well. It seemed with each ecstatic thought of Heather and her new life, a slicing grief would follow for the mother—no, the family that had lost their child.

She hoped God wasn't weary of hearing her "please" requests.

*Please guide the surgeon's hand; please comfort the dev-
astated mother; please warm the heart to beat as soon as it
becomes Heather's; please show me how to pray for the grieving family.* On and on went the alternating thoughts. It was
exhausting and she couldn't stop.

In the middle of a "please let Heather's recovery be as
miraculous as the gift of the new heart," she noticed a man
wearing a clergy collar moving from group to group, making
his way around the room until he sat next to her.

"Hello, I'm Pastor Larson."

"Jenna Montgomery. My daughter is having a heart
transplant."

"How old is she?"

"Twenty."

He nodded, then directed his gaze to the window. "Have
you been waiting long?"

Jenna checked her watch again. "Two hours and twenty-
two minutes."

"Where are you from?"

"North Platte."

"Has there been anyone here with you?"

"No, we had to come immediately. A businessman from
North Platte flew us here in his Learjet, thanks to Dr. Avery
Cranston. He set it all up—I think he's had it set up for some
time, just never told me." Goodness, she was chatty. She usually wouldn't volunteer this much information.

"Sounds like a wonderful man, your Dr. Cranston."

"At the hospital, we all call him 'Dr. A.'"

"You work at the hospital?"

"I'm an RN in the ER."

"Talk about a pressure cooker job." He turned to look at her. "Keeps you from thinking about home too much?"

"How did you know?" Jenna turned sideways and tucked her legs up on the seat. The stretch on her back felt good. She knew she should have been walking around some, but it was like if she moved, she might put a wobble on all the events. If she sat still, the surgeon might come out sooner.

"Good guess." He stretched his head from side to side. "The stress get you in the neck?"

"No, lower back. How long have you been a chaplain?"

He motioned to his silver hair. "Oh, forever."

"Because you're easy to talk with?"

He sort of shrugged. "More because of the need. When we're in crisis, we tend to let our guard down and the Holy Spirit gets a chance to tiptoe in." He smiled at her, a smile that shared love and comfort. "He knows when we are needy."

"That would be me," Jenna said, and told him about her "please" praying. "It seems like it's taking forever."

"Sounds about normal for one in your position. Doctors and nurses not only make poor patients, but they don't wait well."

"I never have waited well. Guess I'm an adrenaline junkie." She watched her hands to see if the internal twitch she sometimes felt had become visible.

"Would you like me to pray with you?" He leaned back in the chair as though he had all the time in the world. "An outside opinion might be helpful."

"I think so."

"You have a church home in North Platte?"

"Yes, but we've not been able to attend much this last year or so. Heather has had to stay away from crowds."

"Makes it harder. But your pastor knows you are here?"

"Come to think of it, no. We had to leave too quickly for me to call him."

"Give me his name and I'll call him." He took a small black notebook out of his pocket, which had a pen in it.

"Adam Bennington. North Platte Community Church." She scrunched her eyes slightly to remember, then shook her head. "Can't think of the phone number."

"That's okay. I'll find it. In my other life, I was a detective."

"Are you serious?"

"Absolutely." He leaned back in the chair. "I was a lieutenant with the Kansas City PD. Was nearly killed by friendly fire, if that isn't an oxymoron, and it was desk or retire. I chose to retire and God led me into the ministry. He never wastes anything. This way I don't have to retire again. Chaplains are always needed."

Jenna shook her head slowly in small motions. "Well, what a surprise. You know to look at you, if you didn't wear the collar, no one would guess you are a pastor."

"Lots of times I leave it off, but here it is helpful. People are looking for comfort. Otherwise, I sneak up on 'em."

Jenna felt a chuckle somewhere behind her tired eyes. "Can I buy you a cup of coffee?"

"Not afraid to leave your post?"

"No, not now. And we won't be gone long."

"And then we'll pray?"

"Try and stop us."

They prayed together at a small table, their coffee half drunk and a packet of crackers shared. It felt to Jenna like Jesus was sitting in the third chair. They talked about the grieving family and how they must be hurting, the fears of Heather's body rejecting the new heart. They talked about peace and how much God loves His children and the power He has that humans so often block. When they said amen, Jenna wiped her eyes with the napkin and took a drink of the now-tepid coffee. "Thanks," she said. "I needed that. Now I'll go back and 'please' pray with assurance. I don't ever want to forget the young person who was my daughter's perfect Christmas."

"I'll walk with you. If I find someone around here who might have need of you, would you be willing to listen and pray?"

Jenna stopped walking and stared at him. Her heart felt like it was thumping in her throat. She chewed on her bottom lip, then nodded. "Yes, I guess I could do that. If you think it could help."

"Oh, it would help all right. You never know who you might meet." His eyes twinkled from between the lines. He reached to shake her hand, but Jenna wrapped her arms around him and hugged him.

"I'll see you again?"

"Lord willing. Here's my number if you need me in a hurry." He handed her a business card with a cell phone number on it. "Anytime, day or night."

Jenna settled back into her chair, wrapping her arms around her legs and resting her chin on her knees. A deep sigh escaped, born out of gratitude and rest, rather than the earlier weariness and frustration from waiting.

Father, let the donor family know how grateful I am. I know we will write letters, but I know that right now, they need comfort. They need someone to come along just like this man. I've not seen you in someone's face before. Not like this.

Chapter Eleven

Nora

"How come you're up on the bed?"

Betsy thumped her tail and rolled on her side for a belly rub.

Nora started to sit up and the reality of the previous night fell on her like a ceiling in an earthquake. She choked on the dust and the pain and burrowed back under the covers. She heard Betsy whining and felt an insistent paw digging at her shoulder. No, it couldn't be. She would walk down the hall and look in Charlie's room and there he'd be, sound asleep, sprawled on his stomach like always. She scrubbed her fingers in her hair and clamped them together, pulling on the strands until the pain registered.

Not that this pain could compare to that assaulting her body, mind and spirit.

She glanced at the other side of the bed. Yes, Gordon had slept there, so the horrific memory from the night wasn't a dream. If only the twenty-four hours before that could be rewound, edited, and the terrible events left on a movie studio's cutting-room floor.

Betsy pushed her nose under Nora's arm and managed to insert her warm body next to Nora's side, so the dog could reach up and lick away the tears that were flowing again. Had they ever stopped? With a fistful of tissues in hand, Nora leaned her head against Betsy's. This was too much to bear. *How do I get through the next hours? I know there are things that need to be done....* She blew out a sigh and mopped again. The tissues grated like sandpaper against the raw skin of her nose and eyes. She should put some cream on her face. "Should." What a terrible word. She should be comforting Gordon and Christi. She should be calling friends and family. She should be planning a—her mind stumbled over the word—funeral.

All she'd asked for was one perfect Christmas. A gift from her to her family, building lifelong memories that they would laugh about years from now: Mom's obsession with a perfect Christmas. Currier & Ives, Norman Rockwell, all the idyllic pictures.

They would never, ever, have a perfect Christmas again.

Life would never be the same again.

She had taken classes at the hospital in helping those who are grieving. She'd learned the five steps of grieving, as if you stepped from stone to stone on a garden path along the grieving trail. Up ahead sunshine shone through a break in the trees, that kind of trail. Not this abysmal pit so dark and dense, with pain shrieking inside and out and no light, no light anywhere.

"*I am the way, the truth and the light.*" The Bible verse floated through her mind. She'd always believed what Jesus said to be true. But if He was the light, right now He was totally hidden.

She would follow His lead. She, too, would stay hidden. The world had stopped and so would she. In the next moment, her head slipped off Betsy's flank as the dog jumped to the floor and headed down the hall, nails clicking on the hardwood floor. Her bark announced someone at the door. Nora shook her head; even her ears must be plugged up, she'd not heard the doorbell.

Gordon entered the room in a bit. "Luke is here."

Nora blinked and moved her head hopefully to clear her vision. "Here."

"In the family room. We need to make some plans."

"Plans." If the world had stopped, there was no need to make plans.

"Christi and I would like your input too. I mean, you might have an idea what Charlie would like."

The idea that she might have discussed Charlie's death with her glowing, healthy boy rocked the little understanding she had left. Nora stared at him. Indeed, nothing made sense but to hide. She looked down at her ratty sweats and picked at a fuzz ball on the front of the shirt. Looking at her husband, she realized he was showered and shaved and dressed in cords and a sweater. Other than his eyes, you'd not know something was terribly wrong. How did he do that? She studied her clasped hands, with her elbows resting on her thighs. She couldn't even sit up straight.

"How's Christi?"

"Coping."

That was a lie. Nobody could cope with this.

She rolled back to prone. "Later. Not now."

Silence. She could sense Gordon remained, although her eyes were closed. *You can't see me,* she thought. *I'm hidden. I'm stopping the world.*

"I've made coffee. You want a cup to help get you going?"

As if that would suffice. Anger flared at her husband. How

could he go about living after all this? Shouldn't the whole world stop in memory, in honor of Charlie?

"No, I don't want coffee." She knew her tone cut him, but that was the best she could do at the moment. There was a wave of air from Betsy's tail as she and Gordon left a few moments later. Too soon after, the aroma of coffee entered her room.

"Please, darling, we can use your input." He set a steaming cup on her bedside table.

"Later," she managed before another flood of weeping. Later, never. What was the difference?

He left, then the murmur of voices began in the living room, but she didn't care because she had stopped the world and was hiding.

How much longer after that, Nora didn't know, but her eyes wouldn't stay shut, and her ears kept straining to hear a clear word from downstairs. Maybe she would hide out of sight and just listen. Listen to "arrangements." Tears welled up again; she lost more time lying down with Kleenex stuffed in her ears so they wouldn't fill up with the wet.

Then, in what seemed like watching someone's home movie in slow motion, she lifted her legs from the bed and stood up. She put one foot in front of the other to the bathroom, closed the door behind her, and clicked the lock. She would get dressed, hide and listen.

Lipstick didn't bring her eyes to life, nor her skin, nor help her smile. That had died along with Charlie. But at least her hair was combed, teeth brushed and she felt some semblance of order. She debated on staying in her sweats, but after staring into the closet, for who knows how long, she pulled on jeans and a black sweater. She'd never been a sweats person for the whole day. She fingered the red sweater laid out, one with yellow Labs dressed in angel clothes, down to the wings. And stuffed it in the wastebasket. Christmas had stopped, along with the world.

No wonder people wore black for mourning. One could hide in it. Sliding her feet into fleece-lined leather moccasins, she left the haven of her dark bedroom and braved the light.

From her spot against the wall, hunkered down to her knees just outside the living room, she could now hear clearly. At least hear Luke and Gordon.

"So we are agreed then on a memorial service rather than a funeral, and we will have a private graveside service as soon as they release the body?" Gordon asked.

A pause, where Christi and Luke must have nodded. Gordon continued, "And we will go to the funeral home and choose a casket this afternoon?"

We will? Who all is the "we"? A surge of something brought Nora to standing. *I thought we talked about cremation at one time? We don't have a burial plot, because we are too young to worry about that kind of thing. And if we are to be cremated and our ashes spread upon Lake Superior, we don't need a casket.*

Anger propelled her into the room before she realized she was standing. "Why even discuss it? After all, there are pieces of Charlie scattered all over the country, for all we know — why not his ashes too?"

The vestige of the screech, which must have been hers, was the only sound in the room. Nora slid her hands to her mouth and tottered to the chair the kids called "Mom's chair."

Christi's eyes were wide. She had on black sweats, the

sweatshirt a hoodie, in case she needed to pull into her shell like a turtle. How did Nora know that? Because she wished right now she'd done the same. Her daughter was huddled into the corner of the claret leather couch. After a quick glance at her mother, she went back to staring at her hands knotted in the pouch of the shirt.

Luke bowed his head. Gordon disappeared into the kitchen and came back with coffee mugs on a tray, including a plate with samples of the baking she'd been doing, his face the color of fireplace dust. "Christi, I put cream and sugar in yours." He handed her a red mug with Santa laughing on it, then held the tray for the others to take theirs. His gaze hung on Nora's; she couldn't look away. *We just said good-bye. We're moving too fast,* she frantically telegraphed to him.

Nora hadn't realized her hand was shaking, until she had to put the mug down quickly before she dropped it. Betsy came over and sat next to the leather recliner. Her basket of needlework, mostly Hardanger embroidery, sat beside the chair, along with a daylight lamp to make handiwork easier. Drink the coffee. The prompting reminded her to pick up the cup, this time with both hands. As she sipped, she realized Gordon and Luke were talking. About Charlie. She must be nodding in the right places, because every time they looked at her, she was aware they'd asked a question. Asking them to repeat it took too much energy.

Her eyes filled again and she dried her face with one of the Christmas napkins she'd hand hemmed so joyously.

Her mind wandered around on various paths, until Gordon called her name again.

"What?"

"I asked if you will go with me?"

She nodded. "Why did you change your mind about cremation?"

"Because I don't know if that was Charlie's wish. What would Charlie want?" He sounded desperate for her to come up with the right answer.

"Charlie wants to finish his senior year, go to college, save the world," Nora said.

Christi spoke to her lap. "Charlie thought not being an organ donor was selfish. Other than that, I think he thought..." Her voice quivered. "He thought he'd live forever. He had so many things to do, to see." She chewed on a fingernail, something she hadn't done for years. Not since she wanted to wear nail polish and keep her hands lovely.

"So what do you think Charlie would like us to do?" Gordon was pale, yet determined.

Stop, stop, Nora wanted to shriek again.

"I don't think he cares one way or the other." Christi looked at Luke. "Does it matter?"

"Only if you want a place to go to remember him."

"Like we need a place." She waved her hand, indicating things around the room, trophies, ornaments on the tree, Charlie's backpack by the door, all things of his. "Oh, my gosh." She leaped to her feet. "No one has fed his critters." She headed for the refrigerator, where the crickets lived in a container and fruit and lettuce waited for Iggy, the iguana. "How long since Arnold was fed?"

"Charlie always marked it on the calendar." Nora rose to go to the kitchen to check. She drew the line at buying mice or chicks at the pet store to bring home for food for Arnold. They were Charlie's love, not hers. Three days since Arnold ate, so they had a few more days. She braced her arms on the granite countertop. *I can't do this. I can't.* The coffee on an empty stomach made her feel like throwing up. She sucked in a couple of deep breaths and slowly her head cleared. Walking back to the sofa, where the men sat, she said, "I think we should go with cremation."

"Are you sure about this?" Luke asked gently. At her nod, he turned to Gordon. "And you?"

Gordon shrugged.

"No, that's not good enough. You all talk it over and let me know. There's no rush on this. I'll look at the church calendar and see when might be a good time for the memorial service. Again, there is no rush."

"Would it be easier if we got all this over as soon as possible?" Gordon asked, then closed his eyes as Christi and Nora speared him with disbelieving looks. "I didn't mean...I just meant..."

Luke heaved a sigh. "There is no easier way. Grieving is different for everyone. God said He'd walk through the valley with us, but sometimes we can't let Him do that and the valley takes more time."

Nora snorted, but just shook her head when the men looked up at her. She cupped her elbows in her hands and rubbed, trying to get some warmth and life back into her arms.

"Are you still cold?" Gordon asked.

"Still, again, I don't know, I can't seem to get warm."

"I'll start the fire."

"Have you eaten anything?" Luke nodded toward the kitchen. "Several of the women have sent over food. I know there are some cinnamon rolls. I could heat one up for you."

The thought of one of Marion's cinnamon rolls usually made her mouth water. The woman was famous for her sticky-bottomed rolls. But today it made her stomach roil. "No thanks, all I'd do is throw up."

"Some people react that way. You need to drink lots of water, tepid is best."

Are you a doctor now too? Nora hoped her thoughts didn't show on her face. Where had all this negativity and the snide remarks come from? This wasn't like her.

"Come, let's pray before I leave." Luke held out his hands. "There will be people asking if there is something they can do. They'll bring food, because that's tradition and because they want to show you that they care. I'll send Sonja over to mind the door for you and she'll freeze what she can and deal with the rest." He nodded to Nora. "You don't have to worry about being polite at this point. Let's just get through the next few days." As they all joined hands around the coffee table, Nora held on to both Gordon and Christi as if they, too, might be snatched away from her. She heard the words, but as from a great distance and in a foreign language. When the amen was said, she rose, stiff as an old woman with arthritis. "Thank you, Luke, for coming." Her words sounded as wooden as she felt. With Betsy at her side, she tottered down the hallway and collapsed again on the bed, to hide once more.

Chapter Twelve

Jenna

*F*our hours passed, then five.

A woman in green scrubs came out to tell Jenna that while there had been some problems, which the surgeon would tell her about, the surgery was going well now. And no, she wasn't sure how much longer it would take.

Jenna stared at the woman's back as she walked out the doorway. *So many questions, but she cut me off at the knees.* The surgeon would answer. Of course she knew that, but it was different this time. The patient was her daughter.

Six hours, and still no more word.

Jenna had no more prayers to offer, no more patience. Endurance was all she had. After all, what were her choices? She couldn't sleep. She had no one to talk to since Pastor Larson had moved to other rooms. One lady had sat by her and they made polite chitchat, but then she'd been allowed to see the one she waited for. Her relief had been palpable. Jenna tried praying for those that ebbed and flowed around her. Then she tried reading a magazine again, the newspaper someone had left, watching the television. She resorted to pacing the hallway, never out of sight of the arch where the doctors came through.

At times she wished she were a smoker, that would give her

something to do with her hands. After buying a roll of Life-Savers, she sucked on one and it was too sweet. She and Arlen used to fight over the red ones. After he died, she'd not much cared for LifeSavers.

"See how well you're waiting." Pastor Larson sat down beside her. His voice sent a surge of reassurance.

She heaved a heavy sigh. "A nurse came out about two hours ago and said that while there had been some difficulties, they were on track and looking good."

"No news is good news?"

"I guess so."

"Have you eaten?"

She shook her head. "Nothing looks good in the machines, and I don't dare go to the dining room, because they might come out and I'll miss the report."

"I understand. If I go get you a sandwich, will you eat it?"

She gazed at his peace-giving face. "I doubt it. But thanks for trying. Once I know, I'll be all right."

"Where are you staying?"

Jenna paused. That's right, Heather would be in the CCU and they wouldn't allow her to sleep on a chair by the bed there. She glanced around the room. One man was stretched out on one of the padded benches, but she doubted she'd sleep that way.

The pastor chuckled. "I wouldn't recommend these accommodations. There's a hotel right around the corner, where families of those in the hospital can stay. They would call you if there was any change and you'd be here in minutes. There's even a covered skywalk over the street so you don't have to worry about the weather."

"Thanks."

"It's reasonable too. Good beds."

"And plenty of hot water for long showers?"

"Plenty."

Jenna glanced at her watch again. Five more minutes and it would be seven hours. Everyone in the room looked up at the sound of footsteps. When Jenna saw Dr. Walker, with his face mask hanging around his neck, she rose and had to take a step back to keep her balance. Then he smiled at her. She could feel the heat of Pastor Larson standing right behind her.

"Heather is one trouper, you can be proud of her." The surgeon's smile looked as tired as she felt. "She's in recovery now, the heart is beating well, and her color is coming back already. Someone will come for you in a while so you can peek in on her, but she will be sedated to control the pain for the next day or so, depending on how she responds."

Jenna ignored the tears trickling down her cheeks and smiled anyway. And kept on smiling. She sniffed and nodded. "Thank you." All her questions blew out of her mind. Heather had a new heart. Heather had a new life. A Christmas miracle.

"Now we fight the rejection battle." He included the pastor with his statement. "So keep praying and we'll win this one."

"Thank you."

"Merry Christmas, Mrs. Montgomery." The doctor shook her hand. "Bring your list of questions with you when you come back after a good night's rest. Are you checked in to the hotel yet?"

"No, but she will be." Pastor Larson nodded as he spoke.

"Good. Call the CCU and leave your room number."

"Merry Christmas. From thinking this would be our last to a whole life ahead. What a Christmas." She felt like twirling to her own music, but instead she watched him leave and kept on mopping.

"I'll go get your sandwich now. What's your preference?"

The decision was too much. "Surprise me, just not peanut butter and jelly."

"I doubt they serve that. If you're in seeing Heather, I'll wait right here. Would you rather have tea than coffee or decaf?"

"Hot chocolate." There, she had made a decision. Her mind was back on track.

A few minutes later, a nurse came to get her. "She is responding to stimuli, but she's not fully conscious yet."

The two approached where Heather lay. "You're going to bring her all the way around before knocking her out again?" Jenna asked.

"Not all the way."

"Good."

Jenna forced herself into nurse mode as she stared down at her sleeping daughter. The blue tinge was gone from around her mouth and eyes, even her fingernails were a healthy pink. She took Heather's hand and the warmth of it sent spirals of joy dancing up her arm and lodging in her heart. *Merry Christmas. Oh, very Merry Christmas.* Still holding her daughter's hand, she leaned close and whispered in Heather's ear, "Hey, sweetheart, you're doing well."

There was a definite squeeze on her hand and the girl's mouth twitched into a slight smile.

"You sleep now and I'll go next door and do the same. They're going to keep you sedated for a day or so for the pain, but if you wake up and need me, they'll call. And I'll come running. Okay?" Another slight squeeze. Jenna kissed

Heather's cheek and mopped away the tear that dripped on her smooth skin. She turned to leave and saw tears in the eyes of the nurse, who was standing right behind her.

"Merry Christmas."

"Yes, thank you. What an incredible, wonderful Christmas."

"Leave your cell phone number at the desk and go get some sleep yourself. At the moment, she looks better than you do."

"Thanks, I guess." Keeping her feet on the floor took some concentration. She left her number and floated out to the waiting room.

"I don't need to even ask, your face says it all." He held out his arms and Jenna walked into them, only to collapse in sobs against his shoulder. When the tears slowed, she pulled away and shook her head.

"That's what being nice to someone gets you." She used her tissue, smiling through her tears. "A wet shoulder."

"Not the first time, and—please God—not the last. Let's sit here so you can drink this and take a few bites. Then I'll show you the way over to the hotel."

Between sips and bites, Jenna filled him in. "She has more color than she's had for years, other than when fighting a temperature. They gave her a good, strong heart." She wiped her mouth with a napkin. "I keep thinking of the family that lost the one they love. This has got to be the worst Christmas of their lives."

"They'll be glad to hear your good news, though."

"I'm glad we'll be able to send them a thank-you note at least." She drained the Styrofoam cup. "It could never replace their loss, but I want to tell them..." She couldn't continue. "Okay, let's go. I can chew and walk at the same time. You get used to that in the ER."

With him carrying her two bags, she'd finished the sandwich by the time they arrived at the check-in desk. He wrote down her room number in his little notebook, reminded her to call it over to the CCU, patted her shoulder and strode back the way they'd come.

"Hey, did you know you're sprouting wings?" she called after him.

He waved and kept on going, but she was sure she heard his chuckle.

After setting the bags down, and notifying the hospital of how to reach her, she decided to call her own hospital first thing and her mother second, then a shower. After the phone calls, she crawled under the covers and passed out.

When her bleary eyes finally opened, she stared at the bright red 7 on the clock. She'd slept through the night, but neither phone showed messages. She dialed the CCU number and rubbed her eyes while she waited for them to answer. They would be in shift change right now, not a good time to call.

"Hi, this is Jenna Montgomery and I'm calling to check on my daughter, Heather, the heart transplant from yesterday." She caught herself. At least she'd given her daughter's name and not just referred to her as the heart transplant. She hated that about hospital lingo, and here she'd done the same thing.

"Let me give you to her charge nurse. I just came on."

"Thanks." Jenna could hear the laughter and conversations of the shift change. Someone had been to a party the night before and some hunk was there.

"Hello, this is Maddie Harrison. I have good news for you. Heather slept on through the night. We were able to keep her comfortable and that new heart is beating away like it lived in her chest for years. Will you be here in time for rounds?"

"When does Dr. Walker usually come in?"

"Oh, within the hour. Since there are no surgeries sched-uled for today, I'm sure he is hoping for some time off."

Jenna realized the date. December 24. "I just woke up, so I'll be over as soon as I can get dressed."

"Good, glad you got some sleep. I'll see you again this evening."

"Thanks."

When she was beeped into the CCU, she made her way to Heather's cubicle and had to smile at the white teddy bear with a Santa hat that sat at the end of her bed. Picking up the bear, she held his softness against her cheek and took the three more steps to Heather's side. "Hey, Heather sweet, I have something here for you."

Heather's eyes fluttered and a slight smile moved the cor-ners of her mouth.

When Jenna took her hand, she squeezed and received one in return.

"That's all right, you just keep resting and healing. That's your job for now. Tomorrow they'll probably have you sitting up. Amazing how therapies have changed." While she talked, she studied the monitors and nodded her approval. Her daugh-ter was indeed doing well.

"Good morning." Dr. Walker paused in the doorway. "Now, if this isn't what I like to see. A mom hugging a bear and a young woman with color in her cheeks."

Jenna set the bear back on the bed. "He was waiting when I came in."

"Ah, the elves have been at work again." He checked Heath-er's responses, wrote some notes on his pad and nodded to Jenna. "So what do you think will be her first words?"

" 'When can I go home?' "

"Not surprising. All depends on how well she does. Minimum stay is usually a week."

"That's all?"

"Amazing, isn't it? But people heal better at home, and in your case, you already know how to do all the care. Others we have to train." He glanced at her empty hands. "Did you bring questions?"

She shook her head. "Nope, fell asleep and just woke up in time to get over here. I'll do that today."

"We'll keep her pretty heavily sedated today and see how she's doing by evening. The respiration therapist will be working with her to keep the lungs clear. So far she's handling the antirejection meds. And we wait and pray."

"Thank you." The words seemed so insignificant for a life, but what else could she say?

"You get some rest while you're here. Once you're home, you'll be plenty busy."

"I will." She caught herself in a yawn. "Merry Christmas."

"I'll see you in the morning." He turned to leave and patted the bear on his way by.

Christmas Eve day. At home she would be finishing wrapping the presents and fixing the cranberry salad she always took to Dr. Avery's house, where she and Heather had been Christmas Day guests for the last several years. *Oh, my gosh, Randy.* She leaned over to Heather. "I need to go call Uncle Randy. Hopefully, Grandma told him what happened. I'll be back later."

Cell phones could not be used in the CCU.

Her stomach growled as she walked the sky bridge back to the hotel with the phone at her ear. When Randy answered, she paused to look out the window. He whooped and hollered his delight when she told him the news.

"I suppose that means you won't be home for Christmas."

"I'm just glad you hadn't left yet."

"Mom called me with the news. I am so glad, Jenna, I can't begin to tell you."

"I know, me too. Let the rest of the family know and I'll call you again."

While the streets of Omaha were clear, the clouds wore the pregnant look of more snow. Christmas banners hung from the lampposts, and evergreen swags looped across the streets with a wreath in the middle. A gigantic lighted wreath hung above the hotel sign.

She said good-bye and flipped the phone shut. Another errand to run.

Deep red poinsettias, with white splashed petals, were grouped in various places around the hotel, and a tall spruce tree, decorated with tiny white lights, red bows and silver glass balls, took up the center of the lobby. Her stomach would have to wait a bit longer. When she'd checked in, she'd caught a glimpse of a present for Heather in the gift store.

He was still there, a cuddly stuffed cat that looked so much like Elmer, they might have used him for the model. Other than the red bow around his neck. Elmer did not tolerate bows. She paid for the toy and a bag of peanut M&M's in Christmas colors. They'd probably be all gone before Heather could eat them, but she could always buy more. They both loved peanut M&M's. Back in her room, she ordered room service for breakfast, and with a promise of food in twenty minutes, she turned on the shower. She began belting out "Joy to the World"; she could finish the rest of the phone calls later.

Chapter Thirteen

Nora

*W*hat are you doing?"

Gordon straightened up from bending near the Christmas tree. "Turning on the Christmas-tree lights. It's Christmas Eve, Nora."

"I..." She blinked, trying to remember. The last two days had run together like a black and tarry stream that absorbed everything in its path. She stared at the calendar above the built-in desk, where she usually sat to pay bills and update her calendar. Sure enough, December 24. Christmas Eve day. This was to have been the beginning of her one perfect day. She closed her eyes against the blazing pain — pain that made her want to scream and claw at her chest, pain that was burning her heart to a cinder.

"How can we have Christmas when Charlie just died?"

Her words bit; she could see it on Gordon's face. "I just thought, I mean...Nora, we're still a family and we need to take care of Christi too."

Nora paused and turned to stare at him. "Is something wrong with Christi?"

"Nothing but the grief that is with all of us. But you haven't said a word to her since we came home from the hospital."

Christi was her daughter. The other half of Charlie. Gordon's accusation stung. Of course she'd spoken to her daughter. She stifled a groan and headed for the hall closet, where she ripped her ski jacket off the hanger, her headband and gloves from the basket hanging on the door, and boots from the floor. Sitting on a chair, she exchanged slippers for ski boots and, without answering a tentative question that Gordon asked, headed for the garage and her cross-country skis. Since her outburst in the living room, everyone had been tip-toeing around her.

Charlie had teased her that if Christmas Day was the first day with snow deep enough to ski, no matter what she'd planned, they'd all be out skiing. She had to get out; the house was suffocating her, sucking out the remaining trickle of what passed for life. Tiny thoughts of "what if we said good-bye too quickly," which had begun yesterday, were circling faster and faster in her brain.

With her gear on, she took the first glide, first right, then left; she caught the top of the slope and let her skis carry her. The soft swooshing and shushing of skis through powder, the bite of the cold on her face, enough cloud cover that she didn't need her dark glasses. It was only she and the land covered in white. She did a stem turn at the level area before the narrow beach to the ice-rimmed but not frozen-over lake. Using both poles and leg muscles, she set off on the path around the lake. All the landowners on their little lake agreed to leave the pathway clear and maintain it across their land, meaning keep it mowed in the summer. They, like many of the others, had graveled their section of path so it wouldn't get muddy.

Today gravel and mowing didn't matter. The snow covered all the same. Halfway around the lake, she remembered she'd forgotten the cardinal rule. Always tell someone where she was going. How could she tell someone when she had no idea? Would she stay on the lake path or head up the south hill and off into the woods?

Had they been too quick to turn off the machines? The quiet bounced off her screaming mind and the rhythm of arms and legs working in tandem deepened her heartbeat as the cold air pumped into her lungs. That was part of the problem, she'd been feeling like she was hyperventilating ever since the police came to the front door. Charlie was such a fast healer: falling out of trees, getting over strep throat, the various stitches he had for his escapades.

A woof sounded from behind her and she knew Gordon had given in to Betsy's plea to go along. Betsy loved accompanying Nora, no matter what the sport, but she especially loved the snow—and skiing. Nora glanced over her shoulder to see the yellow dog charging along the path, throwing snow behind her with the power of haunches and broad feet. As she caught up with her mistress, she grinned up at her, black eyes sparkling, pink tongue lolling out one side of her mouth.

"Good girl." Holding the handles of both poles with one hand, she leaned over and thumped the dog on her ribs. "Let's go." She pushed off again and lost herself in the rhythm. Stride, reach, stride, reach. Her shoulder muscles first whined, then complained, grumbled, shouted and finally screamed. Her legs were in better shape, due to speed-walking, but still, skiing used muscles that hid out until winter. She ignored the hill and continued around the lake. What if they had waited . . . hours? A day or two? It was all too fast. If they had been too fast . . . her mind made the leap. Then they had . . . Step, glide, step, glide. *Don't think, just move.* Hers were the first tracks other than deer and other wild creatures. A few Canada geese remained on the lake, resting before the final push south. With the grass they grazed covered in snow, they needed to be on their way.

At one point, Nora stopped and stared out over the lake, the newest thought undulating like some bilious screen saver on Charlie's laptop. Charlie loved the lake, no matter what the season. A brisk breeze kicked up mini whitecaps, breaking up the collar of ice that daily pushed out farther into the lake. He'd have been out skiing early this morning, yesterday even. Betsy sat down beside her, also looking over the lake. The cold froze the moisture draining down her cheeks. She brushed her face dry with the back of her wool gloves. "Come on, girl, let's go home." Her mouth was beginning to dry with panic.

Gordon met her at the door, scrutinized her face. "Are you all right?"

She only nodded. Would she ever be all right again? Right now, it certainly didn't feel so. Everything reminded her of Charlie. No wonder some people moved out of the house they'd lived in, the memories were just too hurtful.

"The mortuary called. The hospital released the body to them."

She spun around to stare at him. "Charlie. They released *Charlie*."

Nora sank down in a chair at the bay window. A bird feeder hanging on a cast-iron crook needed to be filled. Her face stung from the cold air and now the inside warmth.

"We need to decide on burial. Shall I get Christi?"

"I thought we decided on cremation."

"I-I'm just not sure she was listening."

She glanced up to see his face start to sag, his eyes tightened and blinked before he turned away to pull a handkerchief from his pocket and blow his nose.

"I'll see if she can come down."

Tail wagging slowly, Betsy clicked her way across the tile floor and laid her muzzle on Nora's knee.

Nora stroked the dog's head and stared out the window. At least she'd been able to breathe out there, even though the air was cold enough to burn her face. Here, inside the house that she'd slaved to decorate just so, where she'd planned for them all to have all their favorite things this year, do all their favorites, build memories to last a lifetime, here the air was so heavy that breathing was torture. Ponderous and mixed with the insidious voice silently asking, *"Are you sure you didn't say good-bye too soon?"*

Gordon returned to the room. "She's sleeping, I didn't want to wake her. I think she was up most of the night."

"Were you?"

"Up and down."

"Maybe we all need sleeping pills."

"Are we going to church tonight?"

"I don't know if I can stand it." She stared outside at the two lines her skis had made down the slope and on around the lake. Another skier just crossed their property line. Betsy went to the window and, ears pricked, stared at the intruder until he moved off their land. While she'd learned not to bark, she kept track of all those skiing or hiking around the lake.

"More people brought food."

She nodded. "Did you put some of it out in the garage refrigerator?"

"Yes. We need to give some of it away." He pulled out a chair and sat down, propping his elbows on the table to hold his head up. "Luke called and suggested the twenty-seventh for the memorial service. He wondered if that gave us time to prepare?"

"Prepare how?"

"Notify family and friends, I guess. Choose what we want in the service. He asked about a memorial."

"A memorial?"

"And we need to get an obituary written for the paper."

"Would you like something to drink? Coffee, hot chocolate, apple cider?" She paused in her rising. "Tea, eggnog?" She had stocked in everything, everything they needed to have a wonderful time.

He shook his head. "I don't know. Whatever you're having."

As she held the teakettle under the faucet, her arm and hand began to shake from an attack of fatigue so intense it was all she could do to stand up. She set the kettle on the burner and leaned back against the counter, rubbing her forehead. The ache behind her eyes intensified, picking up a beat like the native drums that Charlie sometimes played. *What if we . . .* Removing two packets of cider mix from the clear-glass canisters on the counter, she ripped them open and poured the contents into snowmen mugs. But the thought of drinking anything made her stomach roil.

"Here. This is about ready. I need to go lie down." She left the kitchen at a run and barely made it up the stairs to her bathroom before the heaves started. But there was nothing to come up. Sorrow and pain tasted strangely like bile. She rinsed her mouth out with water sipped from her cupped hand and wiped hands and face on the red towel with a carefully stitched band of Hardanger decorating it for Christmas. She threw the towel in the hamper and crawled under the covers.

She could feel her heart pounding in her ears, her throat, her chest. The covers held the sound in and magnified it. In spite of her will, the tears trickled into the pillowcase. *Lord, all I want is Charlie back. Why did You take him like this, without even giving him a chance to finish growing up? Why?*

She felt the bed move as Betsy jumped up and lay tight against her back. The dog's sigh matched her own.

Sometime after dark, she staggered to the bathroom and changed into her nightgown. Without glancing at the clock, she crawled back into bed. At least in sleep, she didn't have to think or feel.

Until the dream crept up and attacked.

Chapter Fourteen

Jenna

*C*hristmas morning. Even though she was alone, she didn't feel lonely.

Dr. Walker gave her a good report. Heather was doing as well as could be expected. Her temp was a bit elevated, but not sufficiently to worry. Besides, she was already on massive doses of antibiotics, along with antirejection drugs and cortisone. The list was as long as her arm. She planned on asking the pharmacist if he could give her the info on all of them now, so she'd be better prepared when they headed home. Many of them she'd never heard of before. They weren't commonly used in the ER.

His final statement, however, chilled her, though she already knew the information: they were approaching thirty-six hours postsurgery. Statistically dangerous for rejection of the new heart.

With Heather cuddled in a deep healing sleep, Jenna wandered down to the cafeteria, where a minimum of staff held down the tables, desultory conversation skimming the clatter of kettles from the kitchen. She filled a Styrofoam cup with hot coffee and added two creamers, plus a sugar; today she needed a massive energy fix, she couldn't afford to let down now. Which would be worse? Losing Heather now or losing her by not getting a donor? Chiding herself for harboring vain imaginations, she took her coffee to a table by a window, which looked out on a bathroom-sized fenced garden. She sat down and propped her elbows on the table. Outside, a flock of chickadees flitted from a feeder to the snow-dusted paving stones underneath it, to the small pine tree and back to the feeder again. A nuthatch hung sideways on a block of suet, hanging by the cedar feeder. The fluttering and flitting of busy birds made her smile. Heather loved to watch the black capped chickadees from the sofa in the living room. On days when she'd been too tired to move, the feeder and its guests were more entertaining than the television that droned in the corner.

Now what? They'd never planned for life after a transplant. While they'd prayed for this day, she'd never allowed her dreams to go on, because the thought of life without Heather was more than she could bear. Had she really thought a new heart would never come? And now, they were given this incredible gift. She stubbornly refused to think of the thirty-six-hour window. Saying "thank you" to God seemed far too weak, but she couldn't think of anything else.

Other than the other mother.

Those at the closest table were talking about the suppers waiting for them once their shift was over. One older woman invited a young male nurse to join her family for Christmas dinner, since he was alone.

Please go, Jenna thought. *Everybody needs to be with someone at Christmas.* She hoped the mother mourning her son had a strong family and a church to comfort her. Jenna felt blessed beyond measure. The person she most wanted to be with was sleeping upstairs in the CCU. Sleeping without fear of her heart stopping.

She finished her coffee and tossed the cup in the trash as she exited the cafeteria.

A shame she didn't knit or crochet or something to help pass the time. She hadn't had this much time to spend for years. It gave her too much time to think. She glanced at her watch. While she waited for Heather to wake up, what was the other mother doing? Having made it through another hour, she could go back up and watch Heather sleep.

"There's a gentleman to see you," the nurse who was in charge of Heather on the day shift said when Jenna walked back into the CCU. "I told him you were down in the cafeteria."

"Really, did he give you a name?"

"Nope, said he wanted to surprise you."

"What did he look like?"

The nurse grinned at her. "Tall, good-looking, blond, wearing a burgundy cashmere sweater to die for."

"Randy?"

"I don't know his name and I'm not giving any more hints away. I'm sure he'll be back up here. Must have missed you in the elevators."

Jenna felt her heart rate pick up. Surely, it had to be Arlen's baby brother—who else would show up on Christmas Day, after she told him not to come? She peeked in on Heather to see that nothing had changed, and all the numbers were stable, then headed for the waiting room.

He was walking back into the room from the exit side and the grin that split his face made her catch her breath. Her brother-in-law had that way about him. He crushed her in a bear hug, both of them laughing and crying at the same time.

"They let me see her. Ah, Jenna, she looks so good."

"I know." She rested her cheek on his chest. The nurse was right, his sweater was soft as milkweed down. "I told you not to come."

"Since when have I done what you said?" He squeezed her again. "You should never have to be alone on Christmas. And by the way, Heather's going to blow right by this thirty-six-hour window. Just in case you're battling being a mom and a nurse right about now."

Jenna rolled her eyes, but felt a tinge of warmth rise in her face. Okay, she was guilty. "You are a saint, I know you are." She locked arms with him and they made their way to side-by-side chairs. "Have you found a hotel yet?"

"Nope. Rented a car and drove right here. I figured some place in Omaha would have a single room."

"I'm right across the street. They give special discounts to family members."

"I'll check in later. Have you had dinner?"

She shook her head. "Not too many places open, and besides, I've not been hungry much."

He gave her an assessing look. "You lose much more weight and the wind will blow right through you."

"Thanks a heap. But the worst is over and we'll get back to some kind of normal."

"I pray that is so."

The concern in his eyes made her throat tighten up. "Yeah, me too."

A few moments of silence passed. Jenna's thoughts drifted back to Heather's new heart. *Beat strong, little heart. Make my daughter well.* Hopefully, the heart couldn't tell time and didn't know one hour from another and would just keep beating.

"Earth to Jenna."

She started. "Sorry. What's in the box?" She motioned to the shopping bag he'd set on the floor.

"Something for Heather."

"She'll love it."

"How do you know? You don't know what it is."

"Because she always loves what you bring her. You are a gifted bringer of presents."

"She is easy to please."

"You want to see if they'll let us both go in?"

"Why not? They let me peek. Surely, the rules can be bent on Christmas Day?"

The nurse who buzzed them in just rolled her eyes, but she started to grin when Randy gave her a box of Godiva chocolates. "You didn't need to bribe me, but since you insist...." She tucked the box behind her back when he motioned like he was going to take it back. "Nah, nah. Don't kid yourself. Just keep the noise down in there so I don't get in trouble." She glanced at the clock. "She should be surfacing from the sedation. We'll try to lighten it and see how she does."

Jenna and Randy nodded and made their way to stand on either side of Heather's bed.

"Hey, sweetie, Mom's here."

Heather's cheeks creased just a bit, in an attempt at a smile. Her eyes fluttered open. Her smile widened. "Hi." The word escaped on a croak.

"There's someone here to see you." Jenna nodded across the bed at the man with suspiciously bright eyes.

Heather blinked, then turned her head slowly. Her smile widened more. "Uncle Randy."

"Good, I was afraid you wouldn't recognize me." He leaned over and kissed her cheek. "You look wonderful."

"Is it Christmas yet?" She cleared her throat. "Can I have water?"

"All you want. The more, the better." Jenna held the glass with a bendable straw for her daughter to sip. "And yes, it is Christmas, and this is our present." She nodded again to Randy.

"The surgery went well?"

"Very well. Dr. Walker said your new heart started beating on the first try and acts like it lived in your chest all its life."

"When can I go home?"

"If that isn't just like the Heather I know and love." Randy patted her shoulder. "I think they may want to keep you here a day or two, just to make sure all is well, you know." He set his shopping bag on the bed. "You up to opening a present?"

She looked at her mother. "No, but Mom can do it for me." She shifted in the bed and gasped. "Ohhhh."

"Major surgery, my daughter. Stay quiet. Randy will open it." Jenna automatically transferred her fingers from woven with Heather's to her wrist, to monitor her pulse. The steady beat reassured her.

Randy nodded and took a red box with a wide gold mesh ribbon and bow from the bag.

"Save the bow."

"Okay." He eased the ribbon off the box and laid it on the bed. From the box, he lifted a book. "Now this comes in two parts." He held it up for her to see, then read its title, *Cross-Country Skiing in Ten Easy Lessons*. "I thought a winter sport would be fun, in honor of the season."

At her delighted grin, he held up a gift certificate. "'To Heather. For all your gear.'"

"Skiing. I'll be able to go skiing, won't I, Mom?"

"I don't know why not." She smiled from her daughter to her favorite brother-in-law. "And I'm sure Randy plans on taking you ASAP."

"And if we don't make skiing this year, you can cash this in for a bike."

"Thanks. Either would be..." Her voice trailed off as she slipped back into sleep.

"Thank you. I told you she'd be pleased."

"Well, I don't usually put girls to sleep with my gifts, but in this case, I'm so grateful I could burst." He stared down at Heather. "Her mind is clear as can be. I thought she'd be all groggy and disoriented."

"Could have been." Jenna heaved a pent-up breath. Relief made her knees tremble.

"How'd she do?" The nurse joined them at the bedside.

"Clear as can be. Only grimaced when she tried to move."

"Good. We'll try to get her transferred to the regular floor as soon as we can. Then sitting up, then up on her feet. Dr. Walker is known for getting his patients moving right away." She checked the machines and used a syringe to add meds to the IV drip. "This should keep her comfortable. The next few hours will tell us a lot. Glad she came to while you were here to enjoy it."

Brother-in-law and sister-in-law looked at each other. *Don't hug me*, thought Jenna. *Don't hug me and talk about the thirty-six-hour window. I just might fall apart.*

"Me too" was all Randy said in response to the nurse as he put the box back in the bag. "Can I take you out to eat?"

"Why, thank you, I'd love to. You'd have to wait until my shift changes, though." The nurse made a bigmouthed O. "Darn, I don't suppose you mean me?"

Jenna chuckled. "You can come if you want."

"You go have a good time. She isn't going to wake up again anytime soon." She started to leave the room. "Merry Christmas."

"Merry Christmas," Randy and Jenna said together.

Jenna hitched her bag over her shoulder. "I'll take you up on the food now." Thirty-six hours and counting. *Please, Lord, keep her safe.*

Chapter Fifteen

Nora

What is it?" Gordon asked when Nora woke with a cry.

"That voice, it won't leave me alone. Every time I close my eyes."

"What voice?"

"In my dreams—it keeps shouting that we killed Charlie."

"It's a nightmare, you know nightmares can't be believed." He reached for her hand in the darkness. "You're cold."

Nora continued as though he hadn't spoken. "The dream is always cold and black and this awful voice, sometimes it shouts, sometimes it whispers, sounds like a snake." She shuddered, then lay stiff, trying to keep the shivers and the pain inside. "I can't find my way out. I can't see anything. My ears hurt." Covering her ears with her hands, she forced the words out. "What if we did?"

They hung in the air, then crashed, sounding like icicles falling from eaves and shattering.

"Did what?"

"Help them kill our son. Maybe they just wanted to harvest the organs."

"Nora, you have to let this go. If he'd still been alive, he would have stayed alive when they turned the machines off. He was gone immediately, you know that." He threw himself back on the pillow with a groan. "You need to ask the doctor for some sleeping pills so we can both get some sleep."

"You think pills would take care of this? My son is killed and I just pop a little pill and everything will be all right?" She could hear the brittle shriek underlying her voice. Surely, she didn't really sound like that. What was the matter with her? Luke said grief played tricks on people.

The bed moved and Gordon sat on the edge. "I'll sleep in the family room. One of us has to get some rest."

"No, let me. I'm the one causing the problem."

"Ah, Nora, it's not you that's the problem. We just have to get through this." He sighed again and lay back down, rolling over to draw her into his arms. "You're freezing."

"I've been freezing ever since that officer came to the door. I thought it was you and my heart nearly leaped out of my chest." Her voice sounded detached from her body. "But when they said Charlie, I couldn't believe it. It couldn't be happening. Your children are not supposed to die before you do." She rolled on her side to face him. "I can't even find God."

"He hasn't moved."

"Then my eyes are blinded, my ears plugged and my soul shriveled." She didn't add, "and it's all His fault." She thought it, though. This wasn't the way life was supposed to be.

She lay still, listening for the accusing voice, her eyes burning until she felt Gordon slip back into slumber. Then she crept out of the bed and made her way in the hall, dimly lit by a night-light in the bathroom, past the closed door to Charlie's room, then down the stairs to curl up on the sofa in the family room, with the afghan she had crocheted several Christmases ago. Granny squares in red, green and white. Perhaps the nightmare wouldn't find her here.

Betsy padded across the tile, her toenails clicking, and climbed up to lay on Nora's feet.

She woke on Christmas morning with her arms around Betsy, the smell of coffee in the air. Christmas morning. She had so much to do. Then...Christmas morning and Charlie was still dead. She stumbled back up the stairs and crawled into her own bed. No more nightmares. Perhaps the answer was not to fall asleep; then the nightmare could not come. The voice, however, seemed impervious to day or night: *"What if you said good-bye too soon?"*

Nora thought briefly of the prime rib she'd purchased and planned on serving for Christmas Day dinner. The thought flitted away as fast as it had arrived. Prime rib was Charlie's favorite. She figured she'd never prepare or probably eat prime rib again.

The garlic mashed potatoes were Christi's favorite and the homemade rolls with poppy seeds on top waiting in the freezer were Gordon's. They'd all voted for pumpkin pie, which she would have baked yesterday.

Yesterday, the day before time telescoped and then vanished, only to reappear cloaked in gray with black blobs. Ugly time that could not be overlooked or forgotten. She'd never look at time the same again.

She started to get up, then collapsed back against the womb of her bed. Rage flicked a forked tongue, sending a hiss that sliced raw tissue in such thin sheets it became transparent. Each sheet exuded pain that multiplied with each breath.

Charlie is dead, and the world dares to dawn Christmas. The words could not yet be spoken, lest they arouse the hiss again. But the thought made her pull the twisted sheets over her head. The silence of the womb. Tears leaked from eyes seared raw. Surely, there could be no more tears. Where did they come from? What well that knew no bottom?

A weight jumped on the bed. Betsy whimpered, nosed the form hidden by the sheets. When Nora failed to respond, she lay down beside her with a sigh.

With no sense of time passed, she heard another sound. Footsteps, Gordon by the weight of them. Betsy's wagging tail brushed her side. Gordon sat down, his hand heavy on her thigh.

Go away. She locked the scream within. *Leave me alone. Maybe if I lie here long enough, I will leave this rotten world behind and find Charlie.*

"Nora, I know you're awake." His voice sandpapered her skin. "We have a daughter too, you know, and she needs you."

"No, she needs her father. You have always been better with her than I am."

"She needs her mother and her father. You have always been there for her — and for me. I can't do it alone."

She could hear the tears in his voice. *But at least he is making an effort.* The familiar voice, which she usually joked about nagging her, intruded now, slathering judgment like butter on hot toast.

"You might feel better if you joined us for a while."

"Joined you where?"

"I started the fire in the living room. We could heat something for supper and eat in there."

"Where the tree is." Her voice broke. The tree, Charlie and Christi putting up the lights. Laughing, teasing each other. "I can't go in there." Every inch of this house held memories of Charlie. At least here in her bed, there weren't so many. At least she could halfway convince herself of the safety here.

"Please, darling." His hand felt warm on her thigh as he stroked gently. "We . . . I need you."

When had Gordon ever said he needed her? She fought through the sludge of apathy, searching for a match for his words.

"Give me a few minutes, I'll try."

"Good. Can I bring you anything?"

"No. Just leave me be."

"I'll heat some sliced turkey breast and stuffing in the microwave."

"None for me."

"But, Nora, you've not eaten for two days." When she didn't answer, he continued, "Susan's been calling."

Why couldn't she make the effort to at least call her best friend back? They shared everything, same prayer group, kids near the same age, both husbands traveled for their companies. They learned Hardanger together, cross-country skied, shared books and jokes. Susan was the sister she'd never had.

Susan who?

The bed moved as Gordon stood up. "You'll come then?"

I said I would. Why did everything want to come out in a growl? A Bible verse flitted through her mind. *"Lo, I am with you always." But, God, I hurt so bad. Where are You? How could You let this happen?*

That was the question. If He was the God of love she'd believed in all these years, how could He let her down like this? Why would He? Maybe He didn't really care as much as she'd always believed? Maybe He wasn't.

She dragged herself from the bed and headed for the bathroom. How she could continue to need the john when she'd not had anything to eat or drink was beyond her. Making sure she didn't look in the mirror, she cupped water in her hands and splashed it on her face. The shock of the cold made her blink. She licked some off her lips and was suddenly so thirsty she could have put her mouth under the faucet and turned it on full force. Instead, she pulled a paper cup from the dispenser, filled and drank it once, then again. Her stomach revolted and she heaved the liquid into the toilet. And Gordon wanted her to eat something—hardly. But she would make an appearance—for Christi's sake, if nothing else. She thought of changing out of her gray sweats, but the act would take far more energy than she could muster. Dampening her fingers under the faucet, she ran them through her hair, lifting the limp strands in the hope they'd fall back where they belonged. Sliding her feet into a pair of moccasins, she headed for the hallway. Betsy jumped off the bed and padded beside her, as if making sure she was really moving.

The smell of turkey made her swallow quickly, but she continued down the stairs, hanging onto the carved oak rail in case her knees gave out like they threatened. She should have brushed her teeth to get rid of the dreadful taste.

Christi and Gordon had set the table in the family room, the game table, where they had spent hours at board games, cards and dominos. She closed her eyes. Could she sit there and smell the food?

"Hi, Mom."

Nora nodded and really looked at her daughter for the first time in the last two days. Christi had lost weight, leaving shadows under her eyes, or maybe the shadow came from her tears. While she'd washed her hair, she'd not put on any makeup, showing her skin was a translucent white, like the snow outside that shone blue in the hollows. At least she'd put on jeans and a sweater, not worn her rattiest sweats like her mother.

Nora clenched her elbows with her hands and went to stand in front of the fireplace. Gordon had built a fire in here too. Betsy sat on the braided rug at her feet, staring into the flickering light.

"Would you like some coffee?" Gordon asked.

Nora shook her head. "It wouldn't stay down."

"Tea? Herbal tea? Hot chocolate?"

"You always say crackers are the best to try." Christi opened the cupboard and retrieved the soda cracker box. "7UP might help." She brought the drink and a few crackers on a plate.

I should be taking care of her, not the other way around. Nora took the offering with a nod. A smile was beyond her. She sipped the sparkling beverage, and when that didn't come up immediately, she nibbled on a saltine.

"How about if we pull the chairs in closer to the fire and eat there?" Gordon stood beside her, rubbing his hands in the heat.

Whatever. Had she answered or just thought it? But when the chair bumped against the back of her legs, she sat down. If she sat any closer, the fire might melt the furniture or her clothes.

Gordon and Christi filled their plates from the food on the counter and each took a chair. Where there should have been laughter and teasing conversation, the crackling fire and chewing took their place.

Nora leaned forward, elbows on her knees, nibbling still on the same cracker. When her throat dried out, she sipped the drink so she could swallow the paste in her mouth. But it stayed down. When her face felt like it was melting, she leaned back in the chair with a gut-dragging sigh.

"Susan called again." Christi spoke softly as if afraid to disturb the eddies of Christmases past.

Nora nodded. "Tell her I'll call her tomorrow."

"She said if you didn't call, she was coming over here."

"There have been a lot of calls. I left them on the machine," Gordon said.

That meant Gordon hadn't wanted to talk to anyone on the phone either. She looked at her husband out of the corner of her eye. He had put his half-eaten plate on the floor and Betsy was cleaning it up. Gordon did not believe in letting the animals eat off the plates for humans.

Nora finished the one cracker and started on another. Maybe hot tea would melt the ice inside as the fire was doing its job on the outside. She rose and moved to the stove. Gordon had set several kinds of tea on the counter and the teakettle steamed on a back burner.

"I'll make it if you want."

"No. I'm okay. Anyone else want some?"

When they shook their heads, she poured hot water over a tea bag that she took without even looking at the label. Hot and flavored, that would do. Returning to her overstuffed chair, she sank into the comfort of its solid form, tucking her feet up beneath her.

When the phone rang a while later, she shook her head. Christi started to rise, then sank back down. Gordon was sound asleep, head resting on the cushiony chair back, mouth slightly open. At least someone was getting some sleep.

She stared up at the mantel, where the Christmas stockings hung limp. Santa hadn't visited this house, nor any of his elves.

At the thought of elves, Nora remembered Charlie's story of the little girl wanting a kitten for her mother.

"Did Charlie pick up the kitten?"

Christi shook her head. "He'd planned to do that...yesterday, just before Christmas." A tremor shook her.

Nora's eyes filled. Would the little girl ever believe in Santa Claus again? Would any of them?

Chapter Sixteen

Jenna

$\mathcal{M}$om?"

"I'm here. Merry Christmas."

"Is it today?" Heather moved her hand to touch her mother's as it lay on the bed.

Jenna slid her fingers between her daughter's. One more thing to be grateful for, the nails without a blue tinge, warm to the touch, with no fever.

"Is Uncle Randy really here or did I dream it?"

"He's here. He and I have been taking turns watching you sleep."

After a few sips of water, mother and daughter eyed one another.

"I really have a new heart?" Heather said, a tiny smile pulling at one corner of her mouth.

"You really do."

The smile faded. "Someone died, then, huh?"

"Yes." Jenna blinked and sniffed. The thought of that other mother hadn't left her. Did she have family to help her through this? A husband, other children? How could she bear it?

"Hey, look who's awake." The nurse stopped at the foot of the bed. "You're looking mighty chipper for a girl who's been through such major surgery." She checked the monitors and laid the stethoscope against Heather's ribs. "Sure enough, beatin' away."

"When can I go home?"

The nurse rolled her eyes. "Can't keep a good one down. You'll have to ask the doctor, but it'll be a few days before you can think of that. First you'll get moved to surgical floor and that just might be today." She smiled at Jenna. "What a merry Christmas, eh? We are all rejoicing for and with you." She turned back to Heather. "Besides, there is a very good-looking man who is asking if he can come in again. You want to see him?"

Heather nodded. "My uncle Randy. Are you married?"

The nurse looked at Jenna. "Is your daughter always a match-maker?" Then she turned back to Heather and held up her left hand. "No rings doesn't always mean no man in my life."

"Oh."

"I'll go get your uncle. You just behave yourself and get stronger by the minute. How's the pain level?"

"Tolerable."

"For now. We want to make sure to keep on top of it. Fighting pain slows down the healing. So, don't be trying to tough it out, okay?"

Heather rolled her eyes. "All right. But I hate to miss out on anything. I have a new heart!" She squeezed her mother's hand. "And we have a new life, huh, Mom?"

"We do." Jenna held the water glass and straw out. "Drink lots."

"So how's my girl doing?" Randy paused in the doorway. "Are you the same Heather I watched sleep for all those hours?"

"I am." Heather flinched when she tried to push herself up higher on the pillow.

"Let us help you." Jenna nodded to Randy, and with each of them taking an arm, they scooted her up a bit.

Heather took in a deep breath and flinched some more. "Okay, no moving and no deep breathing." She let out a sigh. "Now I feel like I just ran a block or two." She stared into her mother's eyes. "I will be able to run, won't I?"

"I imagine you will have to work up to it slowly, but I've read of other heart transplants that run. Not sure you'll want to enter races—and this will take a lot of conditioning—but, gee, maybe we could even run together."

"You used to run?"

Jenna nodded. She used to do a lot of things, but over the last few years, her world had narrowed down to work and taking care of her daughter. Doctor's appointments, hospitalizations, school when she could, physical therapy, home-schooling when necessary and working the ER, her place of respite. What would a normal life feel like? Look like? Taste like? *Maybe...what a magical concept.* She looked up to see Randy watching her and Heather sleeping peacefully with a slight smile. *Lord, give her good dreams to go along with this new life. I know she's been afraid to dream, just like I have.*

When Randy looked back at Heather, Jenna studied him. The resemblance to his older brother was uncanny, and yet two men could not have had more different personalities. Arlen had the oldest-child drive to succeed, to be the best. The U.S. Marines had suited him well with all the challenges—yet one could not have asked for a more caring husband. His shoes would be hard to fill.

While she'd met a few men worth dating, none had passed the test of a handicapped child. She knew Heather had wanted a father, and her mother to not be alone. That had been one of her worries, that if she died, her mother would be all alone.

Jenna blinked and looked down at the white blanket that rose and fell over her daughter's expanding and contracting chest, that protected that new heart. Would this heart be as loving as her other poor, damaged one? What of the young person that gave it up for her? Was he or she loving and kind? *Oh, Lord, visit those parents with extra special love today. Christmas without their child. How can that mother and father bear it?*

Randy came around the bed and stood behind her, his strong hands rested on her shoulders, then began to rub them and work up her neck. "You can let all this tension go now, you know."

"Easier said than done." She let her head fall forward. Ah, how good that felt.

"Do you ever go for a massage?"

"Never have the time."

"We need to get Heather to a good massage therapist. That will help her circulation."

"How do you know all this?"

"I've been taking some classes."

"Really? How come you never said anything?" She turned to look up into his face.

"I don't know. It started as a hobby, but I've learned that I have good hands for it. Mother thinks I'm nuts, if I give up my job and start all over again."

"How is your mother?" She'd had a hard time dealing with the death of her son, even though he'd often tried to prepare her for that possibility, just as he had his wife. While an option in theory, preparing for it didn't hold water in reality.

At least Arlen's parents had made the effort to remain Heather's grandparents, doting on their first grandchild and keeping in touch in spite of the miles. Quite unlike Jenna's own mother.

"She can't wait to come visit."

Jenna leaned her neck from side to side. "I'm going to fall asleep."

"Would that be such a bad thing?" His thumbs dug into the knots at the base of her scalp.

"I think if you want to change directions in life, you ought to do it. Grab whatever makes you happy."

"I'm working on that."

She puzzled on that comment a bit, then straightened when she heard the nurse enter the room.

"Hey, I can find you more necks to work on if you are so inclined."

Randy patted Jenna's shoulder and stepped back. "You look like you have good news."

"I do. We are moving this little chickie out of here and onto the floor. She is doing that well. So, if you two want to go have supper or some such, within an hour or so, we will have her all set up in room 416."

"Isn't this awfully early?" Jenna's nursing instincts kicked in. "All I've read—"

"Dr. Walker feels that the sooner we get her on her feet, the better. She doesn't need our services any longer. I'll tell Heather where you are when she wakes up."

I'm afraid to leave her. Don't be silly. An argument picked up again in her head. Always, mother versus nurse.

"I promise we'll take good care of her." The nurse turned from checking the monitors and the drip and made shooing motions with her hands. "We'll miss you all here, but the next floor is lovely."

"Come along, I'll buy you the finest Christmas supper this hospital makes." Randy picked up the shopping bag she'd brought with the present for her daughter and took her arm.

Jenna leaned over the bed and kissed Heather's cheek. "See you in a bit," she whispered.

"We could go back to the hotel for dinner," Randy said as he punched the down button on the elevator.

"Whichever you want, but we should let them know."

"They have your cell number?"

"Of course, I..." Jenna shook her head. "I'm acting crazy, I know." She leaned back against the side of the elevator. "Let's do the hotel. I'm sure they have better food."

"Only if you promise to really eat and not worry about Heather."

"I don't worry, I..." She glanced up to see a teasing look in his eyes. He did have wonderful eyes. "How come you've never married?" The words popped out without passing through the barrier of her brain.

The elevator stopped at the sky bridge floor and he waited until they were walking across the bridge before answering. "If you really want to know..." He paused.

"I do."

"The woman I fell in love with was already taken."

Jenna tucked her hand through his arm. "That's sad. Surely, you can find another."

"Oh, I think I'm a one-woman man."

She glanced up to find him staring down at her. Smiling up at him, she added, "Just tell Heather, she'll find someone for you."

"Maybe I'll do that." They stopped at the entrance to the dining room and then followed the hostess to their white-clothed table, where a candle in a red globe, surrounded by pieces of pine and holly, lent a festive air. A three-level tier of red-and-cream-speckled poinsettias filled a red-draped round table in the center of the room and Christmas music played softly in the background.

"I should have changed clothes, this looks so lovely." Jenna smiled up at Randy as he seated her. "Thank you." Her mother-in-law had taught her sons well in the manners department. Few of the men she'd dated had their grace. Perhaps that was one of the reasons she'd quit dating. No one ever measured up.

"You look fine." Randy took his seat and spread his napkin in his lap. "Now, I suggest we start with eggnog to keep up the traditions of the season, then turkey with all the trimmings."

"And blue cheese on the salad." How good it felt to have someone else make suggestions. She'd have stared at the menu, thinking that making a choice would take too much effort. "You know, this is the first Christmas Day dinner I've ever eaten in a hotel or anyplace not home or at someone's house." She glanced around the room. "I guess lots of people do this — surely, these aren't all relatives or friends with someone in the hospital."

"I've traveled plenty over the holidays, so this is not unusual." He clasped his hands on the table and leaned forward. "Have you given any thought to how your life will change now?"

"Some. But we're not out of the woods yet, you know. These first three months will be somewhat restricted. That's when the threat of rejection is the highest. We have to get her immune system built back up, but that is the same system that will try to reject the heart."

"Even with as good a match as this one?"

"Even so. The list of meds she'll be taking is as long as my arm. I don't know how people without some medical training get through it."

"They have advisors and visiting nurses and phone lines to call for help when it's needed."

"You've been studying up on transplants?"

"My favorite bedtime reading."

Their waiter came and took their orders and their conversation traveled the world as he told her about the places he'd been.

"I'd love to go to New York City," she said in response to one of his questions.

He finished chewing a mouthful of turkey. "We could do that."

She stared at him. "You mean that?"

"Of course. If Heather would like to go, we'll take her too."

"She's always dreamed of going to New York. This could be a celebration for her and her new heart."

"Just tell me when."

She stared across the table at him. "You really do mean this, don't you?"

"I do."

Those two words sent a shiver up and down her spine.

Chapter Seventeen

Nora

They made it through Christmas Day. Endless days to follow.

Nora took out the thought and studied it again. Perfect civility had been the rule, as if they were all strangers being polite, but at least they were together. If being together meant being in one room. They'd not even gone into the living room, or at least she hadn't, and they'd all gone to their rooms about the same time. Gordon had started the fire in there for nothing. She lay as still as possible, not sure if he was sleeping, but not wanting to talk. Would tomorrow be a better day?

Would there ever be a good day again?

Sometime later, with Gordon sleeping and puffing gently, she slid out from under the covers and grabbed her robe from the hook on the back of the bathroom door. She made her way downstairs. Coals still winked in the fireplace, so she added a couple of sticks of pitch wood and stood to watch the flames catch. Surely, there was a message there. She added a couple of hunks of pine and retreated to the chair she'd hidden in earlier. Not that she was invisible, but the barriers had surely been locked in place. Gordon was right. She needed to help Christi. Gordon needed her. But how could she help anyone when she couldn't help herself? *God, I want my son back.* In spite of her efforts, tears leaked and blurred the flames now licking at the split wood.

Mesmerized, she stared into the fire, too cell-aching weary to even follow a line of thought. She heard Betsy's toenails on the tile and then felt a furry muzzle on her bent knees. She'd sat again with her feet tucked to the side of the chair, not an easy pose, considering her long legs. But she needed to be as compact as possible, pulled in both outside and in. If she could be a turtle, perhaps the pain would bounce off the shell and ricochet off into space.

Betsy whimpered, one little cry deep in her throat. It sounded like a baby crying. Did she understand that Charlie would not be back, or was she just picking up on the pain of all of them? Nora leaned forward and clasped her hands over the dog's ears, rubbing gently.

"Poor girl, you try so hard to take care of us, to comfort. If only we could make things all right again. But this time, I can't. I can't make things all better, no matter how much I wish I could. Only God can, and He isn't doing anything. At least not that I can see." She leaned back in the chair again, one elbow propped on the padded chair arm. The fire crackled and snapped. She glanced at the mantel to see one of the pine boughs hanging over the edge. Out of place, marring the plan of the mantel decoration. A reminder of the endless day yesterday. As if pulled by a master puppeteer working her strings, she rose and pulled the pine bough off the mantel and threw it in the fire. That made another bough stick out wrong. It, too, disappeared into the fire. Then another and another. The fire blazed, voraciously devouring the drying pine needles. When the mantel was empty, but for the candles and stockings, she headed for the staircase and ripped off the garland she'd so lovingly wrapped around the railing. Bit by bit, she threw it in the fire too, not bothering to even remove the wire. The fire leaped and roared, shouting for more.

"Nora, what are you doing?" Gordon pulled the last of the garland from her hands. "You want to set the house on fire? A chimney fire at the least."

"Leave me alone." She headed for the table in the bay window. Everything was out of place. Or too neatly arranged. The table arrangement, which she'd admired as one of her better craft projects, now stood too perfect with its pine and cedar branches. Ripping them out of the Styrofoam base, she carried them to the fireplace, but Gordon stopped her from throwing them in.

"Let it die down first." When she ignored him, he grabbed her around the shoulders and held her against his chest. She struggled, calling him names as if she had no idea who he was. "Nora, Nora, that's enough." His voice softened as she pummeled him with her fists and then collapsed against him, sobbing and making no sense.

"I can't. I can't. I can't."

"You can't what?"

"I don't know. Christi, you, me, I can't. I just can't."

Gordon sank down in the chair, pulling her with him, and watched the fire burn back to normal, the loops of wire blackened and empty. Nora finally curled against him and fell asleep in his arms.

When she woke to find herself on his lap, and him asleep, she pulled back and stared around. The plundered mantel said her frenzy had not been a dream. *What ever possessed me?* She laid her head back down on Gordon's shoulder. If the pain wasn't bad enough, now she'd gone loony tunes.

She started to push herself upright, but Gordon stirred and shook his head, pressing a kiss on her head. "You don't have to move."

"I'm smashing you."

"Remember when we used to sit in this chair together?" He rubbed his arm. "Guess I'm not as pliable as I used to be."

"Last night"—she wanted, no, needed to explain as best she could—"I saw one branch hanging off the mantel, out of place...." Her voice faded, then grew stronger. "When I saw it flare and burn, I could have thrown the whole house in. You think I'm a pyromaniac at heart?"

"No, I think you're a grieving mother who needed some kind of outlet. We could go skiing this morning, if you like."

"All I want is for Charlie to come pounding down the stairs, asking what's for breakfast."

"Me too."

She recognized the desolation in his voice, perhaps for the first time. It matched hers.

"Luke said he'd be by today to finish planning the memorial service. I told him Friday would be all right. He put the notice in the paper."

"Thank God for Luke. How will we get through two days until then?" There would be more waiting....Waiting now for the funeral to be over. Then, after that, waiting for—the exhaustion that dried Nora's bones exhaled deep inside—waiting for each day to hit midnight and become another.

"Perhaps we should check the answering machine. I haven't since the twenty-fourth."

Nora clutched her robe more tightly around her neck. "Where's Betsy?"

Gordon stretched to look around them. "I don't know."

Nora pushed herself off his lap and to her feet. "Betsy?" When there was no sound of the dog coming, she headed up the stairs. Perhaps she was on her bed. But when she came even with Charlie's door, she saw it was partly open. Surely, it had been closed last night. She'd not opened it since…She steeled herself to look inside. There lay Betsy on his bed, head on her paws, tail barely moving.

"Come on, girl, let's get you some breakfast." Nora closed her eyes to the collection of reptiles and slapped her thigh for the dog to come. *I'm not going in there to get you. I just can't do that yet.* "Come, Betsy." The dog rose, stretched and, after looking around the room, made her way to the door. She paused and looked over her shoulder; then with tail and ears down, she came through the door to stop by Nora's side.

Nora closed the door softly, making sure of the click. Surely, there would be someone who would want Charlie's critters. But when she started down the stairs, another wave of grief caught her behind the knees, sucking her down until she sat on a step and buried her face in her knees. He couldn't be gone, he had to be coming back.

Betsy sat beside her, whimpering and trying to push her nose between Nora's head and arms. When that didn't work, she licked her ear and pressed as close as she could.

Nora felt Gordon come up the stairs and sit down beside them, laying his arm over her quivering shoulders.

"Mom?" Christi asked from behind her. Her voice sounded newly frightened.

"Come sit with us," Gordon said.

When Christi took the stair below them, Nora reached out and gathered her closer. "Sorry. Betsy went in his room and that just wiped me out again."

"I fed his critters."

"Thanks." Gordon laid his cheek on Nora's hair. "Come on, honey, I'll make the coffee."

"What happened to the decorations?" Christi stared at the stair railing and the fragments of garland on each step.

Nora dried her eyes on the edge of her robe. "I burned them last night." She could see the scratched streaks on the oak finish from the wire being ripped away. What had possessed her? "What a mess."

"Wow, Mom."

"We can fix that. Don't worry about it." Gordon stood and reached for his wife's hand.

Nora let him pull her up, but all she wanted was to go back to bed. The crick in her neck wouldn't let go even with stretches, and a headache was starting behind her eyes. She glanced up at her husband, reading his concern and his own pain in his eyes. He'd said he needed her. The least she could do was help with breakfast. She reached for Christi's hand and the three of them padded down the stairs behind Betsy.

Later, after toast and coffee, Nora stared at her Bible, journal and devotional book waiting for her on the shelf by the bay window. Would it help to write this all down, or would it make it worse? At least for the moment, her eyes were dry. Gordon had chosen to listen to messages and make notes. She knew she had to call Susan back, but could she talk without descending into the pit again? Journal or Susan? Both promised more tears. Just the thought of tears made her eyes burn again and her throat start to clog. *Call Susan and tell her you can't talk yet, but you will call her again, tomorrow.*

She would, when Gordon got off the phone. He'd started the fire again; looking at the mantel made her flinch. She'd never dreamed she was capable of such destruction. But then, she'd never dreamed she'd lose her son either. With all Gordon's traveling, she'd tried to prepare herself if something had happened to him. After all, planes did go down, terrorists did set off bombs, cars did crash. And he'd been late and not phoned.

He hung up the phone and, closing his eyes, rolled his head around to loosen his neck muscles. Sleeping in the chair last night hadn't done much for him either.

"Gordon, why didn't you call?"

"Huh?" He blinked at her. "When?"

"From Germany."

"My cell went on the blink. I'd dropped it earlier and it worked for a bit, then quit. I was running late or I'd have called from the airport." His expression suggested, *What difference does it make?*

"Oh." She knew better than to let her imagination run away with her. There would always be a plausible explanation for anything Gordon did. She knew that.

"You were worried."

She shook her head, jerky little motions that only built tension, didn't release it. "You know how I get."

"Sorry. I was so intent on getting on that plane that I would have run over anyone who got in my way."

They have phones on the planes these days. But she didn't say that either. He hadn't seen this as an emergency. Why did she let her mind take over like that?

"I'm sorry, Nora, so very sorry."

She knew he was referring to more than not calling. "Sorry." What a sorry word. Instead of trying to talk around the lump building in her throat again, she just nodded. "I'm going to call Susan and then go take a shower. What time is Luke coming?"

"Ten thirty or so."

She glanced at her wrist, but hadn't put her watch on. The clock said nine. This promised to be a long day. If only she could sleep most of it away. Without the nightmares. By the time she climbed the stairs again, she had to lean against the wall. How could she be so tired? She'd always prided herself on keeping in good shape, one of the reasons she chose speed-walking for the warmer months and cross-country skiing as soon as the snow fell. The thought of putting on her gear made her choke. She peeled herself off the wall and entered her bedroom. But instead of turning left into the bathroom, she crossed to the king-sized bed and crawled under the covers. Even fifteen minutes of sleep would help.

Seemingly seconds later, she felt a hand on her shoulder, gently shaking her.

"Nora, Luke is here."

Fighting to open her eyes, Nora shook her head. Every bone and muscle in her body ached. She rolled over with a groan. "I can't face him looking like this." She hoped he'd take pity on her and leave her alone. But he stood there looking at her. "All right, give me ten minutes." She pulled herself from the haven of mindlessness and staggered to the bathroom, shucking her clothes while the shower warmed.

True to her word, she walked down the stairs fifteen minutes later, her hair not fully dried but pulled back in a clip. There had been no time for makeup, but at least she was clean; and navy cords with a cream cable-knit sweater were better than her sweats. She found the others in the family room, sipping mugs of spiced apple cider and playing social chitchat. At least Gordon and Luke were. Christi was curled in one of the overstuffed chairs, hiding behind her hair and the steaming mug. When they saw her, Luke rose and came to give her a hug.

"You're getting through," he said softly, searching her face.

"Not very well." If only he weren't so nice.

"This isn't a contest, there are no judges. We'll get through these next days by the grace of God, like we do every day." His gentle voice made her eyes burn again.

"Right." The word had to squeeze past the boulder that had resumed lodging in her throat.

She shook her head when Gordon raised his mug. "Nothing now, thank you." More strangled words, but they had some semblance of normalcy. Taking the remaining chair, she clenched her fingers together to keep them from shaking.

As Gordon listed the order of the service and the get together afterward, which the women were hosting at the church, Nora felt she had stepped out of herself to watch the proceedings from up in a corner. She'd heard of detachment before, but if this was that, it caught her by surprise. Instead of participating, she was just watching. Strange.

"Do you have any questions?" Luke asked.

Gordon sat with his hand against his forehead, shielding his face. His whole body looked shrunken in on itself. He shook his head. "I got a call a bit ago. The cremation is finished. We can pick up the ashes tomorrow."

Nora stared at her husband. Why hadn't he told her? *"Because you were sleeping and he was kind enough not to wake you,"* the judgmental voice challenged. No longer off in the corner, sorrow hit her like the water surge of a hurricane, tumbling her over and over, then sucking her under.

Betsy nosed her clenched hands, so Nora petted the dog,

trying to focus on short yellow fur and not a container of ashes — all that was left of her son.

Just get through. Please, God, just get us through this, that's all I ask right now. The insidious little voice snickered and changed to a new question: *"Why bother when He didn't answer you when you prayed for Charlie to get better?"* Nora gritted her teeth.

Chapter Eighteen

Jenna

Thirty-six hours and no signs of rejection, other than a slightly elevated temperature, which Jenna knew was often the case after major surgery. Still, she found herself watching the monitors while Heather slept.

"How's she doing?" Randy stopped at the foot of the bed and spoke softly.

"Good." Jenna passed on the latest information.

Continuing around to Jenna's side, Randy nudged her shoulder with his. "I thought we were going to have breakfast together."

"I left you a message. I woke up at five and couldn't go back to sleep, so I came over here."

"Did you eat?"

She shook her head. "I wasn't hungry then." Her stomach growled at this; she blushed, Randy laughed.

"I can stay here while you go eat, or I can go get you something."

"So, either way I'm going to eat? Getting a bit bossy, aren't you?" Her smile said she was teasing. He sounded so much like his brother that she had to shake her head.

"What? You need a third option?"

"No, I'll eat." She glanced at her watch. Nine thirty. "I

didn't realize it was this late. Dr. Walker came by and said she's doing so well, she'll be dangling this morning."

"Dangling?"

"Sitting up, feet over the side of the bed. Precursor to standing on the floor."

"I see. And all of this with plenty of supervision of course?"

"Of course. The duty nurse said to let her know when she wakes."

"Okay, I can handle that. Now, which eating option are you planning on taking?"

Jenna thought a moment. None of them until after Heather's therapy. "How about a bagel and cream cheese?"

"Coffee?"

"They'll bring me all the coffee I want here on the floor."

He shuddered. "I'm pickier than that for mine, but I'll be right back. You'll have to take my choice on the bagel."

Jenna nodded absently, already thinking about Heather's next milestone.

"That your hubby?" the nurse asked when she came in to check on Heather.

"No, brother-in-law." As she answered, she wondered briefly about the unavailable woman he pined for. A loss for that woman. Randy was wonderful.

"Well, he's one good-looking hunk, that's for sure."

"Is she talking about Uncle Randy?" Heather asked, her voice still half asleep.

"Yes, she is."

"She's right. Has he gone?"

"You think he'd leave without telling you good-bye?" Jenna patted Heather's hand. "He just went to get me a bagel."

"You don't have to be here all the time, you know."

"What would you have me do?"

"You could go shopping, to a movie, catch up on some sleep, talk on the phone—cell phones are allowed in here. You are going to have a life now." Her voice perked up. "Like me."

"Good point, how come I never thought of that?" She smiled at her daughter. "Is there someone you'd like to talk to?"

"Grandma M., then Grammie, and..." A yawn caught her. "And I think Dr. Avery to tell him thank you and Merry Christmas."

Strange, there isn't one friend her age she wants to call. That will be one thing to remedy, finding friends for Heather.

"And one other thing. Could you find a computer and tell my group my good news? This all happened so fast I didn't even get to tell them I was leaving."

No, Jenna reminded herself. She would not need to find friends for her daughter. Heather was more than capable. "Of course." Jenna took paper and pen from her purse. "Give me the address."

Heather gave it to her and looked up to see Randy entering the room, along with the nurse, who was laughing at something he'd said.

"Look who's awake." He handed Jenna a small tray with orange juice, plus the requested bagel.

"Okay, m'dear, you ready to roll?" The nurse, hands on hips, looked at Heather over her half-glasses.

Heather nodded. "I get to walk, right?"

"We'll do a little dangling first and see how you respond."

"Do you want me to leave?" Randy asked. Jenna thought he looked like a man whose wife was having their first baby.

"No." Heather stared at him, shaking her head just a little, then glancing down at her hospital gown.

"I think we can preserve her modesty." The nurse looked to Jenna, who nodded too.

They lowered the bed and flattened the head so she was sitting nearly straight up. Heather gasped when she moved her feet toward the edge and sat up with her own muscles.

"No rush now, we'll take it easy."

Jenna tucked the gown around Heather's back and laid a hand on her shoulder to feel her daughter quivering.

"Okay, now swing your legs over slowly," the nurse instructed.

Heather inched her heels toward the side of the bed, hanging onto the nurse's forearm. Jenna held her breath. She'd helped patients do this hundreds of times through the years, but this was her daughter, with a brand-new heart. *Breathe, woman, don't go light-headed. That's Heather's prerogative, not yours.*

The nurse scooted the IV line out of the way. "Good, you're almost there. Feeling faint? Don't forget to breathe, there, girlfriend."

Heather widened her eyes, a tiny smile all that she'd spend on the comment. With her lower lip locked between her teeth, all her focus zeroed in on sitting upright and letting her feet hang over the edge.

When her feet hung straight down from her knees, and she was fairly close to straight up, she let out a *whoosh*. "Made it."

Jenna didn't dare glance at Randy, for if his eyes wore the sheen she could feel in her own, she knew she'd start to bawl right then and there. The victory of the moment felt all the sweeter for sharing it with family. So many lonely days in the past. "Way to go, sweetheart. Way to go."

Randy gave her a thumbs-up sign. "You did it. How's it feel?"

"Wobbly. I don't think I'll be walking yet."

"No, but standing this afternoon." The nurse put her stethoscope to Heather's back. "Good and clear. Just what we like to hear." She looked into the girl's eyes. "You want to hear?" When Heather nodded, she slipped the earpieces into Heather's ears and held the disc against her back.

Heather grinned. "Awesome."

The nurse put the stethoscope back in her pocket. "Awesome is right. You got a real thumper there. How you feeling?"

"Like I ran a mile."

"Okay. Wiggle your toes for me and flex your ankles. Let's get that circulation moving. Good girl, that's enough for now. Next milestone is standing up."

When Heather was lying down again, with the bed propped back up, she puffed out her cheeks and blew out a breath. "You know, tiring as that was, I can tell I'm getting more air than I have for a long time. I've been weaker than this at times at home lying on the couch."

"Well, on that happy note, I have something for you here, and then I need to head for the airport." Randy set a small package next to Heather.

"But you already gave me my presents."

"This is extra."

She oohed and aahed over the delicate heart-shaped locket, but her eyelids were drooping even as she thanked Randy.

He kissed her cheek. "I'll see you again, soon."

"At home?"

"For sure." He turned to Jenna. "Walk me out?"

Halfway through the door, Jenna heard Heather's drowsy voice: "Find a computer, Mom."

"Yes, ma'am."

Jenna stuck her hand around Randy's elbow, something she'd been doing for years. But this time she wished she hadn't, and quickly removed it. Something was different. She puzzled on that as they walked down the hall and waited for the elevator and tried to think of something to say. *Other than don't go?* The small voice chuckled with glee.

Everyone always left her. But not Heather. *Lord, why am I fussing like this?*

Once at the sky bridge, he stopped beside the arrangement of poinsettias. "I'm all packed and checked out, so…" He paused and studied her for a moment. "Is there anything I can send you? Do for you?"

"Cards cheer Heather, your phone calls always mean a lot to both of us." She felt close to tears. All the emotion of the arrival of Heather's new heart, the surgery, Christmas miracles, it was beginning to break her down. She was not a sniffer.

"You let me know when you're ready for New York. If you need me, all you have to do is call."

Jenna nodded. She knew that, but as always, she hated to be a burden. The fear of becoming like her mother nagged at her more often than she cared to admit. She never had liked people that whined.

Randy bent a little so he was looking right into her eyes. "I mean that, Jenna. After all, I have a vested interest in that young lady up there. I have to take her skiing."

Back on safe ground, talking about Heather. Randy's hazel eyes, so close to her own, blazed right through her fatigue to her core. What was the matter with her? "She might not be ready to ski this year, but next for sure."

"Would you come too?"

"Sure. I'm not a skier, but I'd love a trip to just about anywhere."

"I could teach you."

The intensity of his gaze forbade the eye roll she had planned. Instead, she heard her voice adopt a "shut down" mode that people at work knew was her "don't mess with me" voice. "I don't take chances with my health. I am the chief provider here, and if I can't work, we don't eat." *Or have a roof over our heads.* She looked up to find him studying her. Her smile tightened enough for her to notice, hoping he hadn't.

"I thought Arlen's pension…" Randy looked like the next moment he'd be taking his wallet out of his back pocket. Dismayed at how this good-bye was progressing, Jenna hurried to end it.

"It wasn't a great amount, him dying so young. Besides, I put some of that aside every month in Heather's college fund. Now she'll be able to use it." She forced a cheeky grin. "Good news, huh?"

He reached out to hug her tightly; then he stepped back quickly. "See you soon."

She watched him stride over the sky bridge heading to the parking garage and waved when he glanced back. The imprint left by his arms stayed warm all the way back to the elevator. She pushed the up button and then grimaced. The computer. She'd promised to find a computer.

After locating one, with the friendly assistance of a hospital volunteer, she settled into a chair. She logged on with only a minimum of trouble and went to the site, clicking on the chat room icon. Once in, she followed the instructions Heather had her write down and typed in the message.

Hi, everyone, This is Heather's mom. We
have wonderful news. Heather received a new
heart on Dec. 23. Her new heart started
beating immediately, and other than post-
surgical pain, she is doing well. She is
back on a regular floor and asking when she
can go home.

She wanted you all to know and I can't
begin to tell you how grateful I am for all
your prayers. We rushed out without a laptop or she would be able to chat with you
in person.

Again, our thanks,

Heather and her mother

Jenna glanced at the number of posts since December 22, when she knew Heather had been on last, but decided not to read them unless Heather asked her to. Switching to her own account, she wrote a general message and sent it to her family, Arlen's family—at least those who had stayed in contact—and several friends at work. Signing off, she thought longingly of the bed waiting for her at the hotel. Surely, Heather would sleep for a couple of hours at least. She flipped her cell phone open and called the nurses' station on four. After leaving a message for her daughter, she made her sleepy way to her room and collapsed on the bed, which had already been made up.

Chapter Nineteen

Nora

The memorial service went well, someone told Nora. Whatever that meant. Since she'd ordered herself to remain frozen so she wouldn't wail or collapse, she just nodded her thanks. Some of Charlie's friends had told stories about him, one girl unable to finish because of her tears. If she didn't look at people's faces, she could hang on to her control. Shredding tear-soaked tissues helped. When a young man on crutches stopped in front of them, Nora tried to smile at him, but her cheeks refused to move.

"If he hadn't been taking me home, he wouldn't have been on that road at that time." He leaned on his crutches to blow his nose. "I'm so sorry. Charlie was the greatest."

"It's not your fault," Gordon said gently as he patted the boy's shoulder. "Some things just happen."

Nora nodded. *Say something. Help him.* But she couldn't think of a word to say.

After he stumped away, she clung to Gordon's arm, and they stayed close together, holding each other up, thanking people for coming and listening to Charlie remembrances. They moved through the crowd, gracious on the outside. But Nora was screaming on the inside. They found Christi huddled with two friends on the steps to the altar. While their eyes showed they'd been crying, Christi said she'd be right with her folks.

"Thank you, Luke," Gordon said as they were slowly making their way to the door and their pastor stopped in front of them.

"This was one of the harder ones." Luke shook his head. "God has gotten us through this far and He won't quit now."

"Are you sure?" Nora blinked repeatedly, anything to stem the sobs now burning at the back of her eyes and throat, dangerously melting her icy resolve.

"Yes, Nora, Gordon, my dear friends, I am absolutely sure. I know that right now you are struggling with that, but when one of us is hurting, we all are and the Holy Spirit has promised that when we can't pray, He will pray for us."

Susan Watson, Nora's best friend and a fireball in human form, barreled through the door. "I'm sorry, Benny is sick and I couldn't find anyone to watch him until John came home."

"That's okay." Nora steeled herself for the hug she knew was coming. So far, she'd maintained, but this was Susan, with whom she'd shared much of her life in these last few years.

"What a mob."

"And many have already left." Luke shook Gordon's hand. "Call me any time and if I don't hear from you, I'll call."

"Thank you."

Someone she didn't remember hurried by, squeezed her arm, then said, "Let me know how we can help."

If one more person says, "Let me know how I can help you," I will run screaming or fly in their face. Nora kept her muscles stiff to keep from doing either.

Susan studied her and seemed to understand how fragile

her control was. She hugged Gordon and squeezed Nora's hand. "I'll be over tomorrow."

"Take care of Benny first."

"He'll probably be all better by then. You know how little kids bounce back." Benny had been her surprise child, after she'd already started early menopause. She patted Nora's shoulder. "Can I bring you anything?"

"No, but if you'll take home some of the things others have brought, that would be a help." Nora looked toward the door where Christi waited. She tapped Gordon's arm and nodded toward their daughter, then told Susan, "I'll see you tomorrow."

"I see." Gordon guided her toward the door with a gentle hand in the middle of her back.

When they were finally in the car, Nora buckled her seat belt and slumped against the door. How she had gotten through it was beyond her. She glanced over her shoulder to see Christi with her head pillowed on the seat back, eyes closed, her jaw clenched. One tear squeezed from beneath her eyelid and trickled down her cheek.

Nora reached between the seats of the SUV and patted her daughter's knee.

"Mom, don't." The words came out strangled.

"Okay." She rolled her lips together. Even one small act of kindness was too hard to accept. It shattered the hard-won control, and with that, the tears would come back; this time, they might never stop. Gordon pulled into the garage, and after turning off the car, he leaned his head on his hands on the top of the steering wheel. He heaved a soul-thrashing sigh, sniffed and opened the door. The empty place where Charlie's Jeep usually sat looked big enough to park a semi. Gordon shuffled as he came around the car and opened the doors for Nora and Christi.

They hurried to the door of the house, hearing Betsy's yelps of welcome, doing their best to ignore the emptiness.

Betsy greeted each of them, then looked for Charlie. She paced beside Nora as she hung her wool coat on a hanger, making sure the long scarf lay flat around the neck of the coat under the collar, then placed her lined leather gloves in the basket hanging on the door, each action precise, controlled. She took Gordon's coat, treating it the same way, and watched Christi go up the stairs.

"Would a cup of coffee help?"

How worn her husband looked. She shook her head. "I think a nap is the best idea. Maybe I'll sleep for a year." She'd heard the first year was the hardest. If Christmas never came again, she'd not mind.

"Think I'll fix some anyway." He stared at her.

She could tell he wanted her to join him, but right now, she had nothing left. She looked into his eyes and saw the glisten of tears. Choking back a sob, she turned, but Gordon wrapped his arms around her and the sobs broke through, leaving her crying against his chest, his tears watering her hair.

When the storm passed, they climbed the stairs, steps matching, and followed Betsy into their room. Nora hung her black suit in the closet and slid into cranberry sweats. She joined Gordon, who'd hung his suit on the butler, under the covers. She rolled on her side and her husband pulled her into his arms. They lay together, spoon fashion, letting the communal warmth send them into slumber.

She felt him get up sometime later, thought about doing the same, ignored the thought and fell back into sleep so deep that even the nightmare, if she had it, failed to rouse her. Gordon had not returned when she got up to use the bathroom, Betsy had taken his place on the bed. She could hear music from Christi's room, but instead of investigating the strange phenomenon, she crawled back into bed. For a moment, she'd thought the music was Charlie's. He was the one inclined to play loud rock—Christian rock, but still loud—not Christi.

Sometime during that night, she heard Gordon snoring beside her. The sound brought some comfort. She rolled over and patted his shoulder before falling back into the deep, dark well.

In the morning, Gordon was gone, his suit hung up and the bathroom set back to rights after his shower. Nora pushed the hair out of her eyes and staggered down the stairs, expecting him to be sitting in the kitchen. No Gordon. But a note on the black marble counter caught her by surprise: "I've gone back to work. I can't stand staying home and doing nothing. G."

She read between the lines: *And think about Charlie.* At least he had a job to go to. She set the machine for one cup, listening to the beans grind and the coffee process, then carried her mug to stand at the bay window, looking down toward the lake. New snow hid former tracks and frosted the pine trees again. The blue spruce that had been their Christmas tree years ago wore the snow coat with ease. Black-capped chickadees flitted about the feeder. Gordon had taken the time to fill that too.

Go skiing or go back to bed. She sipped her coffee and watched the birds. Or write in her journal. She shook her head. Not that. Oblivion with bed, exhaustion with skis and then oblivion. She eyed two baskets of cards sitting on the counter. One of Christmas cards, some read, but none of the latest; the other, sympathy cards. No chance she was going to open those today. Nada on the journal too. All she would do is cry, and so far this day, she'd not succumbed to tears.

When the phone rang, she thought about letting the answering machine pick it up, but instead, she crossed the room and put the receiver to her ear. "Hello."

"Good, you're up. I'm bringing my skis over. We can go around the lake." Click.

Nora stared at the buzzing phone. Leave it to Susan. If she locked the doors and refused to answer, she could go back to bed. No, Susan would storm the house somehow. She climbed the stairs, checked on Christi, who was sleeping soundly, and dressed for outside. Forcing herself to ignore the lure of the covers, she made her way back downstairs.

Betsy heard the car drive up and went to stand at the front door, tail wagging.

Nora pulled open the door before Susan could ring the doorbell. "I'll go on one condition. You will not ask me any questions or make any comments about—" She almost lost her morning's record of no tears.

"Whatever." Susan shrugged, her navy headband holding her hair back, cross-country skis over her shoulder.

"Fine." Nora turned and stomped into the mudroom, where she slid her feet into her boots. All geared up, she lifted her skis and poles from the rack Gordon had hung by the outside door of the garage and joined Susan at the top of the slope. Betsy barked her delight and plowed through the small drift that always formed off the deck.

At least someone is happy today. The thought made Nora clench her jaw. She stabbed her poles in the snow and pushed off, not bothering to see if Susan was right behind, but knowing she was.

Charlie would have whooped his delight in the slope to the lake on fresh powder.

Why does everything have to go back to Charlie?

She turned right at the flat and commanded her body into action. Reach, stride and glide. The rhythm settled into her muscles, her puffs of breath fogging the way in front of her, leaving moisture on her face that on a colder day would have turned to ice. Gray clouds hung low, threatening more snow. She picked up the pace. If they had a whiteout, they at least had Betsy to guide them home. Skiing back across the lake was not an option yet. While the lake was iced over, it had not been cold enough, long enough, for deep ice to form.

"Hey, take it easy." The shout came from somewhere behind her. She waggled a pole and kept on going, all her concentration on getting the next breath. With her lungs on fire and her legs screaming, she finally stopped and bent over to catch her wind. Sweat trickled down her spine and from under her arms. Heat radiated from the neck of her ski jacket and burned her wet skin.

She looked behind her, to Susan poling after her, but obviously not even attempting to keep the pace that Nora had set. Betsy sat in the snow, her ribs pumping, panting hard. Nora set off again, this time tempering her pace. Should one push a broken heart with such a pace?

Again she ignored the south hill and continued around the lake, pushing herself as hard as she could, and then a little more. When she reached the back door, the stitch in her side doubled her over. Gasping, and her eyes blurring, she swallowed repeatedly to keep from vomiting.

"You'll pay for this tomorrow." Susan huffed her way up the rise. "What kind of an idiot are you?"

"Do you want coffee or not?" The words staggered between gasping breaths.

"Yes! I earned it!" She leaned over and snapped the releases on her skis.

"The rule still holds."

"Fine, we'll talk about Hardanger," Susan snapped back.

"And don't be nice to me."

"Am I ever?"

"Just trying to survive." Nora leaned her skis against the wall inside the garage and kicked her boots over the hedgehog brush to leave the snow on her boots in the garage. Betsy bounded before her through the open door and headed for her water bowl, where she drank and drank and drank.

"See, you nearly killed the dog too." Susan pulled her headband loose and cinnamon curls fell to her shoulders. They both left their outer gear in the mudroom and padded into the kitchen on wool-stockinged feet.

"What happened to the mantel?"

"Off-limits question."

Susan raised her hands in surrender. "Where's Gordon?"

"Gone to work."

"Already?"

"He can't stand it here any more than I can. But at least he has a place to go." Her glare warned her friend not to pursue that line of discussion. She set the coffeemaker for two cups and crossed to the refrigerator for the cream for Susan's coffee. "If you must know, I burned the pine boughs and cedar swags."

"Intentionally?"

"Like some pyromaniacal freak."

"Did it help?"

Nora shrugged. "Gordon saved me from myself."

"Oh, Nora, I—"

Nora held up a hand, palm out. "Don't. I said don't, remember?" She handed Susan a steaming mug of coffee. "Be careful, it's really hot."

"Yes, Mother."

The fire had burned to ashes, so Nora ignored the chairs in front of the fireplace and set her cup on the table in the window bay. Knowing Susan's sweet tooth, she retrieved one of the plates of cookies someone had brought and set them in the center of the table. The forlorn arrangement left over from her burning mocked her, so she removed it to the pantry.

"Part of the frenzy?"

"Yes." Nora sat down and propped her elbows on the table to hold her mug at mouth level, a good barrier to hide behind. "So how's Benny?"

"Playing over at Judy's." Susan nibbled a lemon bar from the plate. "I'm sorry I missed yesterday, I—"

Nora shook her head. "Off-limits."

"Sorry, I forgot."

Nora glanced over at the phone, where the red light announced someone had called. She had no intention of finding out who.

"You have to talk about it, you know."

"I know. I will, but not yet."

"That's not healthy."

"Too bad. I am just trying to get by." She rose and went to make more coffee. Anything to get away from the love and compassion in her friend's gaze. She turned when she heard

Christi coming down the stairs, but the smile she wanted to wear to greet her daughter died between heart and mouth. Instead, surprise caught her and she blurted, "You've been painting?"

"Yeah, so?" Christi's voice sounded wary, on guard, and ready to fight.

"Nothing, I mean I-I'm glad for you."

Christi shrugged. "Any more coffee?"

"Well, I can make some." What was the matter? Looking at Christi was like looking through an old window that had faults in the glass, leaving her feeling like if she squinted, perhaps the scene would clear up.

But it didn't.

"Are you all right?"

Christi stared at her, dark eyes hooded, her mouth a straight line.

"I mean, are you sick, catching a bug?"

The straight line bent down slightly. "Oh no, I'm just fine and dandy."

"That was a stupid question. I'm sorry." Nora handed her daughter the cup that was ready and pushed the button for two more. Good thing they had such a complete machine, for the way her hands were shaking, she couldn't have poured water into the reservoir if her life depended on it. Where had the sarcasm come from? Christi never did sarcasm well. Nora closed her eyes for a moment as the follow-up thought reverberated in her head. *Most likely from the same place mine does.* Here was a new problem: how could she help her daughter when she couldn't help herself?

Chapter Twenty

Jenna

Mom, remember what you said one day when I asked about a dog?"

Jenna stared at her daughter. "Which time?" Day four post-surgery and already Heather was making plans. Her daughter had always wanted a dog, but Jenna had begged off, saying, "Someday when you are stronger." Besides, they had Elmer and he was a notorious dog hater.

"Oh, a few months ago."

"As in 'get a dog when you were stronger' or 'when Elmer exited this life'?"

"The first. We can train Elmer to accept a dog. I read some articles on bringing a new puppy into a house with other dogs or cats even. How to help them adapt to each other."

"Really." Jenna knew it wasn't a question, but was marking time. "You know I'm not a big animal person. Let's let Elmer remain king for a while longer before we make any decisions."

"Are you sure Matilda is taking care of him?"

"Heather, she adores that cat."

"He's probably sulking because I'm gone so long."

"Probably."

The nurse breezed in with a happy smile. "Good news, today you get to walk down the hall." The afternoon before,

Heather had hobbled to the chair and was certain she'd never make it back to the bed.

Heather groaned, then grinned at her mother. "That was just for effect, because she says all her patients dread walking because it hurts. Not me, I know I'm stronger today because I've been standing twice already this morning."

"You are not supposed to get out of bed without supervision." The nurse wagged her finger. "But I might forget I heard that if you tell me that good-looking uncle of yours is coming back. Talk about eye candy."

Heather looked at her mother, who shook her head. "How do you know?"

"Because he called last night to say he is being sent to Florida for a meeting."

"Now, that's really a shame, having to go to Florida in the middle of the winter for a meeting. Warm weather, balmy breezes, blue water, I feel so sorry for the man, to have to make sacrifices like that." All the while she was talking, she switched the IV bag to a pole with wheels, clipped off the catheter and lowered the bed. "Okay, here we go."

Heather swung her feet off the side of the bed and rolled into a sitting position with only a flinch. She took in a deep breath and let it out before using her arms as leverage, then stood up with the nurse watchfully in front of her.

"Very good." Jenna tucked the hospital gown around her daughter's back. "We need a belt here."

"Hmm, how about a strip of gauze?" The nurse bustled out of the room and returned in an instant with a roll of two-inch gauze. She cut off a strip, tied it around Heather's waist and set a walker in front of her.

"Do I have to use that?"

"Yep. If you fall, you might sue us, and then where would we be?"

Heather shook her head and stared at her mother, as if asking her to intervene.

Jenna shrugged. "I'm not the nurse here."

"Come on, let's get this show on the road. I got a good-lookin' guy down the hall that wants to see you."

"You do?" Heather's hand crept up to see how her hair was. "Oh sure, he's probably forty years old."

"No, more like twenty-two. He got a new kidney."

"From my donor?"

"Nope, from his brother." She walked backward, motioning Heather forward. "I figure he needs some cheering up."

"Why?"

"Oh, he's feeling guilty, you know, what if his brother needs a new kidney sometime."

At least no one had to die for him to get a new chance at life. Jenna stood right behind Heather, ready to catch her if she did fall.

"Okay, one foot at a time. Put them forward, sister. Keep your back straight, let that walker roll forward, nice and slow."

Heather made it to the doorway before she had to stop. "Whew." She braced her arms on the walker and leaned forward. The nurse braced the walker in front of her.

"You're doing great. Maybe we better postpone that visit for now."

"How far down?"

"Two doors."

"How good-looking did you say he was?"

"Very."

"Then let's go."

Jenna stared at her daughter. Where had that come from? Heather enjoyed other people's jokes, but it had been years since she made a funny of her own. Jenna glanced around, looking for a wheelchair in case they needed it. Her daughter's new heart seemed to give her more courage than ever. More and more, she wished for knowledge of the family that had lost their child—what did she or he like, what was she or he like. This morning she'd brought messages back to Heather from her chat room buddies. Heather had laughed when she read them, then sucked in a deep breath. Laughing hurt.

The three of them did the three-step walk to the bench.

"Okay, while you're resting, I'm going to answer a light. Don't move until I get back."

"You all right?" Jenna asked softly.

"Not sure how I'll get back." Heather leaned against her mother. "But I'm up and walking, and while I feel weak as anything, I can breathe." She sucked in a breath and let it out. "And not get dizzy." She stared down at the hospital socks on her feet. "We shoulda brought my slippers. Does my hair look all right?"

"You're beautiful." *I could go buy her some, but she has perfectly good ones at home.* Even with the discounts at the hotel, the bill was mounting. She'd be paying her 10 percent of the hospital bills for the rest of her life. Thank God she had good insurance, but if she let herself think about it, she'd dread the bills coming in. As if a pair of slippers would make a blip on the screen of indebtedness.

"Mom?"

"What?"

"Will I really be able to go skiing?"

Jenna knew Heather had dreamed all her life of swoosh-ing down the slopes of a mountain, of riding the lift to the ridges and skiing down. The television never went off when the winter games and winter Olympics were being shown. "I truly believe you will." *I also truly believe I will have a heart attack due to extreme fear for your health and well-being, but that is neither here nor there.*

The nurse stopped in front of them. "You ready to go again?"

Heather stood. "Yes, ma'am." She might have saluted if she dared raise her arm away from the walker. They entered the next room.

"Jared, this is Heather. Heather, Jared."

Jenna recognized the moon face of cortisone meds, but even with that, this was one handsome hunk. "Hi," she said.

"Hi," he replied, but he was looking at Heather. "You made it down the hall. Congratulations."

"Thank you."

"Can you sit and talk?"

The nurse pushed a chair in behind her. "Sit."

Heather did. "I do 'down' and 'stay' too."

Jared stared at her a moment before a deep laugh burst forth and he clutched his middle.

We're in for a wild ride, Jenna informed herself. Who would the healthy Heather be? The nurse backed out the door, chor-tling as she went.

"'Down' and 'stay,' I gotta remember that."

"Oh, you shouldn't make me laugh." Jared's eyes crinkled at the edges in a most appealing way. "Ouch."

Jenna retreated and waited outside the door, leaning against the wall, still delighting in her daughter's joke. This one she would write up and send to Randy. He would love it. What if this new heart had changed Heather's personality? Was that a possibility? Although she was not trying to eavesdrop, she heard the two young people lower their voices. Jared's deeper voice confessed to "feeling like he's in a hole and can't get out. I should be happy," he muttered loud enough for Jenna to hear. "But all I can think of is 'what if I screw up in life and my brother's kidney is for nothing?'"

A while later the nurse came back and beckoned her into the room with her. "Okay, missy, time to head back. Too much at one time might wear you down and we sure don't want that to happen."

Heather stood and moved her hand in a low wave. "See ya, Jared."

"Thanks for coming, Heather."

"When will they be walking you?"

"I don't know."

"I'll come again tomorrow then." She turned and rolled the walker to the door, paused and then made it to the bench, where she nearly collapsed.

"I'll get the wheelchair." When the nurse returned with it, she helped Heather in and said, "Hang on to that pole and away we go."

Back in bed, Heather lay against the pillows, while everything was hooked back up, including the oxygen levels monitor on her left index finger. "Could I go see him this afternoon if Mom pushed me in the wheelchair?"

"I guess you could. Why?"

"Because he's bummed out and afraid."

"True."

"And I can make him laugh."

"You certainly can." She patted Heather's shoulder. "You go, girl."

After Heather was sleeping off her exercise, Jenna toyed with the idea that had emerged when she overheard the kids talking. Maybe Jared wouldn't be interested. *Well*, a clearer voice interjected, *maybe you should give him the chance?* That did it. She headed down the hall to the nurses' station. "I have a question."

"Yes?"

"Has Pastor Larson been up on this floor?"

"Not recently. Why?"

"Well, he helped me so much when I was waiting for the surgeon during and after the surgery, that I think he might help here. Should I call him and ask?"

"Can't hurt." The nurse glanced at the door to Jared's room. "Might be a real good thing."

Surprised at her own boldness, Jenna dug the business card out of her purse. Wandering down to the visiting room, she dialed his number and left a message on his voice mail. Was Jared one of those people he'd said might need praying for and possibly with? A little old lady would be far easier. Just what was the line between ministering and butting in?

Chapter Twenty-one

Nora

*W*hat are you doing?"

"Taking the tree down. What does it look like?" Nora swung around as if ready to do battle. *Trying to live after Charlie, if you must know,* she answered internally.

"It's not even New Year's yet. We never take it down this early. Plus, we haven't opened our presents. I was hoping we could do that tonight." Christi slumped down on the stairs and leaned against a spindle.

"They're over there." Nora indicated the stack of gaily wrapped packages in the corner. She had removed those with "To Charlie" tags and put them in the closet. One day she'd ask Gordon and Christi what they wanted to do with the ones from them. Right now, she just wanted Christmas over.

"How can you do this?"

Nora paused in placing one of the family heirloom balls in its own box. "I thought it might make it easier for all of us."

"Thanks for not asking anyone else."

Nora felt a simmer about her midsection. Christi was speedily becoming accomplished in her sarcasm. "Who usually takes down the tree?" Icicles dripped from her words. "I take it down all by myself because no one else is ever around to help me with this part of the job." *And this might be the last time I have to do this because I don't care if Christmas ever comes again. I give up. There is no perfect Christmas anywhere, and there never will be one for this family again.* Controlling the urge to drop the glittering ball to the floor and stomp on it, she tucked it in the box and closed the lid.

"You could have asked."

"Yes, I could have. But you've been hiding in your room and your father went back to work, and so..." She frowned when Christi abruptly got to her feet and stalked back up the stairs. What was happening to them? They never fought like this. Two more days until New Year's and then school would start again. That might help Christi get back to normal, whatever that was. She stared at the half-empty tree. She'd not turned the lights on since the accident, and Gordon hadn't again either, after she'd jumped all over him.

Betsy looked up the stairs, glanced a reproof over her shoulder at Nora and padded up to whine at the door to Christi's room. The door opened and she went in; then it slammed behind her. Nora was alone with the tree. With a sigh, she turned back to work. The needles were starting to drop anyway, most likely because no one had bothered to pour water into the stand. Down to the lights and all the unwinding from each branch. They'd had such fun decorating it the other night, in that other lifetime.

Do not think. Do not remember. She wasn't sure how many times she'd ordered that of herself in the last two days, but constantly wouldn't be far off. Dusk was bluing the snow when she hauled the tree out to the backyard, where she would put suet and seed blocks on it for the birds.

Charlie usually did that and...

"No!" She let the tree fall on its side and hurried back into the house. Maybe Gordon would put it up. No sense mistreating the birds because she couldn't control her body, let alone her mind.

Gordon had awakened her sometime in the early hours, saying she was sobbing in her sleep. Sure enough, her pillow had been wet. Again. At least she could control herself during the day. But at what cost?

She needed to do two things: talk to Christi and make supper. The latter was simple, just pull another casserole someone had brought them out of the freezer and put it in the oven. Susan had brought over homemade rolls and Nora had cabbage to make coleslaw. She turned on the oven and went out to the freezer to stare at the still-daunting array of food that people had brought. Someone had labeled every dish with name, date and description of the contents. She pulled out one labeled "spaghetti" and carried it into the house.

Christi stood staring into the open refrigerator.

"Spaghetti sound good for supper?"

Christi shrugged. "Is there any chip dip?"

"I think so. It was on the third shelf." She stared at her daughter's back. "If you eat now, you'll spoil your supper." Nora wished she could take the words back as soon as she said them.

Christi glared at her over her shoulder, took the bag of chips and the container of dip and headed back up the stairs.

Gordon came home to find Nora staring into the fire in the family room. He inhaled the dinner fragrances and crossed to stop behind her chair and drop a kiss on the top of her head. "Smells good in here."

"Supper is ready, we can eat anytime."

"Let me get changed first." He glanced around the room. "You put all the Christmas things away already?"

"Christi wants to open the presents tonight, but I already had the tree half undone."

"I take it she's hiding out in her room."

Nora nodded and continued to stare into the fire.

"Where's Betsy?"

"Comforting Christi. She's disgusted with me too."

"The dog?"

Another nod. She could feel him staring at her, then heard him turn and head for the stairs. Perhaps he would talk with his daughter, she should have suggested it. Someone had to help Christi and he seemed far more together than she felt. Could she bear opening her gift from Charlie? She had stared at the package, fighting the tears when she saw his signature. "To Mom, with love from Charlie." Her eyes burned, but if she stared hard enough into the fire, she could keep them at bay. As long as she was alone and not watching someone else dissolve in tears.

Fighting with Christi helped. Perhaps Christi had discovered that secret too and it explained her obnoxiousness. Attack. The adrenaline kicked in and the tears dried up. Perhaps there was a chemical reaction going on. Nora heaved herself out of the chair, turned on the light above the table, which she'd already set, and prepared to serve the meal. The casserole, hot from the oven, set on a trivet, the cold salad from the fridge with a serving spoon, the rolls she popped into the still-warm oven to be just right when the two of them came down. Then, after a moment's hesitation, she removed the fourth chair from the round table and set it against the wall by the fireplace.

When no one appeared, she went to the foot of the stairs. "Supper's on the table."

"Just a minute." Gordon's voice came from Christi's room.

Nora returned to her chair in front of the fire, curling her legs underneath her, leaning an elbow on the rolled arm of the chair and propping her head up. While the spaghetti smelled good, she could care less if she ate or not.

When they finally came down the stairs, she knew the rolls would be hard, but she never said a word. She laid her hands on the sides of the casserole dish and figured it was warm enough. With the rolls in a basket covered with a napkin, she sat down at the table and waited for them to take their chairs.

Christi looked around the table and flipped her a puzzled look. "Why did you take his chair away?"

Nora raised her shoulders and dropped them again. "I just thought it might be easier for everyone."

"For you, maybe."

"Christi," Gordon said.

Nora ignored her daughter's comment and started to pass the casserole dish around, since it was no longer too hot to handle. Making small talk took far more energy than she possessed at the moment. How could she be so tired all the time?

Sure, she'd read the books on grief when she attended the class on helping those who mourn. The books said that grieving took a lot of energy, Luke had reminded them of that, but that certainly didn't give her a good excuse to sleep all the time. She looked across the table at Gordon. His face seemed to be melting into his neck. The sweatshirt he'd put on looked to be ready for the ragbag, but the one time she tried to dispose of it, he'd dragged it out of the bag and folded it back in his drawer.

Like the sweats she wore. Surely, there was comfort in old clothes, perhaps that was it.

"Would you like dessert?" she asked. When they both shook their heads, she picked up the plates and carried them to the sink. "Coffee or cider?"

"I'll take a cup of cider." Gordon looked at Christi. "How about you?"

"I guess."

Gordon picked up the serving dishes as he stood. "You get the silver."

Nora filled the teakettle and set it to heat; then she opened three cider packets and poured the contents into the mugs she'd set on the counter. She should have made real mulled cider, she had the bags of spices all prepared, but this was far easier.

"You want me to bring the presents in here, where the fire is?"

"I guess so. Ask Christi what she'd like to do." After all, she's the one who insisted they do this tonight. Her heart rate zipped up. No, Nora would decide. She didn't want to go in the living room. "It's warmer in here, though."

She set the mugs on a tray and included a plate of the Christmas goodies she had made, sandbakles, brownies, fattigman, walnut-studded thumbprints. She couldn't bring out the Rice Krispies cookies without Charlie here to tease her about taking forever to make his favorite treat. She swallowed fast and hard. *No! I will not cry!*

The pile of presents grew as Gordon made several trips. His eyes glistened and he sniffed once or twice. As they each took a chair, Nora passed the tray and set the plate on the square table between the two cordovan leather chairs, hers and Gordon's. Christi had brought over the wingback chair from the bay window. Betsy lay on the rug closest to the fire, watching Gordon stack the boxes.

Nora huddled into her chair. "You go first, Christi, you're the youngest."

Charlie loved—had loved—to play Santa, reading off the name tags and handing around the presents. Each one opened his or her gift before the next box was given out. They'd always done it that way.

Christi knelt by the stack. "One for you, one for Dad and one for me. We can all open them at the same time."

Nora started to protest, but she cut her words off before they hit the air. Anything to get through this the quickest.

She opened her present from Gordon. "Tickets to the Bahamas?" They'd always talked of going to a warm place during the winter.

Christi held up hers. "How can I skip school?"

"I looked at the school calendar and you have a two-day break for some reason. This way you'll only miss one day of school."

"Charlie would have loved to go."

"I know. I had a ticket for him too."

The fire snapped, the only sound in the room.

Nora rolled her lips together and, with a sigh, blinked back the tears. She'd known this was not a good idea.

He pulled the fleece robe Nora had bought him from the box he'd opened. "I suppose you want me to do away with the old plaid flannel?"

"That's the general idea." She set her box beside her chair and standing, studied the boxes to find one for each of them. The ones from her mother would be safe.

Gordon chose the next round, being careful to not give out the ones from Charlie either.

"I'll be right back," Christi said when her turn came.

Nora knew Christi had painted something for her father, but she had yet to see it herself.

"You know what's going on?"

"Sort of." She sipped her cider, now growing chilled, then got up to put more wood on the fire and close the hanging screen, which protected the rug and the dog fur from sparks. Anything to keep her hands busy.

Christi returned with a three-by-four canvas, wrapped in Christmas paper and tied with wide red ribbon and a bow in the middle. She handed it to her father.

"For me?"

She nodded, her face all serious, none of the little-girl delight she used to show when giving her gifts. "Open it."

"You want me to ruin the ribbon?"

"D-a-d."

He pushed the ribbon off the sides and ripped the paper, then held the canvas in front of him and stared at the picture. "Oh my..." His voice crumbled. He blinked hard and smiled at his daughter. "Oh, Christi, this is the..."

Nora leaned over as he turned the picture so she could see. Christi had taken a photo of Charlie and Gordon in front of the icehouse out on the lake last winter, holding their strings of Northerns, and had painted it. Nora remembered the day and the photo.

Seeing the tears in Gordon's eyes did her in. She fought hard, but the tears won.

Gordon set the painting beside his chair and gathered his daughter into his arms. She began to cry and he rocked back and forth with her, as though she were again a tiny girl. "That's the best present you could ever give me and the best painting you've done. Thank you."

She gulped. "I thought you could put it in your office, but now..."

Nora huddled in her chair. Surely, this time the tears would never quit.

Chapter Twenty-two

Jenna

She's in his room more than in her own."

"Now, Jenna, surely you are exaggerating." Randy's chuckle made her smile into her phone.

Jenna had called Pastor Larson and he called on Jared too—in fact, right now, the three of them were in Jared's room and laughter could be heard clear down the hall. "The nurses might have to go in there and calm down the party."

"How come you're not in there?" he asked, sounding so close, even though she knew he was miles away.

"Because you called."

"So . . . I am keeping you away from a party?"

"Randy, even her laugh is different. Or else I've not heard her laugh like this since she grew up." Jenna thought back and switched the phone to her other ear. Laughter took a lot of lung power and Heather hadn't had that to use. But she hadn't cracked jokes to make others laugh either. She thought back further—Heather coming home from school with knock-knock jokes. She even dreamed up ones of her own.

"What are you thinking about so hard? I can hear the wheels turning from here."

"Back when she was in kindergarten."

"She was so blond, her hair was white. Remember when she wanted a pony and so I took her out to a friend's place to ride?"

"Yeah, and she was allergic to the horse and came home sneezing her head off."

"Are you sure?" He sounded so chagrined, Jenna chuckled. "I forgot that part."

"Scared me so, that's why I remember." She'd been in nursing school then, so she could get a job that earned enough money to support them. Arlen had been gone two or three years by that time. "You were still in college."

"Felt like I was always in school. By the time I got my MBA, I figured — Dad did too — that I was a professional student."

"But look how well you've done."

"I know. Good thing." He chuckled. "One Christmas I went to him and Mom and told them I was thinking of changing my major. He about had a heart attack."

"Did you really want to do that?"

"No, not really but I was frustrated with so many years in school and probably tired from exams or something. I'll tell you about it . . . someday."

"Who you talking to?" Heather paused in the doorway, pushing her walker, but not leaning on it.

Jenna moved the mouthpiece away. "Randy. You want to talk to him?"

"Sure, but let me get in bed first."

"You okay?"

"Just tired." Heather sat on the edge of the bed and turned, lifting one leg first and then the other. She lay back against the pillows and closed her eyes for a moment. When she reached for the phone, she smiled her thanks. "Hey there, Uncle Randy, when you coming to visit?"

I wanted to ask him that, but figured it sounded pushy. Heather could get away with it, though. Jenna thought about his last visit. Was she the only one aware of a different feeling, or had he been too? Back when they were younger, their five-year age difference had seemed a lot, but no longer. *So what difference does that make?* she asked herself. *The two of you are good friends, he's your brother-in-law and he loves being uncle to Heather. Why these "am I too old for him" thoughts all of a sudden?*

Maybe because now that Heather can have a life of her own, you can too. Scary, huh?

If she weren't sitting down, she'd have had to. She tuned back in to the phone conversation.

"Maybe the day after tomorrow." Heather listened with a smile. "Would you really?" She caught a yawn and suddenly looked like a deflated balloon. "No, just tired. I start to feel good and then I guess I overdo it, but Jared really needed some cheering up. His body is trying to reject the new kidney." She said it as matter-of-factly as if she were telling Randy how many sutures her surgery took.

Jenna closed her eyes. *Please, Lord, bring health back to that young man. His family has given so much.* They had met the brother the day before. He was heading home and came in to say good-bye. He'd only been in the hospital two days after surgery. Jenna had met the mother too. Not everyone could spend the days with a child in the hospital, which made her even more grateful that she could. She still had another week of vacation she could use to take care of Heather. After that, she'd be on leave, but without pay. But she refused to worry about the future. Somehow they would manage. At least that's what she told herself.

"Okay, I'll give you back to Mom. Yeah, I am feeling kinda tired." Heather handed the phone to her mother and closed her eyes.

"Hi, I'm back."

"Let me know for sure when you will be home again. I have a business meeting in Denver, so I could drive up for the weekend."

Just the sound of his voice made her heart skip a beat. What was the matter with her? This felt more like teenage angst and hormones than a forty-two-year-old woman with a twenty-year-old daughter who was just beginning her new life. Actually, both of them were beginning new lives. "That would be great. I'll let you know." She mentally looked at a calendar. Tomorrow was New Year's Eve already.

"How are you getting home?" Randy asked.

One thing she didn't have to think about. "Dr. Avery said to let him know, he'd take care of it."

"He must have friends in high places."

"Well, some of them fly, does that make for high places?" She realized she'd yet to thank the man who flew them to Omaha. Right now, she couldn't for the life of her remember his name. Or did she ever know his real name?

Randy's laugh came warm in her ear. "Driving would be pretty exhausting for Heather, wouldn't it?"

"If we had a place where she could lie down, it wouldn't be so bad. She still sleeps a lot."

"Who wouldn't?"

"True. I'll call Dr. Avery and see what he says."

"Talk soon, then?"

"Yes. Thanks for calling." As she clicked her phone shut, she thought she heard him say something else. Or perhaps her imagination was running overtime.

Since Heather was sleeping, Jenna wandered down to the nurses' lounge, where she poured herself a cup of coffee, tasted it, made a face and poured it down the sink. She'd learned where the supplies were kept, so she started a new pot. The other had been sitting far too long, no one needed sludge like that—no matter how necessary the caffeine fix. While she waited for it to drip, she studied the notes on the bulletin board. Someone was selling Avon, someone else had a litter of kittens to give away. Saturday everyone was invited to a bridal shower. A letterhead from the hospital board advised all nursing staff of a union meeting coming up in mid-January.

The light flashed and she poured her mug of coffee. What if she were to think about working somewhere other than the ER? Where she could have normal shifts, even work days if she wanted. The stress level in the ER, even in a small town like North Platte, was wearying—though sometimes she figured she thrived on the rush.

How was she going to find out?

Back in Heather's room, she unfolded the blanket she kept on the back of the recliner/bed/chair and covered herself with the blanket, kicked the chair back one notch and sipped her coffee. She'd slept almost as much as Heather. Should that tell her something?

That evening, when Dr. Walker made his rounds, she asked, "Do you have an estimated day we will be released?"

He studied his paperwork. "Would the day after tomorrow be all right, meaning, of course, we continue to see no sign of rejection?"

"New Year's Day?"

"I can't think of a better way to start the new year, can you?"

"Not at all." She smiled at Heather, who grinned back. "Guess I better start the transportation wheels in motion."

"Do you have a car here?"

"No, but Dr. Cranston said to let him know when and he'd take care of it."

"Having him available to you is one reason I'm not asking you to stay around here in a hotel for a few more days. He's one of the best. Wish we could talk him into coming back here."

"That would take something cataclysmic, I think. He likes being able to go fishing when he wants."

"Does he really only work part-time?"

Jenna nodded. "Three days a week and on call only for select patients. He says if you have good staff, you can let go of the day-to-day comfortably."

"Well, good for him. I know he'll be speaking at a conference I'm attending in Chicago. Be good to catch up." He patted Heather's leg. "You can tell him you are one of our star patients. I hear you've been spreading some of that beautiful smile around this place."

"I still haven't won a game of UNO with Jared. Even with Pastor Larson there, he wins every time." Heather raised her eyebrows. "You want to take him on?"

"Nope, my ten-year-old son beats me all the time. Started with Go Fish when he was really little. He's a card shark."

He went out the door, leaving Heather chuckling.

"I get to go home in two days." Her eyes widened and she blinked several times. "Just think, Mom, I can go back to college."

"Not right away."

"No, but I can finish those online classes and actually start spring quarter at North Platte Community College."

Oh, it was difficult, but Jenna kept her mouth shut. *Take it easy, don't push, don't set such big dreams and get disappointed,* she silently admonished Heather. *You've been ill for so long. . . .* "Think I better call Dr. Avery and see what he has up his sleeve."

"You want to come play UNO with us? Maybe you could beat Jared."

"I'll walk you down and come in later." Jenna heaved a sigh and fetched the cotton robe with a belt from the closet. At least Heather didn't have to wear only the hospital gown. One of the nurses had brought in the robe, since she went down the hall so often.

Earlier this morning, they had walked clear down to the end of the hall and back to the other end before joining Jared in a hand of UNO. Heather went to physical therapy after that and then took a nap. Jared, on the other hand, did not look good in Jenna's estimation. She wanted to ask the nurse, but she knew that with all the privacy laws, it would put the nurse in an uncomfortable position. Heather had said Jared's body was trying to reject the kidney. She wondered how far that process had progressed. And how could she ask her daughter without giving away her suspicions?

Lord, I don't know what to do but mind my own business, I guess. Protect Heather from . . . from what I don't know. But this concerns me and I know it must You too. Please heal that young man, he has so much life to live.

Jenna walked on down to the lounge, where a man and his family were visiting in one corner, the television in another corner on mute. She stood by the windows so she could look out on the snow-covered ground. Sun and blue sky immediately cheered her up as she punched in the numbers, knowing that Dr. Avery would be glad to hear her good news. The answering service picked up her call.

"Dr. Avery Cranston is not in today, but you may leave a message on his voice mail if you like." A number for immediate help followed.

Jenna thought a moment. This was a day he should be in the office. Unless, of course, he'd taken extra time off for the holidays.

"Hi, Dr. Avery, it's Jenna. Heather is being released on January 1. You said to call. She has done remarkably well. I look forward to talking with you." She left her number at the hotel, as well as her cell, clicked her phone shut and stuck it in her pocket. *Now we wait.*

The darkling fingers of "what-if," so rarely positive, began tickling Jenna's mind. What if Dr. Avery was not able to provide transportation? With all she'd tried to keep in mind, how to get Heather home had not made the list, since Dr. Avery had taken care of that. She started racing through options. Rent a comfortable car and drive home, stopping as often as needed. It could take a long time, with the need to frequently unbend Heather from the static position in the car, have her breathe deeply while she walked a bit. Then, the longer that took, the more stress on Heather. Option one didn't sound so hot.

She decided a coffee cup in her hand might help her think. Book a flight—but could Heather sit up that long? Short of taking a private plane, Heather would have to sit on the way to the airport, sit at the airport, sit during the flight and then during the ride home. So, she reasoned, what about medical transport? Not as expensive as an ambulance, but still pricey.

Heading into the nurses' lounge, she began to worry. *Please, Dr. Avery, get back to me. You made the trip here such an easy thing. But that was an emergency, this isn't.* Another thought, born long of habit, popped in. Instead of worrying—which, according to a coworker, "never does nothin' for nobody, 'cept itself"—she forced herself to keep thinking *options.* Options and "yeah, but" scenarios swirled round and round and up and down, like the octopus ride at the local fair. Ask the social worker assigned to their case? Call Randy and ask for his suggestions? Jenna stopped short with the coffeepot in her hand. Now, why would she consider that? She'd stood on her own two feet for more than seventeen years, what was different now?

One of the nurses stepped alongside and offered her own cup. "We're going to have to keep you here, we've not had fresh coffee this often for, well...who knows?"

Jenna turned and filled the woman's cup. "I hate drinking dregs."

"Me too, but sometimes there's no time for anything else." The other nurse leaned against the counter. "You got good news."

"I know. I can't thank all of you enough for the good care you've given Heather."

"She's an easy one. She's made it through the first couple of hoops. Others aren't having it so easy."

In the midst of her transportation troubles, Jenna remembered Jared. *Ask, don't ask.* Jenna leaned against the other counter. "I know you're not supposed to share medical information and I won't feel bad if you don't answer, but is Jared doing all right?"

"You've noticed it too?"

Jenna nodded. "It's not rejection, is it?"

"We're praying not, but the numbers will tell us after this last blood work." She stirred creamer into her coffee. "He and Heather sure have hit it off."

"I know. The friendship has been good for her." She began to tuck away the prayer need for Jared that his new kidney would kick in and act like it had always been there—when she received her own spiritual kick. *Pray for him now.* She did. The other nurse seemed unfazed by the silence as she sipped her coffee.

When Jenna raised her head after a silent amen, the nurse poured more creamer into her coffee. "Have they given you all the protocol for when you go home?"

"Not yet."

"Make sure you get all your questions answered." She set her coffee down and turned away to answer a light from down the hall.

Jenna watched her go. Maybe working a floor like this would be a really good thing. Or maybe pediatrics. *New life, here we come.* Oh. Right after she figured out how to get them home to *start* this new life.

Chapter Twenty-three

Nora

An empty house is a lonely place. Especially a house where drama had erupted moments before.

Nora set her coffee cup in the sink. It was the fourth day into the new year of "Living After Charlie." Arnold had once more escaped from his cage. Nora had shouted at Christi to contain the reptile, Christi had rudely told her to chill out. Gordon, caught between his two women, had waited to take Christi to school on his way to work. He was probably afraid what they'd do to each other in the car.

After her daughter's outburst, as was the norm now, came the faultfinding for Christi's school problems—and anything else she could think of—as though it were Nora's fault that Christi's twin would not be graduating with her in the spring. Then the silent treatment and acting as though her mother did not exist.

Nora could not deal with reptiles any longer. Betsy padded beside her as she made her way upstairs, steeling herself to open Charlie's door, to pack up the critters. Continued hints that the reptiles were better off elsewhere had glanced off Christi's rapidly hardening armor. Nevertheless, today, Nora would pack up the creatures and call Mr. Morency at the high school. He'd offered to find homes for them. She picked up the scrap of paper with the phone number and shoved it into her sweatpants' pocket.

Pausing at the closed door to Charlie's room, she reviewed the steps: pack, call, finish. But when even the thought of turning the doorknob brought the dreaded burning to eyes and throat, she passed on and entered the master bedroom. She would call first, then deal with packing them up. The bed yawned its persistent invitation.

"No, you have to adopt out reptiles, actually accomplish something today." She'd thought to write in her journal, ordered herself to do so, but had passed it up again. The ringing phone brought her across the room to sit down on the bed and answer it. At the sound of Susan's voice, she flopped backward, phone to her ear.

"You want to see if you can kill me off on another trek around the lake?"

"Not really."

"What are you doing?"

She felt the paper crinkle in her pocket. "Nothing much. I have to make a phone call." *I have to go in Charlie's room.*

"Then what?"

How did she know? She wasn't sure she was going to get through the reptile thing. But she answered as positively as she could. "Going to strip the bed, do laundry and someone needs to go to the grocery store."

"Call in your order and have them deliver."

Nora made a noise somewhere between a snort and an assent.

"There's a storm coming in by tonight, so this might be the last time we can go for a while."

Nora shut her eyes, wishing she hadn't answered the phone

after all. "Thanks, but I just don't want to go out today—at all." Tears seeped closer to the surface. "I gotta go." She set the phone in the charger and crawled under the covers, suddenly so cold she couldn't bear the light and emptiness any longer. She shivered, felt Betsy jump up on the bed and heard the phone ring. No way was she going to answer it again. Maybe she could sleep a couple of hours and wake up feeling better.

Maybe it would be eighty degrees by morning.

Several times she ignored the phone and lay curled under the covers in the no-man's-land of half awake, half asleep and too sad to force herself awake. When she heard the front door open more than an hour later, she sighed and sat up.

"I know you're here," came the familiar voice from down-stairs. "Your car is in the garage. Your cell is off, so Gordon called me to see if you were out with me. Ready or not, here I come." *Susan.* The words accompanied footfalls on the stairs. Betsy went to stand at the door, tail wagging. "Hi, girl, did you get her up?"

"No, she likes to sleep as much as I do."

"Liar, you don't like to sleep, you just can't seem to find a reason to do anything else." Nora scrubbed her hands through her hair. She'd washed it the day before yesterday, or was it longer than that? It was sure to be glued in odd places to her scalp.

"Nice hair. Okay, I have a list here to choose from." Susan's cheeks were pink from the cold, and fresh air surged around her like a life force. Life. It invaded the soporific atmosphere of the room, poking Nora to get up and join in.

Nora's groan meant nothing to her friend as Susan plowed onward, plopping on the bed and bouncing Nora.

"Skiing. Out to lunch, we can do both of those. I haven't

been out to lunch with you in forever. You could talk with Luke, that could come after lunch. Go shopping, everything is on sale. Build a fire downstairs and have a heart-to-heart and prayer session. Read this book I brought you — start today while I read my own book. Yes, here in your house. Now. We can accomplish all these today or we can spread them out."

Nora glanced up from studying the dust bunny laced with dog hair on the carpet. Susan bounced on the bed again. The compassion on her face and in her eyes set the burning alight.

"I don't want to cry anymore."

"The more you cry now, the less you'll cry later."

"How do you know, it wasn't your son that died." The pain wrenched the words from her.

"No." Nora's tone had no effect on Susan's expression of determined kindness. "I know that, but I took that class with you, remember? Just after my mother died. I don't know how much worse it is when it is your child, but I know that it hurts." Her friend rolled to a standing position by the head of the bed. "I have another option for that list. Let me call Lois."

"Lois? I don't know a Lois."

"Remember, she lost a little girl to leukemia? She said she'd be honored to talk with you."

"'Honored'?" Nora stared at her friend through tears.

"I talked with her this morning. She tried to call you a couple of times, but you didn't return her call, which she said didn't surprise her."

Nora rested her chin in her hands, elbows propped on her knees. "I don't feel like talking to anyone." Not even God. Most definitely not He who took her son.

"That would be a lie. See? You're talking to me." Now Susan squatted next to the bed and clasped Nora's hand. It was warm to her oh-so-cold one. She let her friend keep the grip. "So, do you want me to recite my list again? Add anything to it? By the way, you and Gordon are being prayed for right now, as the prayer group is meeting today."

"Gordon is doing just fine, going back to work, talking with people, coming home to a dreary house." She knew her words wore a patina of bitterness.

"Gordon just hides things better than you do. He's also talking with Luke."

Nora raised her head. "He didn't tell me that."

"Maybe he figured you didn't want to know. Listen, I brought in your mail. You have a stack of cards."

Nora groaned again. How did other people respond to memorial gifts right away? That was another thing they had to decide. What to do with the memorial money? What would Charlie want? Christi might have an answer there, if Christi would talk with her without snarling. Thinking of her daughter reminded Nora of her mission.

"I know what I need to do. I need to call Mr. Morency at the high school."

Susan handed her the bedroom phone. "Great."

Taking the phone with one hand and digging into her sweats for the number, Nora wanted to say she was too tired, too foggy to think. She sighed. She was tired of saying she was too tired. Plus, she knew Susan wasn't leaving anytime soon.

In less than fifteen minutes, the reptile transfer details had been worked out. The biology teacher would pick them up after school today. Nora had a little time to figure out how to tell Christi before she picked her up.

Susan shooed her toward the shower. "Take a shower, that hair sculpture doesn't work for you. To demonstrate what a great friend I am, I'll pack up the critters while you're doing that." Susan bent over to scratch Betsy's back. "Then I'll take you to lunch, my treat."

Nora ran her tongue over sticky teeth and sighed. "All right, I give up." She heaved herself to her feet and headed for the bathroom. She stuck her head back out and hollered. "But not out to lunch, there's too much food here that is going to waste. You can eat leftovers." Susan's laughter ended as Nora closed the bathroom door.

Sometime later as they sat at the round table in the bay window, bowls of chili laced with cheese and tortilla chips for crunch before them, Susan bowed her head for grace. "Father, thank you for food, for friendship, for Your grace to get through these hard and dark days. Thank you that You have a plan for good for Nora, Gordon and Christi, not a plan for evil. You promised and we trust You to keep Your promises. Amen."

Nora's amen was silent. "Thank you." She meant for more than the meal, and the smile Susan gave her said she understood.

After taking her first bite, Susan rolled her eyes. "This is great. Who made the chili?"

"I have no idea. Gordon took this one out of the freezer and heated it up last night."

"And you were?"

"Sleeping, I guess. I lay down for a little nap and suddenly he was shaking me to wake up and come down and eat." She took a bite from her spoon, then used the chip to scoop out the next. "Most likely, the name is on the bottom of the dish."

She nodded toward the counter. "We are getting quite a collection."

"You want me to take them back to church?"

Nora shook her head. "Some are from neighbors and other friends."

"Fine, I'll sort through and take the ones from church. I'm going by there anyway." She crunched on a chip. "Isn't Christi's big eighteenth birthday coming up?"

Why did her saying "Christi's birthday" set Nora's teeth on edge? Because it had always been the *twins'* birthday. Charlie was being left out. "What date is today?"

"January fourth."

"*Their* birthday is the eighth."

Typical of Susan, she switched subjects. "This may be too personal for you right now, but I think you're sleeping too much."

Nora considered telling her she was indeed too personal, but surprised herself by agreeing. "Maybe so. It's so easy."

Susan shrugged. "It happens a lot, I guess. I'm not sure there is any such thing as normal. Each person is different, each situation is different." Susan leaned forward. "I think you should talk with Lois."

"Maybe I will."

"What if I ask her to call you?"

Nora stirred the chili left in her bowl. At least she'd eaten part of it. What good would talking to Lois do? What could it hurt? She'd probably end up crying again. Were there a certain number of tears that needed to be cried out? Did everyone who lost a child feel like she did?

"If you want."

"It isn't what I want, it's what will help you. I don't know how to help, other than praying and coming over here to bug you."

"Well, you're good at that."

"That's what friends are for."

"Don't."

"Right. Far easier to deal with someone who is being un-nice," Susan replied briskly, balancing a disproportionate amount of chili on a tortilla chip and then inserting it into her mouth. After chewing and swallowing the mouthful, she cocked her head. "Un-nice? That's not even proper English." She stood and, after setting her dishes in the sink, started searching for names on the stack of returnable serving containers. She found a box in the garage to pack with the ones she knew. "You want me to deliver these to your neighbors?"

Nora shrugged. She stared at the baskets still on the counter, now stuffed and overflowing with cards. All those needed to be opened, read and answered, if there was a gift inside. Maybe if she and Gordon did them together, it wouldn't be so painful. Maybe Christi would address the replies in her beautiful calligraphy. "Maybe," a heavy word that drove her farther into her chair. She glanced at the clock. Half an hour and she needed to pick Christi up from school.

She forced herself to leave the safety of her chair and join Susan in the kitchen. Putting the dishes from lunch in the dishwasher kept her hands busy, but not her mind. "I'm not looking forward to Christi's reaction to the critter removal. Susan, why do you suppose Christi hates me now?"

"Nora, what a dumb thing to say. You and Christi have a pretty amicable relationship." She held up her hands in warning. "I know, I know, she and Gordon are closer, but then you and Charlie were closer. But still, you've always gotten along."

"If I say something is white, she'll say it is black." Nora opened a tin of cookies and offered them to Susan. "We can't be in the same room without snapping."

"Give it time. You're both hurting so bad, you can't stand it, and then take it out on each other."

"I don't attack her." Nora thought for a moment. "Not intentionally anyway."

Susan picked up the box. "I'll take this out to the car and be right back."

Betsy whined to go out and Nora opened the door for her. At least the dog was polite. Dog back in, Nora headed for the closet for her jacket and gloves. Being late would only add fuel to the fire. Perhaps being back in the school routine would be the best thing for all of them. She glanced at the calendar. Four days until the birthday. How would she get through that day?

"Call me in the morning, and if we can't go skiing, we'll go mall walking." Susan snagged her purse off the counter. "And if you don't call me, I'll be here to pull you out of bed."

"What about Benny?"

"As soon as I drop him off at preschool."

"Thanks for coming. It helped." Nora backed away when Susan started to hug her. "Not yet."

"Not un-nice enough?" Susan waved as she went to the front door, leaving Nora to head for the garage, dog at her heels.

Waiting in line with the other mothers in their warm cars, Nora leaned her head against the back of the seat. Before school started, Gordon had mentioned a car for Christi.

Christi had not particularly wanted a car then, and, besides, she didn't need one. Charlie made sure she got where she needed to go, or her mother did, or a friend. She had her driver's license. Nora thought they might as well stab a knife into her chest, the thought of her remaining child out driving bit so sharp. Even though she'd learned the accident that killed her son was due to the other car skidding on black ice, it could happen again. Or any number of things—no matter how good a driver Christi was. The police had followed up with the details of the accident, and asked if she and Gordon wanted to press charges. But nothing would bring Charlie back, and she was sure the other driver had nightmares about the accident as it was.

Betsy's routine of whining and whimpering and the opening of the car door broke her terrifying thoughts. Nora turned to say something, but the remote look on her daughter's face stopped her. What ever happened to "hi" or "how are you" or "how was your day"? The door slammed and Christi slumped in the seat, her eyes closed.

"That bad?" Nora asked softly.

Christi's nod barely moved her head. Had Nora not been watching, she would have missed it.

"Care to talk?"

A small shake. Then a muttered "Everything. Just everything." A tear forced itself loose and meandered down her cheek.

The sight of it made Nora roll her lips together and blink fast. *No tears. I cannot drive with tears.* What if she had to face school as Christi was, feeling the way she did? They probably didn't allow naps at the desks. Dealing with sympathetic faces that made you want to cry, others avoiding you as if you had something they could catch. She hadn't placed her daughter so vividly in her world, her new world after Charlie, until now. Christi suffered on a much more public stage than Nora did. She reached over the console and patted Christi's arm.

"Do I have to go to school tomorrow?" Christi twisted and untwisted her long, artistic fingers.

"Can we talk about that later?" *After you have some time to decompress.* She eased her way into the traffic, keeping an extra careful watch on pedestrians and cars alike. Never had she been so aware of danger all around as she had since the accident. She gripped the wheel tightly. Feeling so vulnerable was a new experience.

They were nearly home before Nora summoned the courage to mention Arnold and company. "Mr. Morency is coming to adopt Charlie's critters. Susan packed up all their things so we don't have to. Wasn't that nice of her?"

Christi whipped her head around and glared at her mother. "Why are you doing that? You just want to get rid of all his things. You never even asked me what I want."

The venom in her voice blindsided Nora like a car slamming into hers. She gasped involuntarily and jerked the wheel, overcorrecting, then finally reestablishing control. A horn sounded behind them.

"What is wrong with you!" Christi shrieked.

"But . . . you don't even like his snakes and reptiles. You never have."

"I didn't complain about taking care of them, did I?" They were in the driveway now. Christi opened the door, leaped out and slammed it behind her. Betsy whimpered. So did Nora. No matter what she did, it was wrong.

Chapter Twenty-four

Jenna

They sure were nice," Heather mumbled as her mother tucked her into her own bed. Elmer, snuggled in the curve of her arm, his purr in major crescendo, blinked at Jenna as if to say, *Just try and move me.*

"If you mean our pilots and Dr. Avery, you are double right." Jenna had breathed more than one sigh of relief since the phone call that told her she had nothing to worry about, the plane would be at the airport and the ambulance was already reserved to take them there. An aide car had met them at the airport in North Platte and delivered them to their apartment.

"We're lucky, huh."

"'Blessed' is more the word." A wave of weariness washed over her, battering her against the sand of responsibility.

Heather forced her eyes wide open when it was obvious she'd rather drift off. "You don't have to worry about me now, Mom. I'm getting better every day. Call Uncle Randy and tell him it's okay to come visit this weekend."

"I will."

Heather lost the battle to keep her eyes open, and her hand stroking Elmer rested on his fur.

Jenna sat on the edge of the bed and reveled in the privilege of watching her daughter breathe, seeing the healthy color in her face, actually hearing the air moving in and out, in spite of the motor rumbling beside her. She stroked the cat's head and down his back. At first, he'd given her the aloof nose, refusing to look at her, but never Heather. She set the monitor so she could hear Heather from her bedroom and dragged herself across the hall, collapsing on the bed. *Call Randy.* Obedient to the thought command, she picked up the phone and dialed his cell. The question of why she was so tired bugged her as she listened to the repeated ringing. When it switched to voice mail, she half-smiled at the sound of his voice inviting her to leave a brief message. She did.

"We are home safe. All is well. I'm going to bed." She should have left the time. The thought lasted only as long as it took to crawl under the covers, clothes and all.

She woke to the sound of the television, even though it was turned on low. Heather was up and she'd not even heard her. So much for the value of the monitor. Was this part of what their new life would be like? Her sleeping through things and Heather doing what she wanted, not just what she was able? One of the nurses asked her if she was prepared for this new life and she'd glibly answered in the affirmative. She'd spent most of her life thinking on and doing what was most important for her fragile daughter. Now, at the age of twenty, Heather could really develop that stubborn streak that most likely had helped her survive the many emergencies. *I'll think about this later,* she promised herself.

She threw back the covers and made her way into the living room, yawning and stretching as she went. Inhaling food fragrances, she picked up her pace. She glanced in the living room, cat asleep on sofa, television on low, no Heather. The Christmas tree they had decorated before they left now twinkled and glowed in front of the window. Good thing they had an artificial tree. She stopped in the arched doorway to the kitchen. Dressed in jeans and a sweatshirt, Heather was pulling what looked like a homemade pizza from the oven. Had Matilda stocked their refrigerator?

"That looks awfully good."

"Hi, Mom, did you sleep well?" Heather smiled and glanced down at the pizza as she set it on the stovetop. "Hope you're hungry."

"Yes and yes. That smells heavenly." She glanced around the kitchen. According to the stuff on the counter, Heather had made the pizza. She'd used a tube of crust mix that Jenna always kept available in the refrigerator, but she'd assembled the remaining ingredients, even grating the mozzarella cheese. *You're doing too much; you should be taking it easy; you'll pay for this by being so tired you can't function.* The thoughts screamed around in her head and beat upon her lips. The urge to take the pizza cutter away and do it herself made her fingers twitch.

"Are you...?" *Sure you should be doing that?* What force of will it took to chop the sentence in half.

Heather glanced up. "You want to eat in here or the living room?"

"How about since you cooked, I serve?" *And clean up.*

Heather rolled her eyes. "Like how hard is it to carry the pizza pan into the living room?" The slight tightening around her mouth would have been missed—had Jenna not been watching closely.

Jenna backed off, inside if not on the outside. "You take the pizza, I'll bring the drinks." She opened the door to the fridge and continued, "You want root beer or...?"

"Root beer sounds good."

They settled on the sofa, cat stretched out on the back, and propped their feet on the coffee table, the pizza pan between them as they inhaled a first piece each.

"This might be the best pizza I've ever tasted." Jenna wound the string of cheese around her finger and sucked it off before biting off the small end of the next triangle. "You done good."

"I know. Been so long since I made one, I almost forgot how." Heather hooked her string of cheese back on top of the slice. "I'd have put olives on, but we didn't have any."

"Sorry." Jenna picked up the remote. "Anything special you want to watch?"

"MTV?"

Jenna took a turn at eye rolling. "Sorry, how about *CSI*?"

"How can you watch that after working in the ER all the time?" Heather nibbled on the crust of her pizza slice.

"I've always thought forensics fascinating." Jenna found the right channel.

"Well, whatever I do, I want to be as far away from anything medical as possible."

"What do you think you'd like to do?"

"You mean now that I might have a life after all?" Heather flipped the rest of the crust back on the pan.

Jenna flinched. "Living day-to-day is not necessarily a bad thing." Had she given up dreams of the future? She sent her mind searching for a dream, other than Heather living, any dream would do. Or were all her dreams tied up in her daughter's probable death and prayers for a new heart? Had she ever thought beyond that? She glanced over to see that Heather was studying the pizza pan as if it were an algebraic equation.

"Can you believe it? I'm still hungry." Heather stared up at her mother.

"So, have another piece."

"I'm going to, but..."

Jenna waited for the rest of the thought, at the same time contemplating a third piece for herself. She usually didn't have time for a third slice of pizza, had she wanted one. Tonight seemed to be moving in slow motion. She didn't have to be preparing to go to work at eleven, snatching a last-minute nap. She didn't have to call Matilda to have her check on Heather. She didn't have to be monitoring Heather's breathing and heart rate.

She reached for another slice of pizza, her hand colliding with Heather's. They both raised their slices as if in a toast and took big bites.

"Oh, I forgot to tell you. Uncle Randy called. He'll be here late tomorrow."

"Oh good." Jenna hoped she sounded nonchalant, but at the same time, she felt like singing. Randy was coming. Not long after that, Jenna dozed off watching *CSI* and listening to the quiet clicking of the laptop computer keys.

Heather nudged her mother's arm. "Mom, why don't you go to bed?"

Jenna blinked and glanced at her watch. "My gosh, it's eleven. You should be in bed."

Heather shook her head. "*Mo-ther,* I..."

Jenna flinched at the emphasis on the word "mother," two syllables, heavy enunciation, long word.

"...I was just going there. Jared said he's doing better."

"Wonderful. I'm glad to hear that." Jenna glanced around for the pizza pan, but all traces of their supper had been cleared away. She stood, stretched and headed for the kitchen. The cooking mess was cleared away. *Heather, you're doing too much. You're going to pay for all this effort.* Instead, she poured herself a glass of water, drank it and headed for bed, leaving Heather closing up her laptop.

When she was ready for bed, she went to say good night to her daughter. Cat and girl were sharing the pillow. "Night, and thanks for supper." She bent down and kissed Heather's forehead. No temp.

"You're welcome. Can we have waffles for breakfast?"

"You know Randy will want them too."

"Two days in a row, I don't mind if you don't. And can we leave the tree up for a few days?"

"I guess." Jenna paused at the doorway. "'Night."

"Don't worry, Mom, okay?"

"God bless." Jenna left the door partially open, in case Elmer needed to go out, and returned to her own room. She picked up the monitor, started to turn it off and changed her mind. A little insurance was not a bad thing. Tomorrow Randy would be coming. Would things be the way they were in Omaha, or would it be like it used to be?

Randy called just after three the next afternoon to say he was about an hour out and asked what he could bring for supper.

"Nothing." Heather had answered the phone. "We have it under control."

Jenna watched from the doorway, wiping her hands on her apron.

"I am resting. On the sofa. You sound just like my mother." She looked up at Jenna. "He wants to know if you need anything from the grocery."

Jenna shook her head. "I got it all. Just drive safely."

Heather repeated the orders and grinned at something Randy said. "Okay, bye."

"What?"

"Oh, nothing." Her arch smile dug at her mother.

"Keeping secrets from your mother is not nice."

"Maybe not, but it sure is fun."

As the arrival time drew closer, Jenna reminded herself for the millionth time that this was just Randy coming. She checked her lipstick in the mirror and debated if she should change clothes—again. When the doorbell rang, she nodded to Heather to answer it. Surely, he could hear her heart beating.

Was the hug longer than usual? Had she made a fool of herself, nearly bursting into tears? She took the shopping bags he handed her as he promised to be right back and headed for the entry door.

"What did he bring this time?" Heather tried peeking in the bags.

"None of your business, since I have no idea what all he brought." She set the bags on the coffee table and headed to the kitchen to check on the lasagna she'd spent the morning putting together. The cheese was bubbling on top and the fragrance filled the room.

"It smells heavenly," Heather said from the doorway. "How long until we eat?"

"Half an hour or so."

"I'm starving."

Oh, the changes. Heather starving, instead of pushing food around her plate. Jenna handed her the heel of the loaf of French bread she had heating in the oven. "Gnaw on this."

Randy opened the door and then paused to pick up more bags.

"Why didn't you say you could use some help?" Jenna crossed the room and closed the door behind him.

"I didn't realize how much there was, guess it grew while in the trunk." He handed one bag to Heather and another to Jenna, who both peeked in the bags only to see wrapped packages.

"But Christmas is over." *I don't have anything for him.*

"This isn't Christmas, this is New Year's. I found some after-Christmas sales that I couldn't resist." He inhaled, his eyes closed in bliss. "Tell me that isn't your lasagna that I smell?"

"Why should I tell you that? I never lie."

"Really?" His right eyebrow arched in question.

"Well"—she shushed her inner admonishing voice by pull-ing a tossed salad out of the refrigerator—"only when neces-sary." She could feel him staring at her, making her neck heat up. Or perhaps that was from the oven. Ha, and she said she never lied. That had to include *to herself.* Handing him the salad bowl, she pointed to the table.

"So how long can you stay?" Heather snatched one of the grape tomatoes off the salad.

"Have to be back in Denver in time for an eight o'clock Monday-morning meeting."

"How come you make them so early?"

"Only time they could get everyone together."

Jenna listened to the discussion, all the while arranging

on a cut glass dish the homemade pickles their neighbor had given them. The leaf-shaped bowl had been a wedding present. One thought leaped to another, and it was as if Arlen stood beside, stealing pickles from the dish, his rear resting against the counter, his twinkling eyes daring her to warn him off. Strange, how even after all these years, he would take over her thoughts like this. While she couldn't see the rest of his face clearly anymore, the sparkle of his eyes always came through. Perhaps that was because she saw his eyes every day in the face of their daughter. The sparkle had returned to hers since the surgery.

Was she feeling so attracted to Randy because he bore such a strong resemblance to his older brother? Or because he was the only man in her life?

Or because the deep friendship they'd always had was truly morphing into romantic love? She closed her eyes and let the warmth wash over her. Quit fighting and let the river carry you where it will. The inner whisper sounded an awful lot like Arlen's voice. Would he approve? What about the rest of the family? What about Heather?

She brushed away the thoughts and pulled the lasagna out of the oven. Setting it on a serving rack on the counter to rest, she removed the foil-wrapped bread from the other oven and set it into a napkin-lined long basket.

"Want some help?" Randy leaned against the door frame.

Her heart ramping up a notch or two, she handed him the basket and nodded at the pickle dish. "You and Heather sit down and I'll bring in the lasagna." She could smell the cheese and tomato that had dripped over the sides smoking on the oven floor, so she grabbed a turner and opened the oven to scrape up the residual. Black smoke burned her eyes.

"You want me to call the fire department?"

She looked up to scold him and fell into his eyes, the spar-kling eyes that, no wonder, she'd never forgotten. Her breath caught in her throat and she blinked against the iridescence. Or perhaps it was the smoke. "Ah"—she cleared her throat and started again—"ah, no, that won't be necessary." Unless they had a method for putting out heart fires.

When he leaned slightly forward, she took a step back and wielded her turner like a sword between them. Anything to keep him from touching her, or her him. Because if he touched her and she couldn't control her body any better than she could her thoughts, she'd be kissing him rather than serv-ing the lasagna.

She sidestepped, tossed the turner in the sink and picked up two pot holders; she grabbed the handles of the rack as if it were a life ring thrown to a drowning woman. "Let's eat." If she didn't know better, she'd think she had run blocks or maybe miles from the rate her heart was going.

After a meal of laughter and lasagna, when their gazes kept colliding across the table, she ignored the table clearing at their insistence and they gathered in the living room to open the packages, the first of which was a three-layered box of Godiva chocolates.

"I couldn't resist," Randy said with a shrug. The three of them studied the confections, trying to remember which ones they liked best. When his hand brushed hers, sparks ran up her arm and burst in her heart. She grabbed a heart, mar-bled in cream and milk chocolate, and tossed it in her mouth. Anything to distract her from the internal fireworks. With a mouthful of candy, she glanced up to see him staring at her.

"What?" The word came out garbled by too much chocolate.

"Nothing." But his eyes continued the dance he'd started previously.

"Mom. Mom!"

She tore her gaze away to answer her daughter. "What?"

"Your box. It's your turn to open a box." She raised another from her bag. "So I can open another one? Hello?"

"Oh, sorry." Confusion was not a comfortable state of being. She dug a flat box out of the shopping bag and glanced at Randy with a question.

"Just open it." Heather rolled her eyes. "You don't have to figure it out first."

"But that's part of the pleasure."

Heather groaned, but her grin belied the sound.

Jenna slid a fingernail under the folded and taped end; then when Heather groaned again, she ripped the paper off a black velvet box. When she lifted the lid, an intricately wrought silver bracelet lay on midnight blue velvet. As she lifted it from the box, she realized it was a charm bracelet with three charms. She fingered the first charm, a silver heart with an *H* engraved on it.

"Heather's new heart?" At his nod, she had to swallow. The gift of life, so perfect. She held the second. The U.S. Marine symbol, with "Semper Fi" engraved on the back. "For Arlen." She blinked back tears. The next charm was twisted behind the link, but when she held it, she smiled at him. Two letters, entwined. *RN*. "Because I am a nurse."

"I thought of doing 'MOM,' but maybe we'll do that another time. I have other ideas to add to it."

"I'm sure you do. Randy, this is just beautiful." She held it out for him to snap it around her wrist, including the safety chain. "You think of everything, don't you?"

"I try." He stared into her eyes. "I try."

She started to say something, then swallowed and whispered a simple "thank you."

"Uncle Randy, you are one devious hombre." Heather pulled out a square box and held it up to her ear to give it a shake.

"Now look who's stalling." She could feel his gaze as if he were stroking her arm. Focusing on Heather, who was alternately shaking and unwrapping the box, she glanced at the man in the recliner, his feet propped on the coffee table, nibbling on another chocolate. She would never have guessed he would do something this perfect, that would make her think of him every time the bracelet jingled.

"An iPod. How did you know?"

"That yours died?" At her nod, he said, with a wink at Jenna, "I guess a little bird told me. I didn't transfer any music to it, though."

"I have plenty to put on it." She pressed the on switch. "Thank you. Your turn, Mom."

Jenna drew out a box that looked like the one Heather had just opened. "I know, rip it." *Please, I don't need an iPod.* But within the box was another smaller one. She opened it to find another charm lying on white cotton. Jenna laughed when she lifted it out. "A cell phone."

"Cell phones are the perfect link between *friends.*" His special emphasis on friends made her swallow again. Maybe it was better not to look into his eyes at this point.

"Where did you ever find such perfect things?"

"He's a magician." Heather caught back a yawn.

"Or maybe not," Jenna said. She glanced in the bags. One more for each of them. She was almost afraid to open the last one. What was he up to?

Heather pulled out a square box and ripped it open. An uncharacteristic squeal leaped from her. "Oh, Uncle Randy! A digital camera! To record my new life!" She opened the box, pulled out a camera, smaller than any Jenna had seen, and immediately began reading the instruction manual.

"I think you scored an especially big hit, Randy," she said, keeping her eyes on Heather. She picked up her last package. Not too big and not too small. It could be about anything. She slid the paper off and lifted the box lid to find a book nestled in the tissue. A one-word title on the cover, *Dreams*. She opened it to find a quote on each thick, rich page, plus room to write.

"I think it is time you learned to dream again."

She laid her hand on an open page. "I'm not much of a writer"—and realizing how ungrateful it sounded—"I mean..."

"Doesn't take a lot of writing to jot down lists, maybe things you want to do or have...or be."

"She wants to go back to school and become a forensic something or other."

Jenna stared at her daughter. "I do?"

"Don't you?"

Jenna thought a minute, then barely shook her head. "Guess I'll have to think on that. I have thought of leaving the ER and working normal shifts without so much pressure. It all depends..."

Heather moved her head around to work out the kinks, then caught another yawn. "This was a great New Year's. Thanks, Uncle Randy. Well, fans, I'm going to bed. All this excitement has worn me out." She kissed her mother's cheek, gathered her cat and stood. "What are we doing tomorrow? Going to the pound to see about a dog?"

"Heather, I didn't mean so soon. I said one of these days."

"You said that about a house too." She walked around the coffee table, dropped a kiss on Randy's cheek and stage-whispered, "Talk her into both." She headed down the hall to her room.

Jenna shook her head, at the same time running her tongue over her front teeth. When Randy grinned at her, she felt the now-familiar warmth in her middle.

"She's growing up awfully fast, making up for lost time," he said.

"I heard that," her daughter's voice floated from the hall. "Why don't you just kiss her good night and leave, so she can get her beauty sleep?"

Jenna trapped her giggles with a hand over her mouth even as her face heated. What would her daughter do next? Or more important perhaps, what would Randy do?

Chapter Twenty-five

Nora

Do you have any ideas what you'd like to do for your birthday?"

Christi shook her head, her dark hair veiling her face. She pushed the food around on her plate with her fork.

Nora sent a pleading look to her husband, who shrugged before taking a deep breath.

"I was thinking of taking you out to choose a car."

Christi's head snapped up, delight immediately tamped down with her prevailing sarcasm. "But Mom will have a fit."

"Surely, you can't mean that, Gordon. Why, what if—" His narrowed-eye look cut the flow of Nora's words.

"See, I told you." Christi slapped her napkin down on the table as she pushed her chair back. "I can't do anything without her worrying and nagging."

"Christi, this caught me by surprise, that's all."

Nora's critical, silent voice snapped, *"Liar. You no more want her to have a car than you want to fly."*

Of course I don't want her to have a car. What if something happens to her, like it did Charlie?

As soon as Christi was out of earshot, she turned on her husband. "How could you do that without talking it over with me first?"

"Look, Nora, you asked me to help. I can't talk with you because you don't want to talk. I've been thinking on this for some time. Christi needs to know we believe in her."

"But a car of her own? Why, she never even asks to drive my car."

"Would you let her? She drives with me."

Nora felt like pounding her fists on the clear glass wall that seemed to divide her from the members of her family. "You've been letting her drive?"

"Of course. She needs the practice." Gordon pushed his plate back and crossed his arms on the table. "Nora, you can't..." He paused and started again. "We can't wrap her in cotton and keep her from growing up because of what happened to Charlie."

"But she never wanted to drive."

"Because we made it too easy for her not to."

"Gordon, I can't handle her having a car of her own." Nora dredged the acknowledgment from somewhere deep where her fears festered. Her hands felt like she'd been soaking them in ice water.

"This isn't about you, this is about our daughter and getting on with living." Gordon's voice was gentle, but with the firmness the children called the "end of discussion" voice.

Nora kept herself in the chair, when all she wanted to do was throw herself across her bed and wail—fists pounding on a wall might help too. Or pounding them on Gordon. How dare he? All these years they'd agreed to talk things over, to make decisions together regarding their children. And mostly they had. Even when he was traveling, she consulted him before agreeing to anything major one of the kids had wanted.

"Are you so ready to forget about Charlie?" She knew that was an unfair question as soon as the words were out of her mouth.

Gordon shook his head and sighed, a heavy sigh that took all the steel out of his shoulders. He pushed back his chair, gathered his dinner things together, and walked over to place them in the sink. Propping his hands on the counter, he leaned on them for a moment, then turned. "It's your choice, you can come with us if you want and make this a family event, or you can cause more hard feelings by staying home. You decide. I thought perhaps we could go out to dinner afterward."

Nora's eyes burned and her throat felt like it might be swelling shut. Heavy, the air felt so heavy and thick she could hardly suck it in. She raised her head and stared across the room at him. *No matter what I do, it won't be right.* "I'll go." *But if something happens to her, I swear I'll never be able to forgive you.*

Sleepless hours never did much for one's attitude, besides giving fears a chance to grow more hideous through the dark hours. She finally got up, not that her tossing and turning had disturbed Gordon. With Betsy padding at her side, she made her way to the kitchen and a cup of herb tea. She propped her straightened arms on the counter and stared into the marble slab, searching for some kind of answers to the questions ricocheting through her brain like the balls in a pinball machine: buy a car, not buy a car, go along, stay home, throw a fit, go to the guillotine quietly. When the teapot whistled, she took down a box and then chose a tea bag as if it were a life-changing decision. She dunked it in the mug she'd filled with steaming water. Letting it steep, she dug out the honey and drizzled sufficient into the water, then tossed the soaked tea bag in the under-the-sink garbage. Each movement wore a mantle of lead that threatened to send her to the floor.

With her mug in hand, she crossed the room to the padded seat in the bay window and sat, knees bent and slippered feet flat on the upholstery. "*... Moon on the breast of the new fallen snow...*" The old line fit as she stared at the black shadows cast by naked birch trees, stark on the pristine white. Tonight would be perfect for skiing. On many nights like this, the four of them, usually Charlie in the lead, had headed around the lake. Once, they'd seen a silver fox, often snowy rabbits and, one year, a snow-white owl, all the denizens of the night.

Of all the family, only Charlie loved cross-country skiing more than she did. Gordon would rather find mountains and schuss with amazing speed and dexterity. Christi followed her father, but only because she coveted the time with him. "Charlie, if only we could go out tonight and I could laugh with you one more time, hear you shout, 'Come on, Mom.'" She rested her cheek on her knees and soaked her sweats with tears. Betsy whimpered and nosed Nora's elbow, then put both front feet on the bench and nuzzled her ear.

"Will the tears never go away? How can there always be more, waiting to leak out?" She wiped her eyes on her sleeve and sipped at the cooling tea. Betsy whimpered, then jumped up on the window seat, insinuated herself under Nora's arm and leaned against her.

At some point, she lay down on the sofa and pulled a thick fleece throw over her. With Betsy stretched out beside her, she finally fell asleep again. Gordon's kiss on her forehead woke her.

"Bye. I'm dropping Christi off. I'll pick her up at school and come by here to get you."

Nora shook her head. Come by for what? Oh, the dreaded car-buying venture. "Okay." *But I don't want to go.*

"I know you don't want to do this, but it will mean a lot to Christi."

There he went, reading her mind. Was she so obvious?

"Bye, Mom."

She heard the door slam behind them and Betsy padded back to sit and stare at her. "They didn't let you out?" A barely audible whimper. Nora sighed and threw back the blanket. Probably a good thing she had Betsy to take care of, or she most likely would sleep all day, every day. The ringing phone made her shake her head. Or not. For sure it was Susan beginning her daily nag fest. One day, she figured, she'd probably appreciate this friend who never let go, but not right now.... She heaved herself to her feet and snagged the phone off the wall on her way to the door to let the dancing dog out to do her business. Yellow circles in the perfect blanket of white.

"Hello."

"You could put a little cheer in your voice, you know."

"I'm fresh out of cheer. Today we are going to buy Christi a car. Gordon's decision, in case you didn't know."

"I thought she didn't want a car."

"Some things change. Charlie isn't here to drive her everywhere and she doesn't like me being the taxi driver. In case you haven't figured it out, she doesn't like even being in the same room with me. I know she would rather I stayed home, and so would I, but Gordon insists we do this for her birthday. Buy a car, have dinner out...." Her voice broke on the rant.

"And you're scared to death."

Nora sniffed. "That's about right." She responded to the woof at the kitchen door; then, with the phone clamped between shoulder and cheek, she opened the plastic container of dog food and scooped the requisite amount into the dog's dish. She used the jug of water they kept on the shelf for this purpose, poured about a cupful into the dog dish and set it on the rug on the floor, where Betsy waited with wagging tail and bright eyes.

"Can I entice you out on the trails?"

"Too cold."

"Come on, it's only zero."

"Too cold, too windy, too bright, just *too*." Nora set the dials on the coffeemaker and waited while it ground the beans and finally filled the mug she'd set under the spigot. Inhaling fresh coffee used to work, but now the caffeine fix had to be drunk to work. "I couldn't sleep again last night. If I dreamed one car crash, I dreamed ten."

"Sorry. When fear gets you, the only thing to do is tell Satan to butt out and take his friends with him. Screaming it at him feels mighty good. You surely know it's not from God."

"Yeah, that would have been a great way to wake up the neighborhood, let alone Gordon and Christi."

"I remember you told me that the best way to kill off nightmares was to pray, sing verses or picture Jesus."

"That was before." Nothing works now. *"Have you tried it?"* There it was again, that nagging little voice that she could well do without.

"Have you tried it?" This time her friend asked the question aloud, but softly.

Nora let the silence stretch. Her throat started the familiar burning, along with her eyes. She sniffed and rolled her gaze at the ceiling. Sometimes that helped stem the tears. She could hear Susan sniff too. "I — I can't find Him." She seized a tissue from the box. "Now, look what you made me do."

"Nora, He hasn't moved. Jesus is waiting for you with His arms outstretched. He said He'd never leave you nor forsake you."

"Sure feels like it. Seems to me He left and took Charlie with Him."

"How long since you looked for the promises in your Bible?"

Nora blew her nose and huffed out a sigh. "Look, if you're going to preach, I'll hang up right now and save you the effort."

"Sorry. I'm backing off. Okay, since no skiing, I'll be over in fifteen minutes and we'll go walk the mall."

"Then Betsy can't come."

"Nora, you can't have it all. Dog means walk or ski. Too cold means mall or fitness club. See you." She hung up.

"As if I ever asked for it all." Nora hung the phone up. Bone-deep weariness, her constant companion, whispered enticements. Lock the doors, shut off the phones, climb the stairs, and sink into oblivion. After all, she hadn't slept much at all during the night — no wonder she was so tired. She sucked in a deep breath and ordered herself to eat something so the coffee wouldn't burn her stomach alive. Opening the refrigerator door, she stared into the interior. Cheese? She shook her head. Bacon and eggs? Another head shake. Betsy appeared at her side and looked up at her hopefully, then joined her in staring into the cavern. Nora sorted through some containers and found a carton of yogurt. Mixing it with granola for crunch, she wandered over to the bay window. A line of deer tracks embroidered the slope. Gordon had filled the feeder, so a mixed flock of birds flitted and fluttered. The chickadees and sparrows picked their seeds off the snow, while a blue jay and a pair of crows fought over the feeder. A nuthatch hung upside down on the suet holder. Finishing her yogurt, she held the carton down for Betsy to get her licks in and then threw it in the trash. Susan would be at the door any minute and she was still in her rapidly aging sleeping sweats.

After we walk, we're going to attack the baskets of sympathy cards."

"Who made you king?" Nora slammed the passenger door and buckled her seat belt.

"Just doing my best to be the kind of friend I know I'd need in your circumstances."

Nora swallowed. "Thanks. But remember, I do better with un-nice people."

"Fine, then. We skip the mall and go straight to the track at Family Fitness. I hope you brought your speed-walking shoes."

"I didn't."

"Too bad."

An hour later, both of them fighting for breath, they slumped on a bench in the women's locker room.

"I think you're trying to kill me." Nora reached down and retied her shoe. Even her toes hurt.

"We do the same thing for a week or two and we'll be getting back into shape. This is awful." Susan rubbed her side and stretched her neck from one shoulder to the other. "You want to do weights?"

"Do you want a black eye?" Nora glanced at her watch. "You want an early lunch?"

"Nope, we're doing cards. There's still plenty of food at your house."

Nora groaned, yet felt one corner of her mouth pull up. "Sadist."

As she had dreaded, the tears seemed nonstop as she read the loving messages in the cards. The stack of checks grew as they opened the envelopes. "Any suggestions on what to do for a memorial?"

"Did you ask Christi?"

"No, nor Gordon. They've been avoiding these baskets like I have and would continue to do so, if it weren't for my pushy friend."

"Well, see how I'm helping you? Now you won't have guilt eating at you too." Susan opened another envelope, this one with lots of signatures. "This is from some of Charlie's friends. They donated a hundred dollars to the natural-science lab at the high school in Charlie's name."

Nora took the card and turned it around as she read all the names. Some she knew, many she didn't. "How do we write one card to thank them all?" She blew her nose and wiped her eyes at the notes.

"Put a thank-you in the school newspaper?"

"Good idea." She set the card up so that Gordon and Christi would see it. The other cards they returned to the basket.

"I'll bet Christi could do a wonderful scrapbook with all these cards and letters. Maybe not now, but someday."

Nora finished addressing a thank-you card and set it in the "to be stamped" pile. "Have we even made a dent?"

"I think we've opened and sorted most of them. Those are the ones that need answering."

Nora got up and set the coffeemaker for two. "I'll ask Gordon and Christi to help with the rest. Starting has been the hardest part." She glanced over her shoulder at Susan and squinted her eyes in mock reluctance. "And much as I hate to admit it, you were right. This was one of those things weighing on me. My mother drilled into my growing-up head that gifts were to be acknowledged within a week—the sooner, the better." She glanced at the calendar. Coming three weeks since Charlie died. It seemed more like months, and like it happened two days ago. Pouring the coffee gave her an excuse to wipe her eyes.

After Susan left, without looking at the clock, Nora gave in to the craving for a nap. She set a timer for fifteen minutes and it was still going off when Gordon shook her.

"You're supposed to be ready to go with us."

Nora blinked, trying to figure out if this was night or day. "Go where?" The memory rushed over her. "Oh, to buy..." She threw back the covers. She needed a shower, wash her hair, get fixed up. Half an hour to an hour. She could hear Christi, and the banging around said she was already in a foul mood.

Flopping back on the bed, Nora shook her head. "You go on without me. She'll like that better anyway."

"Nora, you can't sleep the rest of your life away."

"Sleep my life away? Did you see those piles of answered

sympathy cards on the counter? All the cards sorted. You think they did that themselves?" She could hear the anger in her voice and clamped a lid on it. And here she'd been busy all day except for...she glanced at the clock. She'd slept for an hour.

She heard Gordon mutter something and leave the room.

"Hey, kid, you ready?"

The two of them clumped down the stairs and seconds later she heard the front door slam.

Messed up again. Left alone again. Self-pity brought the tears this time. But instead of pulling the covers back up over her head, Nora forced herself to her feet and into the shower. If she hurried, she could catch up with them. Gordon would start at Olson's. That's where he bought all their cars.

An hour later, she parked behind his SUV and strolled into the showroom. After greeting Carl Olson, their longtime friend and owner of Olson and Olson, she asked, "You know where my two are?"

"Test-driving the perfect car for Christi. A mini SUV—safe, dependable and good on the gas—and only twenty thou on it. She even liked the color, lime green."

Nora made a face. "Lime green?"

"Hey, I just sell 'em, I don't paint them." He motioned to the door. "Here they come now."

Nora watched as Gordon and Christi laughed about something as he held the door open for her. The sporty lime green SUV glinted under the lot lights.

"Cute car," she said as they walked up to her.

"You like it?" Christi looked over her shoulder, her smile tentative.

"The question is, do you?"

"Uh-huh. It drives nice. Dad says it's a good buy."

"And you like lime green." Nora kept a smile on her face and in her voice.

"I know. Like it was waiting here for me."

"Well, let's get the paperwork taken care of." Carl ushered them into his office. "I went ahead and got it together, just in case."

Nora motioned for Christi to take the chair next to her dad and she leaned against the wall, shaking her head when Carl offered to bring in another chair. Gordon had taken Charlie car shopping too. Even though she'd been against buying cars for their kids, he'd been adamant. He wanted his son in a safe car, not something that would break down and eat them up in repairs. She jerked her mind away from that train of thought and focused on Christi. For a change, the frown was gone and she smiled at something Gordon said. Even her shoulders were straighter.

"Well, you can pick the car up tomorrow afternoon." Carl straightened the papers and paper-clipped the check in the upper left-hand corner. He leaned across the desk with a hand toward Christi. "Congratulations, and happy eighteenth birthday."

She shook his hand and nodded. "Thank you." She turned to her mother. "You want to see it?"

Nora nodded. If it took a car to be a peace offering, so be it. "And where are we going to supper?" *If we can get along through an entire meal, it will be a miracle.*

Chapter Twenty-six

Jenna

*J*enna woke in the morning with the kiss still warm on her mouth. Brief as it had been, her lips felt seared. She could hear whistling in the kitchen, surely not Heather. Heather never whistled. When she put her ear to the monitor, nothing came through. But when she heard laughter, both female and male, she knew who was whistling.

She ignored the impulse to leap out of bed and, instead, closed her eyes for ease of remembering. She'd dated a guy for a while, and he'd kissed her once. That was what, at least five years ago. It had been like kissing a fish; not that she was into kissing fish—alive or dead—but she'd never gone out with him again. But last night...suffice it to say, it was not a brother-in-law–like peck on the cheek.

Her lips warmed at the thought. He either felt the same as she did, or he was a good actor, or had lots of practice kissing.

She used to have that. Letting her gaze roam to the picture on her chest of drawers, she silently asked the man with his arm around her if he minded. *Arlen, it's been so long. Is it time to let love come back into my life?*

"Mom?"

"I'm awake."

"Good, we want waffles."

"And not out of the freezer." Randy's deep voice sent shivers up and down her arms.

"Sheesh, just because you two are up and going, can't you let anyone else sleep?" While she tried to sound grumbly, it was hard with a smile stretching the skin on her face. She hit the bathroom for a fast prep, the closet for jeans and a cable-knit sweater in a grayish blue. She knew he liked it, he'd told her so. After pulling on fluffy socks, she slid her feet into loafers. Tucking her still-damp hair behind her ears, she headed for the kitchen. All the ingredients for waffles, including the waffle maker, were lined up on the counter.

Randy handed her a cup of coffee, the smile in his eyes making her toes curl. "Good morning."

"Good morning."

"The pound opens at ten." Heather turned from setting the silverware on the napkins on the table. "I heated up the syrup too."

Jenna took an apron off the pantry hook; with the bib loop around her neck, she tied the strings in back. "I get the feeling you two might be hungry."

"Starved." Heather checked the microwave, which emitted bacon smells when she opened the door.

Jenna separated the egg yolks into one bowl and the whites into the small bowl of the mixer and set it on high speed. As she measured and stirred, she listened to the banter between Randy and Heather. Had her daughter's now-growing quick wit been hidden by the effort needed to pump oxygen into feeble lungs and heart? And Heather being starved? After all these years of nearly forcing her to eat, of making high-protein shakes and snacks—anything to keep life in a frail body. Joy and rejoicings rose from her heart and tap-danced on the ceiling. She'd been cultivating gratitude for years, but now it gushed forth.

"What are you smiling at over your mixing bowls?" Randy leaned against the counter next to her.

"How can I keep from smiling?" She motioned to Heather dangling a catnip mouse in front of Elmer's nose so he would bat at it. The cat rose on his haunches and grasped the mouse with both front feet, making Heather giggle.

"An amazing change for sure."

Randy was the picture of male relaxation, arms crossed, ankles crossed, his coffee mug in his right hand, a smile creasing his handsome face and dancing in his eyes. When he shifted his gaze to her, she almost poured the bottle of oil into the bowl, instead of the cup she used to measure it. She set the bottle down instantly, chiding herself to pay attention.

"Have I mentioned that I want either a yellow Lab or a golden retriever—you know, for when we go to the pound?"

"Only about a gazillion times. Like every time I suggest a small dog. I think Yorkies are so cute."

"So why can't you have two dogs?" Randy drained his coffee mug and crossed to the maker for a refill.

"We're not supposed to have even one in this apartment, but Mom got special permission. I think it's because Mr. Dean wants me to get better and a dog might help. He says dogs are better for people than cats."

"So, buy a house."

"Randy, I can't afford to just go out and buy a house." She didn't tell him how close to flat her finances had become.

"Houses are cheap here."

"That all depends on your point of view."

"I could help you."

Shaking her head, Jenna finished folding the stiff egg whites into the waffle batter and poured the correct amount into the waffle maker. "No."

"Don't be so stiff-necked. That's what money is for, to make people happy. And I can't think of anyone I'd rather make happy than you two."

"No."

"Call it a loan."

"No."

"Hey, Uncle Randy, come here and play with Elmer while I get my camera."

"The waffle is nearly ready," Jenna warned.

"I'll hurry." Heather darted out of the room and returned almost immediately, camera on and ready. Randy dangled the toy and Elmer performed as if he'd been trained. Heather kept snapping, shifting angles and moving around for different shots.

Jenna watched with one eye, while she forked the crispy waffle onto a plate and set it at Randy's place at the table. "Shoot over, get your waffle while it is hot. Heather, get the bacon, will you? Randy, you want a fried egg to go with that?"

"Nope." He sat down and ogled the round waffle. "You could go into the breakfast business and make a mint on your waffles."

"Thanks, but no thanks." Jenna refilled the waffle maker and fetched the bottle of syrup from its hot-water bath.

By the time they'd finished eating, the clock had reached ten, and Heather hurried them out the door, promising to clean the kitchen later. She had the picture of a yellow Lab up for adoption, cut from the newspaper clutched in her hand.

But when they stood in the receiving area of the local

pound, the woman behind the desk shook her head. "A family adopted her yesterday, sorry."

"I should have called," Heather moaned.

"We have plenty of other dogs." She hadn't needed to say anything, as the cacophony of barking hadn't let up since they walked in the door. "Let me show you around."

"This is going to be awful," Jenna whispered to Randy as they followed the woman to a closed door. "I'll want to take them all home."

"You don't just need a house, you need one with acreage. Has Heather mentioned to you she wants a horse?"

"Or two or three. She's never had animals other than the cat, so she wants to make up for lost time." They stepped into a concrete room lined with pens down both sides. Between the smell and the noise, the pitiful looks on the dogs begging to be adopted made her blink to fight back the tears.

Their guide told them the history of each of the dogs, or at least what they knew. "If the dog you choose has not been altered, you have to agree to have that done within a month."

Jenna watched Heather squat down to pet a litter of half-grown puppies that looked to have some black Lab and who-knew-what-else in them.

"Aren't they the cutest?" Two pink tongues were licking Heather's fingers as they curved through the chain-link fencing.

"We agreed, no puppy. We're looking for an adult dog."

"I know, but..." Heather stood with a sigh.

"What's the history on that one?" Jenna pointed to a gray-muzzled mix.

"The family brought him in because he got too old." The tone of voice clearly indicated what the woman thought.

Oh, to be able to help a dog like that. "I'm afraid if I weren't working full-time, I'd take that one and several others home with me."

Heather reached the end of the cages and turned around. "How come I have my heart set on a yellow Lab or golden? Most of these would be good dogs."

"Your choice." Jenna glanced around to see a bedraggled floor mop, with four feet badly in need of a pedicure. "Oh, look." She squatted down and wiggled her fingers through the wire. The little dog, chin whiskers dragging on the floor, tail low and barely wagging, inched his way to sniff her hand.

"Would you like me to bring him out?" the guide asked.

With a deep sigh, Jenna shook her head. "No, we want a dog for Heather." She didn't add the "now."

"I have a Lab/golden cross that we have fostered out. She is two years, had a litter of pups and been spayed. If you'd like to go look at her—"

"Really?" Heather's face lit up.

The guide led the way out. "I'll get you the instructions as soon as I call to see if they are home. You do want to go out right now?"

"If we can." Jenna glanced up to see Randy grinning at Heather's excitement.

"I always wanted a dog, but Arlen was allergic and so is Jessica," he said.

"Good, I'll share. What is the dog's name?"

The guide held up one finger as she spoke into the phone. In a moment, she grinned at Heather. "They are home and delighted to have you come. She said they've been foster failures before and just couldn't do that again."

"Foster failures?" Jenna answered her question before

the woman could. "You mean they adopted a dog they'd fostered."

"Put that as in 'dogs' and you got it right." The woman wrote instructions on a pad and handed it to Heather. "If you decide to keep Goldie, you need to bring her in to be chipped and fill out the paperwork. Oh, and pay the fees."

"Goldie? Chipped?"

"You can change her name. She learns quickly. And chipped means microchipped with your name and address in case she gets lost."

Heather danced ahead of them out to Randy's rental SUV. "I'm going to see my dog."

"She might not be the right one," Jenna cautioned.

"I know. Just think, we don't even have a dog collar."

"I'm sure we can find pet supplies somewhere in North Platte." Randy shut the doors behind the others and climbed in. "Okay, Miss Navigator, tell me where to go."

Jenna rolled her eyes at him and delighted in Heather's laughter.

They drove out into the country and up a long driveway, greeted by three barking dogs.

"Oh, she's beautiful." Heather leaped from the car as soon as it stopped. "Hey, Goldie." While the other two hung back, the golden dog sniffed her way forward, her rear wiggling in delight. She sat in front of Heather and sniffed the offered hand. The two stared at each other; then Heather knelt and the dog walked right into her arms, as if they were long-lost friends just reunited.

"I think we found the right dog." Randy put an arm around Jenna's shoulders and hugged her into his side.

A woman came out the front door, stuffing her arms

into the sleeves of her jacket. "Ah, I see you found each other." The other two dogs, one black and one brown shepherd mix, ran over to her, leaping and yipping until she said "enough" very softly. They both trotted by her side out to the visitors.

Jenna looked up at Randy, in awe at the display of training. She stepped forward. "I'm Jenna and this is my daughter, Heather. My brother-in-law, Randy."

"Thank you for coming and saving me from myself. Goldie is such a special dog, I just wanted the right home for her." She smiled at Heather. "I think she found it."

"Can you tell us any more about her?"

"Other than she's smart as a whip, has a heart big as all outdoors, and only the fact that I already have three dogs, did I not declare foster failure—again." She motioned to the two sitting by her side. "The other is in the house, a dachshund mix who is really top dog here."

"Can we take her now?" Heather asked.

"How fast can you load her in the car?"

"We don't have a leash or collar or anything."

"She has a collar, you can leave the leash off at the pound and I'll pick it up. She eats Purina dry kibble I buy at the feed store. If you want to change to another brand, I'd suggest you mix the two for a while. She's a good eater, we free-feed here, meaning an automatic feeder. She's been wormed and I got her up to date on her shots. The vet gave her a clean bill of health. I've had her for more than a month. We wanted to get her built back up after weaning the puppies."

"How many did she have?"

"Six, she lost two. Poor girl was kept outside, and while they didn't abuse her, they didn't take care of her either." She stroked Goldie's ears. "You have a fenced yard for her?"

"No, we live in an apartment, so she'll be out on a leash."

"But we're going to be looking for a house," Heather chimed in.

Jenna rolled her eyes. "Don't worry, this dog will get good care." She extended her hand. "Thank you."

The woman dug a nylon leash out of her pocket. "Here you go." She patted Goldie again. "You be good, girl."

They said their good-byes and climbed back in the SUV. Jenna glanced in the backseat to see Goldie sitting next to Heather on the seat. So much for dogs on the floor and other myths.

Sometime later, after taking care of things at the pound, shopping for dog supplies at the feed store, and stopping for hamburgers, they hauled all the supplies upstairs to the apartment. Randy carried a sack of dog food under one arm and a cedar-chip-filled dog bed under the other. Jenna carried a sack with chews, brush, food and water dishes, leash, dog shampoo and a couple of toys they couldn't resist.

"For a free dog, this has been rather expensive," Jenna said, plunking the bags on the counter.

"I told you I'd pay for it all."

"Randy, you can't pay for everything."

"Why not? What and who else can I spend money on?"

"You have other nieces and nephews." She hung up her coat and surveyed the messy kitchen.

"You think I don't spoil them rotten? Just ask Jessica." He hung up his coat and pushed up the sleeves of his navy cashmere sweater. "I'll load the dishwasher if Heather will..." He glanced around to see Heather already brushing her dog. "If you want to fix the coffee, I'll clean up."

"We can do it together."

"I like the sound of that. 'Together.'"

Jenna nodded. "Me too." Her whisper made his smile grow wider.

They could hear Heather talking to Goldie and saw the brief camera flash. Goldie would soon be flying through cyberspace to Heather's chat room buddies. With the kitchen cleaned up, a pot roast on simmer and coffee cups in hand, they retired to the living room to find Heather on the sofa, laptop plugged into the phone line and dog snoring softly beside her.

"I think we need some ground rules here. Dogs belong on the floor."

"*M-o-m*. She's all clean now. Besides, her fur isn't too long and I brushed her good."

"Softie," Randy whispered from right behind her. She could feel the heat of him through her sweater. She'd lost that round.

"You in the chat room?"

Heather shook her head. "I've started the search."

"The search?"

"For the donor who gave me my new heart."

Jenna cocked her head. "How are you doing that?"

"Looking for all the auto accidents within a four-hour radius of Omaha for December twenty-second or twenty-third."

"What made you think of that?"

"My chat room."

"You mean the one for those on donor-waiting lists?" Randy sat down beside her. "You know you'll be able to send the donor family a letter through the proper channels."

"I know, but this way I might find the real person."

"How do you know so much about this?"

"Research." Heather fingered the gold heart-shaped locket

she'd worn around her neck ever since Randy gave it to her. "I really want to know."

"Just don't let the disappointment get to you." Jenna took the recliner and kicked it back so she could have her feet up. "Just think, Monday I have to go back to work."

"So soon?" Heather stopped typing.

"You knew that."

"I—I guess, I just hoped you'd stay home longer."

"Do you need me to?"

"The biopsy is Tuesday."

"I'll take you to that."

Heather covered a yawn. "Think I'll take a nap." As soon as she moved, Goldie raised up; then after a prolonged doggy stretch, she followed Heather down the hall.

"Why don't we take the dog for a walk? She probably needs to go out by now." Randy smiled, making her heart skip a beat.

"Better be quick, the temperature is dropping."

They bundled up, clicked the lead on Goldie's collar and went down the stairs and out the door. The wind had indeed kicked up, and dusk already blued the drifted snow. Randy held the leash in one gloved hand and took Jenna's with the other.

"The things I have to do to get you alone." He sighed dramatically.

"About last night…" What about last night? That it was wonderful? Too fast? *No*, she told herself, *not too fast. Simply wonderful.* She didn't continue.

"Yes?" They waited while Goldie did her business.

"Ah…" Why had she started this line of conversation? What could she say? Did that kiss mean as much to him as it did to her? *Is this love I feel or just attraction? After all, I've not spent this much time with any man, other than you, since Arlen left. And came back in a box.*

"You want to try again to see if it was a fluke or... ?"

She shook her head, the smile Randy seemed to encourage peeping out.

"Jenna, what is it?" He bent to lock gazes with her. Randy Montgomery melted her very bones, in the very nicest of ways. After years of being alone, alone with Heather's health, it was heady stuff.

Goldie tugged on the leash, then threw herself into a soft spot and rolled, rolled over, dug her nose into the snow, showering powder, and, shoulder down, rolled again.

When the dog turned to look at them, Randy picked up his end of the leash again. "Remember when I told you I was in love—back at the hospital right after Heather's transplant?"

"Yes." She did. She remembered thinking that woman had a blessing beyond compare. She shivered.

He turned to face her, taking both of her hands in his. "It's you. I've loved you for years."

"We're family."

"Started out that way, but these last years, I've just been waiting for you to be ready."

"You think I'm ready now?" How had she gotten ready? She'd already known Randy's kindness, his character, his sense of fun that helped her remember life could be more than a doctor's visit. When had she slid into love? She didn't know, might never know. But she was there.

He nodded. "For the first time, you've been aware of me as a man, not a brother, ever since Omaha. I could feel it then."

Jenna stood as though the temperature had plunged and

she'd become a statue. Aware of him as a man. Everything that was squishy went off in her. That she wasn't a teenager made not one jot of difference. As stiff as she'd been standing, her knees now threatened to buckle with the intense gaze of the *man* Randy. "This takes some getting used to." It came out too clinical, unfeeling. She turned and started back. "It's cold out here." At least no one could ever accuse her of being a flirt — but oh, if she could begin to convey what was tumbling around inside. He might just run. She had to smile. No, not Randy.

"I'm not cold at all. And, Jenna, I'll wait as long as it takes." His wide smile embraced her as he tucked her arm through his.

Back at the apartment building, they kicked the snow off their boots, brushed the snow off Goldie and entered the lobby.

When he was ready to leave the next afternoon, he asked if she wanted him there for the heart biopsy.

"Thank you, but that's not necessary. We know the process."

"You might, but I don't. How long will the weekly ones last?"

"All depends on the results." She turned at the flash of the camera. "You've created a monster here. Heather and the evil eye."

Randy grinned at them both. "Call me when it's over."

Heather raised an eyebrow. "You want her or me to call?"

"Either, both. I leave for New York on Wednesday, but the cell always works." He kissed them both on the cheek and waved as he went down the stairs.

"I think he loves us." Heather knelt down by her dog. "All of us."

Thursday afternoon, when they returned from a meeting with Dr. Avery, Mr. Dean, the building manager, called them into his office. "I have something here for you." He beamed at Heather's glowing face, as though he were personally responsible for it.

Jenna and Heather exchanged puzzled looks.

Mr. Dean returned with a dog carrier. "This came for you." He handed the carrier to Jenna.

She peeked inside. "A Yorkie." Not only was it *a* Yorkie, but *the* Yorkie mop she'd seen at the shelter, now beautifully washed, combed and clipped. A blue bow pulled up its front fringe.

"There's a card."

She handed the carrier to Heather and opened the card. "'This little fellow needed you. He's been fixed, chipped, groomed and just wants you to love him. Randy,'" she read out loud. Opening the door, she took the shivering little fellow in her arms. "Sorry, Mr. Dean, we now have two dogs. What can I say?"

"Call it therapy for Heather. Just don't tell the other tenants or we'll have dogs all over the place."

"What are we going to name you, little fellow?"

The exquisite little creature gave her a lick on the nose.

"I think we better begin to look for a house," Heather whispered. "We may find a horse on our doorstep next. You can never tell with Uncle Randy."

Chapter Twenty-seven

Nora

"You have to let me know where you are and be home for curfew."

"But *M-o-m!*"

"Those have always been the rules. Why are you having such a fit about it?"

"Mother, I am eighteen now and not a child."

If the pout on her face and the whine in her voice hadn't been so pronounced, Nora might have conceded her daughter had a point. But the presentation overshadowed the facts. *You act like a child, Christi, you get treated like a child.*

"Sorry."

"No, you're not." Christi slammed her fist down on the counter. "If Dad were here..."

That was the problem. Gordon wasn't there. Several days earlier, the first of February, he'd left on the first business trip since Charlie's death and wasn't due back until Thursday. No Gordon, no buffer between her and her daughter. "He would say the exact same thing I'm saying." *At least I hope he would.* At times Nora wasn't so sure—sometimes she thought Gordon was being more lenient with his daughter because he so missed his son. If that made any sense at all. And Nora realized that she was being even more protective. The fear of losing this child, too, ate at her like a rapacious monster, tearing flesh from bones, then filling the empty spaces with vile poison. If she had her way, she'd take away the car keys so that she knew where she'd left her daughter and when to pick her up.

Had she trusted Charlie more? Christi had thrown that in her face on more than one occasion. She only knew she had worried less about Charlie because she'd trusted God and society to watch out for her son. Trust was a terrible thing to lose.

But how to explain this to her daughter, who absolutely hated anything her mother said or did?

"When is Dad coming back?"

Nora heard the question only vaguely as the mere thought of Charlie had loosened the demons of grief again. "What?" She mopped her eyes and dug in her pocket for a tissue, something she'd learned to keep near at hand.

Christi's sigh, fueled by impatience, lashed across the space. "Dad, your husband, when is he coming home?" The tone snarled around her.

Nora sucked in what was hopefully a draught of patience and turned to look at her daughter. The sarcasm was becoming entrenched. "I don't appreciate the tone of your voice. Would you like to try again?" She hoped her own tone was civil—that had been her goal.

Christi stomped out of the room and up the stairs, slamming her bedroom door hard enough that Betsy slunk out of the room.

"I don't blame you, girl, I don't want to be around her either." Nora went to the cupboard and reached for the bottle of port she'd purchased a week or so ago. Anything to help her calm down and be able to sleep at night. After a fight like this, she'd be replaying it in her mind for hours. "What could she have done differently" would segue into "if only" and disintegrate into tears. "If only" never got her anywhere.

She poured the tawny liquid into a glass and took it over to the chair in front of the fireplace, where Betsy now lay on the rug. Warmth settled in with the first sip. Was she using port as a crutch? Probably, but at this point she needed something. Even the Bible suggested a glass of wine to settle the stomach. What would it take to settle the heart?

"Go talk to her." The voice in her head was insistent. *"Go talk to her."*

What good will it do? She'll get more upset, and neither one of us needs that. She heard the voice again. *What are you, voice—on autopilot?* Susan said Christi's behavior was a cry for help. *How can I help her when I can't help myself?* When she sipped again, the warmth of the port brought tears to run down her cheeks. *Christi, how can I convince you that I love you? Gordon, how can you be gone at a time like this? God, what am I to do?*

"Go talk with her."

Nora set the glass on the table between the two chairs, pushed herself to her feet and started toward the door. Betsy rose to accompany her. "No, girl, we're not going to bed, at least not yet. No matter how much I want to." Each riser on the stairs fought to imprison her foot, like slogging through a swamp. When she reached the top of the stairs, she clung to the banister. This was insanity.

Pausing at Christi's door, Nora sucked in a deep breath, hopefully inhaling courage, along with the necessary oxygen. She tapped gently.

"Go away." The tear-thickened voice reminded Nora of her own.

"Please, Christi, can we talk?"

"No."

"Please, may I come in?"

"No."

Nora leaned her forehead against the door, one beseeching palm flat against the wood, reaching high above her head. Short of bashing the door down if it was locked, what were her options? *"Wait."* That voice with no sound, but ringing with such compassion that she could do nothing else.

Time stretched, quivering like an overused muscle.

Sitting at Nora's feet, Betsy scratched behind her ear with her back foot. The thumping sounded against the door like a bass drum at full volume. Nora stroked the dog's head and stretched her own from side to side.

Say something? Be still? Wait? What to do? Was she doing not only the right thing but the best thing? She knew she'd been so locked in her own grief that she'd not helped her family, but where was the strength to do anything else? Just getting through moment by moment drained her dry.

"Wait."

She heard shuffling and the turn of the knob. The door swung open, and without looking at her mother, Christi motioned her inside.

Nora's arms ached with the desire to gather her suffering daughter into her and just hold her. But when she moved toward Christi, the girl stepped back, her hair a hanging veil in front of her face.

Christi turned and made her way through discarded clothing, stacks of finished and half-finished canvases, shoes, schoolbooks, finally shoving things off the bed to have room to sit.

Those paintings. They could not be called art. Her stomach coiling into a knot, Nora stared at them, the lamp from the bedside table casting shadows on what could only be art from shadowed places. Misshapen monsters in black and red leaped from the two-by-three-foot canvas on the easel, sending ripples of horror and fear up Nora's spine. She wanted to turn and run, out the door and back down the stairs, pretending she'd never seen these products of her daughter's mind. Half pivoting, she saw one of her favorites that Christi had painted last year, an Easter painting with an empty cross, ripped down the center, one half hanging. She closed her eyes, screaming at her heart to keep beating, in spite of the hole where Charlie had been cut out.

"I'm sorry, Christi." The words came from someplace inside of her, not of her own volition.

The veil swung as Christi nodded. "Me too."

"I don't want us to fight. I love you and I'm afraid I'm losing you."

Christi raised her tearstained face. "Mom..." She covered her face with her hands. A slash of black paint stained the back of one of her hands.

Nora waited, resisting the urge to pick up the dirty clothes, sort through the paintings. Christi, who had always been so particular about her clothes and possessions, now lived in this mess. Or, like her mother, did she only exist?

"Why did Charlie have to die?" The words burst forth like a lanced boil.

"I don't know." Nora wrapped her arms around her middle. "I don't have any answers."

"It's not *fair.*" The final word turned into a wail.

"No, it's not." She omitted the "who said life was fair?" which her ever practical mother had often told her.

"But you don't understand, Charlie was my twin."

"I know. He was my son." Nora could no longer hold back. She sank down on the side of the bed and gathered her daughter into her arms, where their sobs rocked the bed. When the storm had passed, like it always did, even though Nora feared it would stay forever, Nora looked around for a box of tissues. When she didn't see any, she dug a crumpled one out of her pocket. Used. So, instead, she picked a corner of the sheet to mop Christi's face and then her own, keeping one arm tight around her.

When she felt Christi sag against her side and the girl's catchy breaths deepen into sleep, Nora eased herself out and laid her daughter back on the pillow, picking up her legs and swinging them up on the bed. With an incoherent murmur, Christi turned on her side. Nora smoothed the long hair back from Christi's face and bent over, kissing her cheek. "I love you, Christi, I will always love you." After tucking the comforter around the girl's shoulder, she turned out the lamp and carefully made her way around the stacks on the floor to the door. She turned at the sound of the cat leaping up on the bed. Wondering where he'd been hiding through all the storm, she shut the door behind her.

The need to crawl into her own bed ached throughout Nora's body and mind. But she had to let the dog out for a last run, check the doors, turn out the lights—all the things that Gordon usually did. The red light flashed on the phone. Hoping it might be Gordon, she punched in the numbers for the answering service and listened to Gordon tell her good night and he hoped she and Christi were doing better. He'd left some messages on e-mail for them both. He would be home Thursday evening. Knowing the time difference, she didn't call him back.

With all the evening chores finished, including a load of clothes in the washing machine, she and Betsy padded back upstairs and got ready for bed. She began to pull on sweats, hesitated, then retrieved pajamas from a drawer and put them on. She brushed her teeth. Betsy would warm up her feet.

A nightmare with "Guilt" riding hard, spurs slashing, woke her up at five. Shaking and shivering, she wrapped a fluffy robe around her and went downstairs to turn up the thermostat. Setting the coffee to start, she crumpled paper for the fireplace, added kindling and split wood, then lit the paper with a match. When the paper flared, she turned on the gas lighter. Standing, watching the flames sneak around the wood and lick the small bits, she tried to figure out the dream. The coffee machine dinged and she fetched her mug, curling up in the leather chair, with her hands cupping the heat of the mug.

Christi. How to help her daughter? Gordon. How come he was handling this so well? Or was he just stuffing things? She got up and added more wood to the fire, then propped her elbows on her knees, stroking the dog with one hand and holding her coffee cup in the other.

Why am I such a failure, hiding out, unable to function? I've always handled crisis well. I thought I was capable, a strong woman of faith, and now I can't make myself walk through the church doors. I don't want to talk to anyone. I've let my family down. What a mess!

She heard her alarm going off upstairs. She thought of just letting it ring, but she forced herself out of the chair and up the stairs. At least she could make a good breakfast for her and Christi. But what? Leftovers from the freezer? She didn't even make sure there was food in the house. Back downstairs she studied the innards of the refrigerator. They did have eggs and cheese. A package of bacon in the freezer. Omelets. Country music drifted down, Christi's alarm. Did she have to fight to wake up like her mother did, or...? The sound of the shower running answered that one.

"Your omelet is ready," she called up the stairs a few minutes later, after the shower had been turned off and she'd allowed time for Christi to get dressed.

"Okay."

How about that? An answer. *"Rejoice in small things."* Where had that come from?

She had set both their plates on the table when Christi walked through the door. "Coffee or hot chocolate?"

"Both with cream." Christi sat down at the table. She ate quickly, keeping an eye on the time.

Nora waited, hoping for a return to normalcy, but then she reminded herself that Christi had never been the talkative one in the morning. Charlie was the whistler, a "greet the day with a smile" kind of guy. She ate her omelet in silence, eyeing the stack of journal, Bible and devotional in whose company she used to greet the day. Each day she turned away. There was no way she could praise God for Charlie's death. The verse had floated through her mind more than once, the one about praising God in all things. That seemed like a travesty of sense. A gross impossibility.

"I'll be late, I have a meeting until four, four thirty."

"Be careful in the snow." Nora mentally slapped herself on the cheek. There she went again, overprotecting.

Christi rolled her eyes. "We need cat food." She pushed back her chair, grabbed her backpack and headed for the mudroom, where the winter gear hung.

Nora raised her voice to be heard across the room. "Thanks for letting me know." She waited and added what she always used to say: "Hope you have a great day." Or at least a good one, but then perhaps just better than the day before was as much as she could expect. She thought about the artwork she'd seen. Maybe she should keep it to herself for a while, anything to keep the peace.

Did she even dare go into Christi's room, strip the bed and pick up the dirty clothes? Or would that ignite World War III?

Chapter Twenty-eight

Jenna

"Mom, do you love Uncle Randy?"

"Well, of course." They were sitting in the living room, empty soda glasses on the coffee table. Today was Jenna's day off and they had gone looking at houses.

"No, I mean as 'in love,' are you *in love* with him?" Holding still-miffed Elmer on her lap, Heather leaned back against Goldie, both of them on the sofa, and stretched her arms over her head. "Well?"

"I'm thinking."

"*M-o-t-h-e-r.* Either you are or you aren't?"

"What makes you an expert on love?" Jenna stroked the little dog in her lap, earning her a quick lick kiss on the hand. Oscar had settled right in, understanding the value of a forever home, just as Goldie had. They'd all fallen into a routine, both dogs ignoring the cat. Heather and the dogs waited for Jenna to get home so they could all go for a walk. Afterward, breakfast, and then Jenna went to bed, with Oscar curled right beside her, while Heather hit the books, Goldie at her feet.

"Shouldn't you be studying?" Why was she having a hard time answering Heather's question? She knew the answer. Of course she loved him, was in love with him, but that didn't make everything easy. Five years her junior wasn't bothering her, but it might bother the rest of the family. Not hers, but his? He wanted to take care of them, but did they need him to take care of them? And the biggie — she was pretty much beyond childbearing age. Randy would have no children of his own, unless they took a chance on the newer treatments.

Didn't he deserve the joys of rearing children? Yes, he'd been around for much of Heather's life, but visiting and being a live-in dad were two different lifestyles. She looked up to see Heather studying her rather than the book on her chest. "What?"

"You didn't answer my question."

"Why do you want to know?"

"Aren't you the one who said it was impolite to answer a question with a question?"

"Did I say that?"

"M-o-th-errr" made it to four syllables that time. Jenna nibbled her bottom lip. Why was she worrying about marriage, when he'd not even mentioned such a thing yet — other than saying he'd loved her for a long time and would wait until she was ready. How would she know when or if she was ready? After all, this wasn't teenage raging-hormones time.

"I think I'm going to marry Jared."

Although if Jenna thought about kissing him, or even touching his hand, something in her middle melted.

"And we're going to have fourteen children."

And they could talk for hours, Randy made her laugh. So many years since a man had made her laugh.

"And live on motorcycles."

Mrs. Randy Montgomery. See, she wouldn't even have to change her driver's license. How about that for a bargain?

"With ten dogs."

"Dogs can't ride motorcycles, and you are a goof. You thought I wasn't listening." She tossed the blue plaid pillow from behind her back at her daughter, who collapsed in giggles. Jenna joined her.

"But, Mom"—Heather leaped in when she could talk again—"I was serious."

"Right. Yes, of course you were."

"About Uncle Randy. I hope you are in love with Randy, because he loves you and he has for a long time, and I think we would be a real good family, and I'm too old to be adopted, so he'd still be more like my uncle, but, Mom..." She paused and blinked back tears. Her voice dropped to a whisper. "I want you to be happy."

"You think I'm not happy?"

Heather rolled her eyes and shook her head. "There you go again."

Jenna scooted forward in her chair, until she could turn and take Heather's hands. "Daughter mine, I am incredibly happy and I want to savor every minute of it. I look at you and I want to sing and dance and throw confetti out the window. I think of Randy and I get all warm and mushy inside, and I know I'm sort of scared to think of marriage again, but when he asks me, I'll say yes."

"Why are you waiting for him to ask you?"

"Because I'm an old-fashioned girl who believes that is the way God wants it to be." She sniffed and swallowed, along with a slightly damp smile. "Anything else?"

Heather nodded, rather emphatically. "I think he should help us pick out a house."

"So does he."

"Will we need to move away from here?"

Jenna paused. "We've not talked about that. But he can fly in and out of the airport here. It means one more stop probably, but—well, we'll see."

"I don't want to leave Dr. Avery."

"I know, me neither. And I do like my job, you know?" Would the Montgomery women be too set in their ways to allow Randy what he needed, wanted? Jenna wondered.

Why are you being cranky?" Jenna asked several days later. "Are you feeling all right?"

"I'm fine, Mother. All I asked was to take my driver's test. Other kids got theirs years ago." She stomped across the room to throw herself on the sofa. "Twenty years old and my mother is still driving me around."

"Well, first of all, you need to get a permit and then you have to take a driver's education class."

"You could teach me."

"As I said, you have to take a class, then drive with a teacher who knows more about cars and laws and teaching driving than I'll ever know."

"But if I get my permit, I can drive."

"With an adult, meaning me, in the car."

"Uncle Randy would let me drive with him."

"Most likely, but before any of this, you need to get clearance from Dr. Avery." Jenna shuddered inside. Heather had never insisted like this before. Next she'd be saying she wanted to move out, get an apartment, go away to school. Sure, all those things should happen in the future, but right now, they were still in a waiting mode. Waiting for Heather to grow stronger, to get past the most dangerous times of rejection, for all the medications to learn to work together and her body to accept them.

She watched her daughter stare down at her fingers. She turned her hand, fingers bent, and studied her nails and cuticles. After nibbling off a hangnail, she sighed.

"And when he says I am cleared to go?"

Jenna heaved a deep sigh. "Then we start the process, I guess." She hated to give names to her fears, but her daughter driving was one of them. Did she not trust the miracle of the new heart? Yes and no. The visible evidence was out there for all to see, but what was happening on the inside?

"Guess I better get busy. I'm about due for another test. The school said I can take it at the library."

Jenna still had trouble with Heather going out into public places. Who knew what kind of germs she might contact there? A cold could turn into pneumonia, there were always flu bugs floating around. Building up resistance again was difficult with all the drugs to fight rejection. They trod a fine line.

With this class finished, Heather would have completed her freshman year of college all online, not bad considering all her health problems. Sheer dogged persistence, that's what it took. One time, Heather had told her that studying helped take her mind off her incapacities. In the weeks since the surgery, she'd made amazing progress. No one ever accused her daughter of being slow in the brains department. It was her body that hadn't cooperated.

Jenna set Oscar on the floor and headed to the kitchen, hearing his tiny nails as he trotted after her. After all, she might drop something while she was cooking. The kitchen remained a land of possibilities.

As soon as Dr. Avery acquiesced, she needed to add Heather to her automobile insurance. Next she'd be wanting a car of her own. The thought struck horror in her soul. She knew the time was coming for Heather to be more independent. She knew it was her job to foster that. But between the knowledge and the doing lay a Grand Canyon–sized chasm.

"How's the search coming?" Randy asked when he called later.

"Ask Heather, she's not talking to me much right now."

"Is she feeling all right?"

"Says she is." Jenna was trying to decide how to ask Heather if she could listen to her heart, although the doctors had said that the biopsies were the only diagnostic tool for rejection. If it had gone far enough to be detected with a stethoscope, it had gone way too far.

"I can't come for the weekend, but I could be there Monday and Tuesday, or whenever you have days off."

"I'm working the weekend, but off Tuesday and Wednesday."

"Perfect. Have you seen any places that are possibilities?"

"Not really. There's not a lot for sale around here." And fewer in her price range. Randy's perspective on what was available would be quite different.

They talked about his traveling, the family news and the weather before he said where he was calling from.

"Mexico City? What are you doing there?"

"Looking at a company as a possible acquisition."

"Does that mean you would spend a lot of time down there?"

"Possibly, well, most likely. For a while, at least, to make sure everything runs smoothly in the transition."

Jenna knew he was in the financial division of a communications firm that was expanding worldwide. Like his older brother, he liked living a bit on the edge. Traveling to less advantaged parts of the world was his equivalent of his brother's marine service. Was she making a mistake in thinking he'd be home more if he were married?

"I miss you." The timbre of his voice deepened.

Jenna closed her eyes. She could feel his voice clear down to her toes.

"Four days."

"Four days. I'll be counting," she said. The hours, the minutes.

"I'll be praying for the biopsy."

"Thanks."

They said good-bye and she set the phone in the charger. Phone calls used to be sufficient, a good break. Now they were not enough. Was that a sign of being ready?

After the heart biopsy on Monday, Dr. Avery came into the room where Heather lay dozing. Jenna sat near a window, reading a novel.

"So how's our girl doing on a daily basis?"

"Loves walking the dogs a couple of times a day. If the weather is too cold, the walks are short."

"Good. Do you both use the gym when it's too cold outside?"

"She does more than I do."

"How's her attitude?"

Jenna smiled. "Try keeping her down. Pulling A's in her classes, chatting with her group, searching for the accident that gave her a heart."

"Wanting a driver's license." Heather sounded drowsy but adamant.

"A driver's license, eh? Have you ever taken driver's ed?"

Heather snorted. "Like when?"

"I see. So, are you asking if I approve?"

"Mom thinks we need a release signed by you."

"Perhaps you do for insurance purposes. I'll look into it." He smiled at Jenna. "But let's see how this test turns out."

"I'm fine, can't you tell?"

Dr. Avery tweaked her toes. "Patience, Heather, patience. Are you staying out of crowds?"

"Yes. I only shop online, we rent movies, I haven't been to a theater for years. Mom does the grocery shopping, the only other person I see, other than in passing, is Uncle Randy. I really could use a social life, you know?"

"I know. You've been faithful and I'm proud of you. We'll call you with the results. I'll send the nurse in to disconnect that IV."

"Thanks." Jenna smiled at her friend. "I hear you went ice fishing."

"I did. Only caught one walleye, but he was a fighter." He patted Heather's foot. "You take care now."

Jenna watched him go out the door. How blessed they were to be in his care so they didn't need to go to Omaha every week.

But when he called with the results the next day, his voice was somber. "Bad news, I'm afraid. There are signs of rejection. We'll need to see her ASAP."

Jenna closed her eyes to shut out the fear. Rejection. They had been so fortunate so far. *Please, God, take this away.*

Chapter Twenty-nine

Nora

*N*ora, it's Easter, we need to go as a family." Gordon locked his hands behind his head, the picture of relaxation in the light from the bedside lamp.

Nora closed her eyes against the onslaught prompted by his request. She hadn't been to church for—well, ever since just after New Year's. She did nothing but cry there, and when people asked how she was, she cried some more. That made them uncomfortable and her more miserable. Easier to stay away. Easier to not have to talk to God. He could have kept this from happening—had He wanted. As far as she could see, He'd not lived up to His promise to protect His children. How could you trust someone who let you down so terribly?

"You and Christi can go."

"I know we can, we have been, but everyone keeps asking about you. What can I say?" He crossed his ankles. "Besides, I miss you."

She turned to stare at him.

"It just doesn't seem right without you there with me."

She thought of all the times she and the kids had been in church without him when he was on business trips. What he said was true, it had never seemed right. "All I'll do is cry."

"Is that such a terrible thing?"

"I am so tired of crying, of wanting to crawl under the covers and not come out." She twisted her fingers in the covers. *Of missing Charlie. God, how can I keep going?* While some days weren't quite so bad, others felt like her world had just caved in again. Three steps forward, two back, didn't begin to cover it. Had she gained any ground at all?

"Please."

One word. A word so powerful when asked in love, in sorrow. "We have to sit in the back." *That way I can get out if I begin to make a total fool of myself.*

"Nora, it will be okay, they're our family. They miss you."

Easter. Resurrection. New life. Yes, she believed that Charlie had new life, that he was happy and loving heaven. That wasn't the problem. She believed she'd see him again, but someday was not now. Someday shouldn't have become part of her vocabulary.

"Don't worry, we can sit in the back."

She knew this was a concession on his part. Their pew was on the right, six from the front. Not that they owned it or any such thing, but that was where the Peterson family always sat.

Morning came far too soon, dread making her want to dive and hide. Instead, she put on a gray wool pantsuit. While the calendar said late March, winter had yet to release its hold on the Minneapolis area. Anyone silly enough to wear a spring suit or dress would freeze. As she entered the kitchen, Gordon looked up from his coffee.

"You look very nice."

She answered with a half nod. She didn't look nice, she looked drab and the clothes hung on her. She didn't realize how much weight she'd lost. Instead of wearing the silver silk blouse that went with the suit, she'd dug out a black cashmere mock turtle to help her stay warm. Gordon looked good in a navy suit, with a red-and-blue patterned tie. But then, he always wore his clothes well.

While there was more silver at his temples, he didn't seem any worse for wear after all they'd been through. She knew there was no way to say the same for her. The face in the mirror looked ten years older, in spite of her extra time with the tools of makeup. Christi joined them, wearing cords and a turtleneck sweater, not dressed up but better than jeans and a sweatshirt.

Nora fetched her cranberry wool coat from the front closet, checked to make sure lined leather gloves were in the pockets and added a white mohair long scarf. She always felt cold lately. Did grief even change one's personal thermostat?

Gordon took her hand as they neared the front steps to the sanctuary, as if afraid she might bolt and run. She almost had. She nodded and hoped she was smiling—she'd ordered her mouth to do that—at the couple greeting just inside the door. Easter lilies welcomed them from three-tiered stands and banked both sides of the steps to the altar. She slid into the second-to-last row, with Gordon following her and Christi after him. Immediately she wished she'd changed places with her daughter. Now she'd have to climb over them to get out if she had to flee. Nodding politely to the person next to her, she buried her face in the bulletin. The organ prelude faded as the brass ensemble took their places to herald the risen Christ.

Nora clamped her teeth. This was always one of her favorite services. Easter in the past started with the sunrise service, moved into the Easter breakfast served by the youth of the church and culminated in one of the two main services, usually filled to the needing of extra chairs. Not today. *Just get through this,* she ordered herself. *You can do anything for an hour.*

Gordon took her hand again, something he rarely did in public, but she knew he meant it as a lifeline. Just the thought of his kindness made her eyes burn. The trumpets and coronets finished and Luke stood before the congregation. "'Christ is risen.'"

"'He is risen indeed,'" responded those in the pews.

Nora focused on her hymn book as the service proceeded. She felt like a little girl with her hands clapped over her ears, muttering to herself to drown out the voices, the music, the silence. *Just get through.*

"'I am the resurrection and the life. He who comes onto Me shall not die.'"

The words of Jesus broke through her barriers. Sobs clawed at her throat, tears bursting past her control. She stood and pushed past her husband and daughter. "I'll wait for you in the car." The usher, one of their longtime friends, tried to catch her arm, but she pushed passed him and fled out the door.

The icy wind felt cooling on her hot cheeks. She reached the SUV, climbed into the driver's seat and turned the ignition to get the heater going. She should have gone downstairs or into the choir room, where it was warm, but getting away had been all she could think of. As the storm abated, she slumped against the seat. When she saw the first people returning to the parking lot, she climbed out and back in on the passenger side. Surely, they wouldn't stand around visiting today.

"I'm sorry," she said as soon as Gordon climbed into the car.

"It's okay. That was a hard service to go to."

"Where's Christi?"

"She'll be here in a minute." He rubbed his hands together,

then reached over for his driving gloves. "Looks like it could snow."

To keep from crying again, Nora read the list of donors for the Easter lilies. When she saw that one was dedicated to Charlie, from his loving mother and father, she crumpled the paper and succumbed to tears too strong to resist.

"Sorry, guess I should have warned you."

The heat blasting from the vents turned on high covered the sound of her recalcitrant sob. She shook her head, blowing out a deep sigh.

"Luke said to tell you that he's praying for you, us, and will come over any time of day or night if that would help."

"I couldn't stay. Tears are one thing, but bawling is quite another." She leaned back against the headrest.

"It will get better." He leaned over and patted her knee. "At least that's what they tell me."

"And you believe them?"

"What are my choices?"

Looking out the window, she saw Christi walking with a boy, not one of the kids Nora knew. Since the teens from church had often been at their house, she knew them all and their parents too. "Who is that Christi is with?"

Gordon leaned forward and stared out the window. "I don't know."

"Has she mentioned a boyfriend to you?"

"Nope."

Nora had heard tales of Charlie and his friends vetting the boys that Christi could go out with. Not that she'd been too interested in the opposite sex, so far her art took first place.

Christi waved good-bye and strode on toward the family car.

Questions rose for Nora to battle down. She couldn't ask

Charlie about the new guy. Charlie, who'd kept her up to date on all the goings-on with the kids both at church and school. She'd overhear as the twins had sat at the counter for snacks after school talking of their day. How she missed those times, often kicking herself in the wakeful hours of the night for taking so many things for granted.

"So who's your friend?" Gordon asked as he backed out of the parking space.

Christi scooted forward and leaned her crossed arms on the back of her father's seat. "His name is Brandon McCafferty, he was in Sunday school the last couple of weeks. They moved here from Rochester, but he goes to school in Savage. He's cute, huh?"

Was this the same Christi who wouldn't string three words together the weeks her father was gone? The girl who'd have snarled or flat-out ignored anything her mother had said and here she was Miss Chatty Cathy. *You should be grateful she has a good relationship with her father,* Nora reminded herself. *She needs someone to talk with too. You at least have Susan.*

"The Styvansents invited us over for dessert, about four. I told them I'd ask you."

Nora shook her head. "I can't." All the energy she'd started the day with lay splashed over the sidewalks from the church to the car, fluid drained from a transmission. Without that fluid, the car did not run. All she could think about was a bed, a pillow to soak up her tears and a warm comforter. "I'll put the ham in, we'll eat about two."

"Maybe Susan and John would like to come over for a game of cards tonight," Gordon suggested.

"She probably can't get a sitter on Easter Sunday."

"I'll go babysit. Ben is a sweetie," Christi offered.

Nora closed her eyes. Was everyone ganging up on her? Couldn't he tell she was at the end of her rope with no knot to hang onto? "I'll see."

"You want me to call?"

"Anything you want." Now she sounded like Christi. Speaking through gritted teeth was not exactly conducive to warmth. Once in the house, she hung up her coat and let Betsy out for a run. After peeling the sealed plastic wrap from the ham, she set it in a pan, the pan in the oven, and turned the dial to 250. She scrubbed the yams, splashing water on her suit jacket. Slamming the yam in the sink, she grabbed a towel to brush dirt and water off, muttering words she might have thought often but did not speak. Why didn't she change clothes first or at least put on an apron? She knew why. If she went up to her room to change, she'd have crashed on the bed and not moved. At least this way, she could say she was taking a nap, not checking out of life.

"Anything I can do," Gordon asked, coming into the kitchen in khakis and a navy cotton pullover sweater. "I called Susan and left a message."

"Good. If you'll make your special coleslaw, that would be great. I got all the ingredients."

"Anything for dessert if they come?"

"There's an apple pie in the freezer. Wake me in an hour." Without waiting for his response, she dragged herself up the stairs, hung up her clothes, slipped into sweats and crawled under the covers. When Betsy jumped up on the bed and snuggled against her back, the cold gave way, muscle by muscle, to warmth, and blessed sleep took over.

She could feel her mind returning to that no-man's-land of neither asleep nor awake when Gordon sat down on the edge of the bed. She yawned and stretched, then reached for his hand. "Thank you."

"You're welcome. For what?"

Gratitude welled up, overwhelming her with the force, not like a wave crashing but a surge from below, lifting her into sunlight. "For being so steady, for being there for Christi, for making the coleslaw."

"You haven't tasted it yet." He stroked her hair back. "I want you back, Nora. I want our life back."

"Me too." She turned on her back so she could look at him more clearly. "But so far, I'm just doing the best I can."

"I guess we all are. But maybe you can get some help."

"Maybe. Susan wants me to talk with Lois."

"I'd hoped you could talk with Luke."

"Maybe." She traced the back of his hand with her fingertips. "I-it seems like I'm walking, staggering in this empty land, and there's no end, no help, nothing. But if I stop"—she shook her head—"something terrible will happen."

He picked up her hand and kissed the palm. "Dinner's about ready."

"Where's Christi?"

"On the phone. Brandon, I think."

"One more thing to worry about."

"Give her a break, honey, she's trying her best too."

Nora nodded and threw back the covers. "I'll get dressed and be right down. Did you think to stab the yams to see if they are done?"

"Yup, and turned off the oven."

"Are we playing cards tonight?"

"Susan said they're willing if you are. Christi will go babysit."

Nora shucked her sweats and pulled navy cords and a turtleneck, along with a knit vest, from the closet. "Here it is Easter and we're still wearing winter clothes."

The two of them walked together down the stairs.

An envelope lay beside each of their places. Nora looked at Gordon, but he shrugged. Together they put the food on the table and Gordon called Christi to come eat. They had sat down by the time she entered the room.

She slid into her chair. "Open the cards."

Nora slit open the envelope and pulled out a hand-painted card of Easter lilies. Inside she read, "Happy Easter, Mom. I love you, C." She looked up to see tears glistening in Gordon's eyes. An empty cross decorated the front of his card. He showed it to Nora: "Happy Easter to the best dad ever. I love you, C."

They turned to their daughter. "Thank you." Gordon reached over and patted her hand. "These are beautiful."

Nora set hers up in the center of the table and then Gordon did the same. He bowed his head. "Father, we thank You for our daughter and her many talents, for this blessed Easter day, for the food we have, and the friends. In Jesus's name, amen."

Nora wiped her eyes and reached for the ham platter to start the dishes going around.

This feels like old times." John glanced around the card table.

Nora caught Susan's slightly rolled eyes. She had probably coached him on what and what not to say. Nora hoped she was wearing some semblance of a smile. Sometimes it was hard to tell, her face felt taut from all the tears, or rather fighting against the tears.

"How about UNO?" Gordon laid the deck on the table. "Or Hearts?" A regular deck joined the first. "Or Crazy Eights? Any preferences?" When they all shook their heads, he tapped the UNO deck. "All right?"

"Ben was thrilled to see Christi walk in the door. She's always been the best babysitter. Unless, of course, one of the girls is home." Susan took half the deck and started shuffling, then handed hers to Gordon to shuffle with his.

"Can I get any of you something to drink?" Nora glanced at each and shrugged at their nos. "There are chips and dip on the counter, along with cheeses and crackers."

"I'm fine." Gordon gave each of them the proper number of cards. "Remember, when you get down to one card in your hand, you have to say 'uno,' or if someone catches you, you draw four."

Nora stared at the cards in her hand. Surely, she could concentrate enough to follow a simple game like this. But her mind kept wandering and she could tell the others were getting frustrated with her for playing the wrong cards. Soon she had so many cards in her hand from having to draw that she needed a basket to hold them. John won the first hand, Gordon, the second and Susan, the third. Nora had so many points against her that she'd never catch up.

"How about we have dessert now?" Susan suggested. "This needs to be an early night for me."

Nora stood immediately. Just a simple game and she couldn't even do that. Was she going crazy or what? "Do you all want ice cream with your pie?"

As she and Susan prepared the dessert, the men spent the time talking in front of the fire. "I saw you come to church, I was really happy for you."

"And then I was gone. Sorry, I just couldn't handle it."

"Nobody minds if you cry."

"How about wailing and gnashing of teeth?" Nora slid a slice of pie onto a plate. "It wasn't just tears pouring down my face. I had to get out of there. Sometimes I wonder if I'm going stark raving mad." There, she had said it, admitted one of her deepest fears, second only to losing another member of her family: Gordon flying across oceans, terrorists in other countries, Christi and the car. Charlie had been a good driver, a careful driver. But what about the other drivers?

"I really think you need to talk with someone who knows about grieving. Lois, Luke, a counselor, someone. I feel so inadequate, with no answers."

Nora pushed her tongue against the roof of her mouth. Somewhere she had read that could help stem the tears. Amazingly, it worked. "Charlie loved apple pie. I put all these in the freezer this fall. Other than Thanksgiving, this is the first I've used." She swallowed hard. "You really think Lois could help?"

"If she can't, I'm sure she knows someone who can." Susan carried two plates with forks over to the men, Nora followed with mugs of coffee. The women took theirs over to the table in the bay window.

"I sure hope she can help, because I don't think I can keep going on like this. Freaking out at church, hiding in bed, can't even concentrate on a stupid card game." She watched a blob of ice cream slide off her warm pie.

Susan reached over and covered her hand. Nora heaved a sigh as a tear ran down her cheek. Three months since Charlie died. Shouldn't things be getting better? "Maybe I'm having a nervous breakdown."

Chapter Thirty

Jenna

"You're not looking too good, my friend." Dr. Avery pulled out a chair and sat down beside her.

Jenna nodded. "Guess I was foolish enough to believe we'd made it through all the bad possibilities and we were home free."

"Don't go giving up on me now. This is just a blip on the screen."

Jenna stared at him. Had he been reading the same numbers she had? "Do you know something I don't?"

Avery shook his head. "Nope. We both pray to the same God, we both fight to not only keep people alive but to get them healthy again. The big difference? I've seen far more of this than you have, and I absolutely believe Heather is one of the victorious ones."

"How come you don't do like most doctors and hedge your bets?"

"If I weren't sure, I most likely would do that too. But I believe God has some mighty plan for our girl here and I can't wait to see what He is going to do." He clasped his hands behind his head and swung his elbows from side to side. "We'll lick this attack, for you know that's what it is, and rejoice in the victory. Remember who won the war, we just put out the brush fires." He spread his hands on his knees and pushed himself upright. "You go on home and get some rest, so you don't frighten her when she wakes up."

"That bad?"

"No, but I got a rise out of you." He glanced at the monitors. "They know your number. Satan would like nothing more than to get you discouraged." Patting her shoulder, he headed out the door.

Jenna took out a pen and paper and wrote a note to Heather. "Dr. Avery sent me home. He says not to worry, this is a blip on the screen. I love you, Mom." She laid the paper on the tray table and grabbed her down jacket off the back of the chair. Best do what the doctor ordered. That's what she always told Heather. She leaned over to kiss her daughter on the forehead and headed for the exit and the parking lot. Hopefully, Matilda had taken the dogs out. That was one thing about a cat, the litter box was always available.

"So, God"—she continued her conversation, aloud, on the drive home—"the word is 'trust.' You realize, of course, that is easier said than done, especially in the matters of my daughter's health. I know, I know, *our* daughter. Thank you for Dr. Avery. I just have to tell You, and I know You already know it, but this really scares me. So, I choose to trust You with the most precious thing I have, Heather." She gritted her teeth. "She is Yours." Jenna stared around the inside of her car. No one had turned on a light, but it sure felt like it. The warmest light she could feel, but not really see. She parked the SUV in her slot and slung her purse over her shoulder. Glancing up, she could see a light in the living-room window. Matilda had indeed been on duty. Probably praying too, like all their other friends. And Randy, he'd be here tomorrow. She took the stairs to the second floor, two at a time. Sleep quick, so tomorrow could come sooner.

Once she'd calmed the exuberant greeting from the dogs, mollified the cat and read the note on the table, which said they'd been out at eight, she checked the answering machine—no red light—and slipped into bed in less than five minutes. Oscar joined her and Goldie stretched out on the floor beside the bed. The three of them sighed in unison, making Jenna smile. Amazing how these animals made the apartment more of a home.

The ringing phone woke her at six thirty. Randy's number flashed on the screen. Letting her heart settle back into place, she propped the pillows behind her as she answered.

After the greeting, he continued, "I'm just getting on the plane, so I'll see you in a couple of hours."

"You're in Denver?" She let his voice wrap comfort around her.

"Yes. You heard anything?"

"No, Dr. Avery kicked me out about ten. Left her sleeping like a baby. He says the worst is passed."

"How does he know?"

"Years of experience, I guess. Says this is a blip on the screen."

"But you said—"

"I know, that she was having a bad reaction to the new meds. Wish you could have heard him."

"I gotta turn this off, the stewardess is frowning at me. I love you."

Her heart skipped. But before she could answer, Jenna

heard the phone click off. He'd not said that on the phone before. Goldie whimpered at the doorway. She threw back the covers and dragged on her sweats. "You guys better make it quick. It's cold out there."

While the eastern sky was lightening, the stars shone clear overhead. Snow had melted some yesterday, and from the south breeze on her face, she judged more would go today. If all went well, Heather would come home tomorrow. And Randy would be here soon. What more could she ask for? She fingered the charm bracelet, which she only took off when showering, caressing the dangling heart, which represented Heather's new heart. Hearts could signify all kinds of different things.

The dogs raced her up the stairs, poor little Oscar leaping from riser to riser. She scooped him up and let Goldie help pull her the last few feet. Once inside, she dialed the hospital, asked for the nurses' station and fed the dogs while she waited for someone to answer.

"She is grumbling that we never let her sleep, that's how she was a few minutes ago, but I just checked on her and she's out again. Been that way all night, so I'd say that was good news, wouldn't you?"

"Sure do. I'll be in pretty soon. Thanks." She hung up the phone and danced her way to the bathroom for her shower, "Thank you, Jesus," her theme song.

She had brought Heather's laptop; so when Randy arrived, Jenna was listening to Heather read messages from her donor friends, all of whom said they were praying and not to let this get her down. Some of them made her laugh, others brought on a sniff or two.

He rapped on the open door with his knuckles. "Anyone home?"

Heather leaned back against her pillows and crossed her arms over her chest. "What took you so long?"

"Now, is that a friendly greeting or what?" He leaned over and kissed her cheek. "Wish I could have come sooner." Tapping the computer, he asked, "How's the search coming along?"

Heather shook her head. "Narrowed down to four possibles, but can't get any more information. I'm going to write a letter and send it through the donor organization."

Jenna blinked. "When did you decide that?" She took the hand that Randy offered her and enjoyed the shock waves going up her arm at the contact.

"Before I got slammed in here again."

Jenna started to say something, but Randy's hand on her shoulder squeezed.

Heather made a face. "Sorry. I know I should be grateful we caught this in time, but I am so tired of hospitals."

"I heard that." Dr. Avery stood in the doorway. "Maligning our magnificent facilities. You must be feeling better."

Heather had the grace to look ashamed. "When can I go home?"

"How about this afternoon? But you'll need to take it easy. IVs daily. Another biopsy in two days. Think you can handle that?"

"What are my choices?"

He shrugged and winked at her. "You could stay here."

Heather held up her hands, in mock surrender. She dropped the gesture, then gave him a studying look.

"What now?"

"You couldn't, by any chance, bypass the system and find out who my donor was?"

"Not a chance. All I know is that a healthy young male gave you a new lease on life."

"Never hurts to try."

"You still looking?" He shook his head. "Just write the letter, like we discussed, and send it through the channels. What difference does it really make who it was?"

"Doesn't make us related, huh?"

"Nope. But I know that a letter like that makes a difference to donor families. I sometimes get to hear both sides, you know?" He patted her foot. "Later."

Heather leaned back against her pillow. "How's Goldie?"

"Missing you. She had to sleep on the floor."

"Mean Mom." She set her computer on the tray table. "Why don't you two go get coffee or something, so I don't have to entertain you."

Jenna snorted and Randy shook his head. "Yes, Your Highness. Can we get you anything, Your Majesty?"

Heather closed her eyes and scrunched up her face. "Ah, let me think. Something with chocolate."

"Your wish is my command." Randy pulled a box out of the bag he carried and set it on Heather's lap. "I couldn't find Godiva."

Heather giggled. "I like See's just as well." She dug into the wrapping around the flat box. "There's a plastic knife in that drawer, if you can find it." She waited and watched him dig. "Mess, huh?"

He held up the plastic-wrapped knife and, without unwrapping it, sliced through the clear wrap around the candy. "You have to share with your mother."

Heather made a face, pulled the lid off and studied the contents, settling on an almond cluster, then handed the box to Jenna and crunched half the piece. "Um. You bring good presents."

"Glad to oblige. Now we'll leave you to your decadence." He made a half bow and stage-whispered to Jenna, "Let's get out of here while the getting's good."

In the elevator, Randy put his arm around Jenna and brought her closer to his side. "She looks all right."

"It's what's on the inside that counts. Dr. Avery said we got this one early, thanks to those miserable heart biopsies, but she reacted to the meds. They had to take her off the new one that is best and build her a cocktail of the others." The elevator opened, a nurse stepped on, saw his arm around her and stepped back off, with a nod and a smile.

"Sheesh, now this will be all over the hospital in a heartbeat."

"This?"

"That I was making out on the elevator."

"An arm around you is making out?" He leaned close and kissed her quickly as the elevator opened again. They strode past two giggling candy stripers and headed for the cafeteria, Jenna's cheeks flaming and Randy chuckling.

When he carried their coffee tray to a table in the far corner, Jenna sat across from him and rested her elbows on the table, propping her chin on her laced fingers.

He glanced up to see her studying him. "What?"

"I'm not used to someone waiting on me like this."

"All I did was carry the coffee tray."

"And come running as soon as you could get here. And buy See's candy, because you know Heather loves chocolate."

"According to my mother, every female loves chocolate."

"And men don't."

"Not as obsessive."

"Puh-leeze," came out as a two-syllable word, emphasized by upward-seeking eyes.

Randy pushed her cup of coffee closer to her. "Do you want something else?"

"No…"

"I hear a 'but.'" He reached across the table and took her hands in his, thumbs stroking the backs of her hands. "Sorry I couldn't get here sooner."

"You couldn't have done anything either. That's the frustrating part. That helpless feeling. I am having a difficult time trusting God to get us through this."

"But you're doing it anyway."

"How do you know?"

"Because if you weren't, you'd be muttering and pacing and stewing and you wouldn't have left that room to come down here with me."

Jenna thought about what he'd said. He was right.

"Hey, even Thomas had doubts."

"True."

"By the way, Mom said that she's put Heather and you back on the prayer chain at church."

"I called my friend in Omaha too, you know the chaplain at the hospital? He said he'll keep praying and that Jared finally got to go home with his family. He beat the rejection."

"As will Heather."

"Sometimes I think about the mother of the donor. A male, Dr. Avery said. Someone's son. I would be so angry at God, at everything. Makes me feel guilty for being so happy." She paused with a half shrug. "Well, most of the time."

"I have something I want to show you."

"What?"

He hesitated. "I was going to wait, but . . ." He squeezed her hands, released them and picked up his coffee mug. "Drink up and call the floor to tell them you'll be gone an hour or so."

"Randy."

"No, I was going to wait for Heather, but"—he glugged his coffee—"let's go."

They set their mugs and the tray on the moving belt and headed for the elevator, Jenna fumbling with her cell phone. She left the message and only hung back a little as he dragged her out the doorway. "Where's your coat?"

"In Heather's room. I didn't know I needed it."

"Here." He shucked his leather jacket off and put it around her shoulders. "Don't worry, I have a sweater on and another in the car." He held the door of the rental open for her and slammed it as soon as she cleared the door frame. He fed some numbers into his portable GPS and drove out of the parking lot, heading north.

"Randy, if you don't mind, what is going on?"

"I have to show you something." The voice told him when to turn west, then north and west again. When he pulled under a log-framed arch, she stared at him.

"Have you gone nuts?"

"Do you know this place?"

"Not at all. Do you?"

"Pretty much." He stopped the car at the top of the rise and inched forward until they could see a small valley on a bend of the North Platte River. Red willow bushes lined the banks of a creek that fed into the river. Wood fences framed a gambrel-roofed barn and a house sheltered by several old deciduous trees and a windbreak of pines and mixed trees.

Rolls of hay lined one side of the barn, several smaller corrals the other.

"What do you think?" He kept his arms crossed over the steering wheel and looked at her over his shoulder.

"Well, it's beautiful, even now. Why?"

"There are four bedrooms in the house, a remodeled kitchen, two-and-a-half baths, big stone fireplace in the living room, an office and a family room, sort of a great room around the kitchen."

"So?"

"The barn has been kept up, they've been running horses and beef cattle on the place, along with hay and dryland grain."

"Okay."

"Do you think you could be happy here?"

Jenna sucked in a deep breath. "Randy, I can't afford a place like this."

"No, but I can." He turned sideways to look at her. "I think I'm doing this backward. Jenna, will you marry me?"

Her heart stopped and picked up again, a thudding against her ribs. She searched his eyes for any doubts. "You're sure of this?" All her excuses flew right out the window when he leaned across the space and gently placed his lips on hers. Her hands stroked his cheeks, then locked behind his head. When he drew away, she blinked.

"Did that feel sure?"

She nodded. "Perhaps we should try it again to make sure we got it right."

"Oh, we have lots of time to practice. Is that a yes?"

She nodded. "Yes, I love you, and yes, I'll marry you." She swallowed the butterflies that rampaged around in her middle. Had she really agreed? Or was she dreaming all this? Talk about a whirlwind, picking her up and putting her down in a new life.

He rested his forehead against hers. "Good. Now that the most important things are settled, how would you like to go look at this place? I think we could all three be really happy here. You're not too far from the hospital, I'm not too far from the airport and—"

Jenna put a finger on his lips. "One thing."

"What's that?"

"If you buy this place, will you have to give up your dream of becoming a massage therapist?"

He shook his head. "I'm not sure if I really want to do that, but buying this won't break the bank." He kissed her again. "I think Heather will approve."

"Of what, the place or our marriage?"

"Both. Since it is vacant, we could take possession as soon as escrow closes."

"So."

"So what if we had the wedding and then moved in, after a honeymoon, of course?"

"I hope you don't want a big wedding." Jenna stared at the man beside her. So much had changed since Christmas. But they'd had years of friendship, so it wasn't like they were rushing into the unknown.

"Nope. So, do you want to go look at the place or go tell Heather?"

"Tell Heather."

"I figured." He backed the SUV to a wider spot and wheeled it around, then parked and leaped out of the rig. Throwing his arms in the air, he shouted, "She loves me! She really loves me!" He climbed back in and grinned at her. "Just couldn't hold it all in any longer."

She stared at him, her head wagging slightly from side to side. Life with Randy would certainly be an adventure. "How'd you find this place?"

"On the Internet, virtual tour, talked with the Realtor. It just seemed a good fit—for all of us."

"Us"—such a small word that covered so much. She'd not been an "us" for so long. She turned to stare at his profile as he watched the road. When he stopped at a stop sign, he grinned at her. "I love you, Jenna Montgomery, for now and forever."

The words curled around her heart and danced in her mind. She had learned that forever could be long or short, but she resolved to love him, forever, one day at a time.

Chapter Thirty-one

Nora

$\mathcal{G}$ordon, are you sleeping?"

A gentle snort. "Almost."

Nora hesitated. She'd been wanting to talk to him for days, but he'd been gone on another business trip and come home fighting some kind of bug, which had left him coughing his head off and exhausted. He even missed church. She sucked in a huge breath and felt her shoulders drop as she exhaled. "Have you seen any of Christi's recent paintings?"

"No, how would I?"

"I thought maybe she offered to show them to you."

"Come on, this is Christi we're talking about." He was silent so long, she thought he'd fallen asleep again. Then he spoke, nearly slurring his words with sleep. "She never shows her art to anyone, until she is absolutely satisfied with it. How did you see any?"

"I was in her room apologizing to her a week ago. It's a disaster."

"Her room? The art? Christi?" There was a shade of irritation in his voice. The man wanted to sleep.

"Yes." She left out the information that she'd gone in the room again and the paintings were no better. "I wish you would talk with her."

"Come on, Nora, she's dealing with a lot right now. You worry too much." He turned over on his side, obviously cutting off the discussion.

"What if she is suicidal?"

But his soft snores told her he'd already fallen asleep.

What would Lois have to say about this? Nora had finally taken her misery in hand and called Lois right after Easter. They'd been meeting one morning a week. The first time she came to the house, Nora had spent the time crying and crying about crying. Lois had held her as she cried and told her over and over how normal this was.

"But I thought I was getting better." Nora gulped.

"This is an up-and-down journey, or back-and-forth."

"But I hurt so much."

"True, but that terrible pain will eventually abate. I'm sure you find times now where you can actually think about something else, at least for a few minutes."

"Like my husband and daughter?" That brought on another freshet as she cried about what a terrible wife and mother she'd been.

But Lois had been right. Talking and crying and hearing that she wasn't going crazy and that God was not punishing her finally penetrated, and helped. Now she looked forward to the time they spent together. Thoughts of death being the only surcease were fading away.

The next morning after Gordon and Christi were out the door, Nora sat down with a cup of coffee, her journal and Bible. Even with her new car, Christi sometimes rode with her father and asked her mother to pick her up. Shaking her head over how to read her daughter at the right moment, Nora put her mind to what Lois had suggested. Go back to journaling, she'd said, giving her specific instructions to read through the Psalms, stopping to re-read places that spoke to her. Here she was, to meet with her friend the next day, and had yet to open either Bible or journal.

She stared at them, her hands trembling as if she were reaching for fire. She closed her eyes. Betsy laid her head on Nora's knee, a good interruption. Nora stroked her dog's head and stared at the black leather-bound book with gilt-edged pages. Worn spots on the cover spoke silent witness that she used to read and study this book a lot. Her wire-bound journal held the pen in the coil, ready and waiting. Her stomach clenched and the urge to leap up and run made her sip the coffee, now gone cool. "This is silly." She brushed away incipient tears. "Just write something for Pete's sake."

She ripped the pen out of the wire coil, flipped pages until she found a blank one and slashed the date across the top: "April 20." Charlie had died almost four months ago. "These have been the worst days of my life," she scrawled in large, untidy words. She threw the pen on the table, leaned her head in her arms and cried. When the phone rang, she wiped her eyes and blew her nose on the way to answer it, knowing her voice would creak and croak. Hopefully, it would be a solicitor and would think her ill.

She tried clearing her throat. "Hello?"

"Uh-oh. Bad time?" Susan paused; Nora blew her nose again.

"Yes. I tried to do as Lois keeps suggesting and read the Psalms and write in my journal."

"Well, that's a step in the right direction. You tried."

"I guess. I'm so drained I can hardly stand."

"Sit down, then. You want to walk?"

"I guess." Nora turned to look at the books on the table. "Too wet to go around the lake."

"So we do streets. I'll be there in a few."

Nora flipped the journal closed and the Bible open. It fell on Psalm 91 and she read about God hiding His children under His mighty outstretched arms. She closed the book and went to change her shoes. Should she tell Susan about her fears for Christi, or just wait until she could talk with Lois? Or never tell anyone? Let it slide, like Gordon said. But what if Christi was indeed suicidal?

The one thing she knew for absolutely certain: if she said anything to anyone, Christi would hate her.

Speed-walking kept Betsy trotting, and set Nora puffing and her body screaming long before they made it back home. If she was going to keep this up, she had to get back to a consistent routine. An article she'd read on grieving strongly suggested working out on a regular basis would be advantageous. Of course, exercise seemed to be the panacea for all of life's challenges.

"Thanks, I think," she puffed out, bent over, spread hands on her knees. "This was worse than cross-country skiing."

"We're not usually so out of shape, come spring." Susan walked in small circles to get her breath back.

"I know. Blame it on Charlie." Nora's mouth dropped open. What had she said?

"You know that's the first joke you've cracked in months."

"Guess my smart mouth is coming back." She blinked back the tears, which sprang to the front like soldiers to an order. "That's one of the things I miss the most, Charlie making me—us—laugh. There's been no laughter at our house."

Susan nodded. "He made us all laugh. That was one of his gifts. I bet he's making the angels double over at times."

Nora used her shirt hem to dry her eyes. "Thanks."

"Tomorrow?"

"Early. I have my appointment with Lois at ten."

The phone ringing when she entered the house sent her hustling away from it. Gordon needed to catch an afternoon plane; he'd be gone a couple of days. While she packed his small suitcase, she dreaded his being gone again. The female emotion in the house grew thick as fog with her and Christi at odds most of the time. Now she had further problems to deal with.

Perhaps Lois would say, "Do and say nothing."

Lois sat with her hands folded, her eyes on Nora's face as she explained the paintings and the changes in Christi. "I'm so sorry," Lois said when the recital was ended. "But I'm not surprised. I don't know an awful lot about painting, but images like that, and changes like you say, sound like a cry for help, to me. I think you need to talk with her counselor at school. If she is suicidal, we have to get her help before it is too late. I think many people think of suicide when someone they love dies, but it is a passing thing for most. If this is getting worse, like you say..." She paused. "Has Christi said anything to you?"

"Complains about most anything I do or say, but she doesn't talk about herself. I thought perhaps things were better, because we've been talking about what all she needs for art school. She was angry, though, even through that, saying it should have all been done sooner. Or at least a lot of it." Nora leaned her head against the back of the chair. "And she was right." She paused. "How can I do this?"

"How can you not?"

"She'll hate me even more."

"But at least she'll be alive."

Nora nodded. *God, I'm so tired of all this. Can't You make it all right?* "Might it be better if I confronted her?"

"Would she be truthful with you?"

Why hadn't Gordon taken this seriously? Resentment burned like holding her finger over a candle flame. He should be the one asking his daughter if she was indeed suicidal. "I doubt it. And if I do this, when Gordon hears about it, he will be furious with me too."

"Sounds to me like you're caught between a rock and a hard place, but if you really believe Christi is in danger, how can you not?"

Nora rubbed her forehead, an ache beginning behind her eyes. How much easier it would be to just ignore this, like Gordon said.

Lord, what do I do? How can I ask for help when I am not doing the things that I know You want me to do? How can I be angry with You on one hand and pleading for help on the other?

"There are no easy answers," Lois said simply. "Sometimes you feel like you're being ripped in half and that hole in your heart is never going to mend. One minute you're mad at God and the next you're asking Him for help."

"I was just thinking that." Nora stared at her new friend. "You felt that way too?"

"Oh, so often."

"But it finally let up?"

Lois nodded. "Slowly, very slowly, sometimes the only way

you can see the changes is to look back at where you were the months before. Like so often, we don't realize God has been working in and through us until we look back to see how things changed."

Nora let the words sink in, like drops of life-giving water into drought-dried earth. "Thank you. I know I keep asking for life to go back to what it was...."

"And you know that can never be."

"I know it, but I don't have to like it."

"Nope, you don't. Acceptance and liking are two different things entirely."

A pause lengthened, but for a change, Nora didn't feel like she had to fill it right in. She leaned her head against the sofa back, peace placing a fleeting kiss on her heart before sorrow shoved its way back in. "Will you please pray that Christi gets over hating me?"

"Of course."

Nora let her mind go back. "I wanted the perfect Christmas this year, planned so carefully and started on things so early. Now I don't care if we ever have Christmas again." She opened her eyes. "Is that such a terrible thing? You know, none of us have even opened the gifts Charlie had chosen for us. I put them up on a shelf, along with those we had for him. Gordon planned a trip to the Bahamas for all of us—I don't know if he canceled the tickets or what."

"There will be a time for all that and you will know when." Lois nodded slowly. "Christmas won't be easy, but perhaps by next year, you will all begin to make some new traditions. I remember the second Christmas after Lindsey died. I hung a little angel on the tree, and thanked her for being my daughter. We had to go on; the younger children needed to know that Christmas hadn't died with Lindsey, so we had Christmas at Grandma's house the first year. But the second year, we decorated and I could finally talk about good memories of Christmases past. Good memories will finally overlay the bad ones and the sorrow." She leaned forward and patted Nora's hand. "I promise."

Nora sniffed and nodded. "I sure pray so." There, she'd said that again. Pray. When she considered it, she was probably praying more than she thought. Luke had said prayer was nothing more than talking with God, just like we talked with our friends and family. And she talked with Gordon even when she was mad at him or disappointed in something he did or didn't do.

After Lois left, Nora climbed the stairs, determined to go back into Christi's room and see if things were really as bad as she thought. She knew that opening that door was breaking her trust with Christi. But if it meant keeping her alive ... *Lord, I will do anything I can to help my daughter, to keep her alive.* She pushed open the door and entered the chaotic room.

While she tried to look at the room as an observer, she felt her heart clench at the paintings stacked and scattered around the room. Paint slashed on canvas screamed fury to her. How could Christi contain all this anger? But perhaps these paintings were what helped keep her from spewing these feelings all over everyone. These later ones had eyes staring at her from gargoyle faces, with curved black claws that dripped red—hideous forms.

She huffed out a sigh. *So, do I just go talk with the counselor at school, or do I take one of these along to show her?* She wished she'd asked Lois what she thought was the best avenue to take. *Gordon, why didn't you listen to me or at least come in here to gauge for yourself?* She left the room, glancing at her watch. She had plenty of time before she needed to pick Christi up. Several times she'd had the feeling that Christi would just as soon not drive herself to school. Perhaps the car had been more Gordon's idea than her own.

Go...wait? Call...wait? Call, perhaps the counselor didn't have time to meet with her today anyway. She dialed the high school and asked to speak to the guidance counselor. While on hold, she chewed on her lower lip. *Please, Lord, please.* At this point, she wasn't even sure what to ask for. She at least knew the people who worked there. Perhaps this was one of the good things about her volunteering at her kids' schools.

"Hi, this is Ms. Jones." The voice came across, rich and cheery, just like the woman behind it. She truly cared about her students.

"Beth, this is Nora Peterson." The last time she'd seen Beth was at the service for Charlie.

"Oh, Nora, how good to hear your voice. I think about you so often."

"Thanks." Nora swallowed around the block that sprang in her throat. "I have a couple of questions, if you have a few moments."

"Of course I have time. How can I help you?"

"It's about Christi."

A slight silence preceded an exhalation. "I'm glad you called. I've been thinking I should call you, but I figured you didn't need one more problem right now."

"Like what?"

"Christi's grades are dropping. A couple of her teachers have mentioned this to me, but since it is not surprising, considering what has happened, we hoped to give her some more time before we intervened."

"I wondered. She doesn't want to discuss much with me right now."

"She's withdrawn a lot."

"Any suggestions?" Nora pulled the desk chair out and sat down.

"I would be glad to talk with her, sometimes it is easier to talk with someone outside the family."

Nora nodded. Wasn't that what she was doing? What Gordon had done? *But do I tell her about the paintings?* "Ah, has her art teacher mentioned anything?"

"Like what?" The tone became slightly guarded.

"Perhaps a difference in her work?"

"What are you observing?"

Nora closed her eyes, but instead of wisdom, Christi's paintings bombarded her. "She's painting horror and nightmares." The words came out on a whisper, air pushed past the boulder in her throat, growing larger by the moment.

"Scary stuff?"

"Big-time scary stuff. Death and dying, blood and black."

"Are you worried about her being suicidal?"

Talk about blunt. Put it right out there. "Yes."

"Okay, I'll work from this end and do my best to keep you out of it."

"But you'll keep me posted?"

"As much as I am able. I'll talk with her teachers and find out what they've observed. We'll do our best for her. Like Charlie, she is much loved here. Thanks for calling."

"Thank you." Nora hung up the phone and rested her forehead against the wall. She'd set the balls in motion—now to see what would come of it.

Two days later, Christi stormed into the kitchen, even ignoring Bushy, who met her at the door and meowed to be picked up. She slammed her backpack down on the chair and glared at her mother. "I got called in to talk with Ms. Jones today."

"And?" Nora kept her back to her daughter, scrubbing carrots and potatoes for the pot roast cooking in the oven.

"She said my grades are falling and the teachers are concerned about me. Bunch of nosy—"

"Well, are they right? About your grades, I mean?" Nora tried to release the death grip on the scrubber.

"Just because I'm not pulling straight A's right now"—Christi reached in the refrigerator for the orange juice and poured herself a glass—"she asked if I wanted to talk about anything."

Charlie would have glugged from the jug. The thought brought the burning to Nora's eyes and made her sniff.

"There's cheese in the drawer if you want some and I bought crackers today." Yesterday she'd been taken to task for not keeping the right foods in the house.

"Any more cookies?"

"In the jar." Christi usually opted for cheese or some other protein rather than carbs. Hard to stay on top of things, especially when the last place Nora wanted to go was the grocery store.

Bushy jumped up on the counter and bumped Christi with his nose. He turned down the bite of cookie she offered and sat to clean his front foot.

Nora watched the byplay out of the corner of her eye as she cut up the potatoes and carrots. "Supper will be ready in about an hour."

"Is Dad coming home tonight?"

"Tomorrow night."

"She said she thinks I need to go to a counselor." Her daughter's tone was tight, spitting out the words like cobra venom.

"So what's wrong with that? I talk with Lois, Dad talks with Luke. We all need help at times." Nora dumped the vegetables in the roaster with the meat and shut the oven door again. "I know you miss Charlie terribly and this could help."

"Like talking to some shrink is going to help. Can they make Charlie come back?"

"No, of course not. How I wish someone could." Nora rolled her lips together and sniffed.

"There you go, crying again." Christi slammed her glass down on the counter; then grabbing her backpack from the chair, she stormed out of the room and up the stairs.

Nora clamped her teeth together. What a brat. She was sure if she looked down, she'd see blood running from the stab wound. What ever happened to the idea that families stuck together, helped each other out when troubles got to be too much? The more she thought, the more the tears flowed. The pull of her bed and the sanctuary beneath the covers and in sleep dragged at her shoulders, fastened upon her feet, willing her upward. Lately she'd been doing so much better at resisting.

She wrapped her arms around her middle and went to stand at the bay window. Gray clouds scudded across patches of blue, the wind chased wavelets across the lake. Tiny spears of green poked up through the winter-browned grass.

Be honest, she commanded herself. *Right now, you want to go up there, break down that door and scream back at her. Rip up those horrible paintings, make her clean up that disgusting mess and order her to apologize.* Rage made her shake as if she were freezing. Fury sent her across the room to grab a jacket off the hook and head out the back door. She stopped a moment on the deck, Betsy's bark penetrating her storm. Letting the dog out, she started down the hill, but instead of hitting the path around the lake, she veered off to the rose garden on the right. Or what was usually the rose garden. By now, she always had the mulch removed so the roses and perennials could send out new shoots of life.

Leaning over, she pulled back some of the straw and tree trimmings she'd used to protect the plants. Instead of healthy new growth, she saw limp white stalks, fighting and dying beneath the heavy mulch. "Oh no." Her breath caught. She pulled off more, ran up to the garage, got out fork and rake, along with the wheelbarrow, and pushed it back down the hill.

After she pulled the mulch back and forked it into the wheelbarrow, she knelt beside one of her favorite rosebushes, Double Delight, one of the most fragrant of her collection. Charlie had given it to her for Mother's Day two years ago. Instead of healthy green shoots, the stalks looked black and dead. "No! You can't die!" She cleaned off more, frantically searching for healthy green stalks with small buds of leaves ready to pop out to greet the spring sun. Her breathing became ragged as she scrabbled in the dirt. "You will not die too!"

One stalk—that's all, but at least there was one. She tenderly examined it. Sure enough, down near the crown, but on the stalk, was one, no—two small nubs, not dried and black like the others, but reddish with bulging life. *Life.*

She dashed her tears away and dug around the anemic spears of daffodils, coaxing them upright with straw and dirt mix mounding around them. Pulling back another patch, she found crocuses, their blossoms spent before they could reach the light. Why had she waited so long? Her garden needed her. Needed her to pull off the protecting mulch and let new life seek the sun.

Like her. It made her pause momentarily. Throw off the grief that so pressed her down and made her want to die. Surely, if her plants could seek the sun after the winter they'd been through, she could also. Betsy lay down beside her and nudged her arm.

Sometime later, when she realized dusk had snuck in and blurred the trees across the lake, she tossed the rake and fork on top of the wheelbarrow load and trundled it over to dump on the growing new compost pile. She'd use the compost from last year's pile to spread a life-giving summer mulch on her flower beds.

"Oh, Betsy, the pot roast." Overwarm with her exertion, she jogged to the deck, and when she saw the dirt on her shoes and knees, she toed off her tennis shoes and hustled into the house. With the roaster on the stove and the oven now turned off, she lifted the lid. Pretty brown, but not burned, with all the water cooked away. Still, the brown drippings in the pan would make wonderful gravy.

Just in time. Just in time for the roast—hopefully, just in time for her plants. With spring bringing new life outside, surely there could be new life inside too. Inside her house, inside her heart. Yes, the hole was still there, but according to Lois, even that would eventually heal. Was the help just in time for Christi? She had to believe it was so.

When Nora reached up in the cupboard for the flour canister, she discovered a note on the counter. "Mom, I'm sorry—again. I guess I do need to talk to somebody. Christi."

Epilogue

*T*wo days after Christi's graduation, and still tearfully savoring the tributes to Charlie the other students brought that day, Nora brought in the mail, flipping through the envelopes to dump the advertisements in the trash. A letter with a return address from Omaha, Nebraska, and a typed address to "Mr. and Mrs. Peterson" caught her attention. She set it, several cards addressed to Christi and a couple of bills on the desk, flipped the applications for more credit cards to one side to shred and dug the letter opener out of the drawer.

Probably another plea for donations, she thought as she almost tossed the letter, then opened it instead. An envelope inside was addressed by hand: "To Donors."

Her mouth dried as she stared at the block handwriting. Should she call Gordon? She went to the stairs and called up. "Christi?"

"What?"

"Are you busy? You got some cards."

Christi, cat on her arm, strolled down the stairs. "What's the matter?"

Nora sucked in a breath and swallowed. "We have a letter." She handed it to her daughter.

Christi stared at the envelope and handed it back. "You open it."

Nora slid the blue plastic opener along the fold and pulled out a sheet of plain paper. She cleared her throat and read it aloud.

To the family who gave me my life,

I know you don't know me, but I had to write to you and thank you for being so generous. All I know is that my heart was failing, or almost failed, and now I have a new heart, which is strong and vigorous. I have been through a rejection episode, but thanks to medications and many prayers, I am able to walk and run, and am learning how to roller blade. I plan to start skiing next winter. I am back to college with a communications major.

My father died years ago and my mother recently married a man who loves us both; actually, he was my uncle first. We have moved to a ranch and I have a horse now, something I dreamed of all my life.

My mother is a nurse and she says that you gave both of us back our lives when you were willing to donate your son's body for organ donations. I know there are others out there who can see better, have had skin grafts and other gifts of life, thanks to you.

I can only guess at your grief and suffering. One thing I've learned is that life is not fair, but God is love and He never lets us go. My mother says He is the original recycler, never wasting anything. I pray that He comforts you and your family every day, and know that there are families who thank Him continuously for new lives and health. Your son's death was not a waste.

                              In God's love,
                              A grateful family

Reading Group Guide

1. When someone close to you dies, what do you learn about grief?

2. Have you ever experienced the loss of a loved one? How did you grieve? How did your family and friends help you? What could they have done to ease your pain?

3. How do you feel about organ transplants? Are you an organ donor?

4. Jenna has built her life to entirely revolve around Heather before the transplant. Is that in her or Heather's best interest? How can a mother love and care for a chronically sick child without losing herself in the process?

5. How does grieving for the death of a young person differ from grieving for an older person?

6. Trauma and death can either drive us toward God or away from Him. How does your faith help you in times of trouble?

7. Jenna has to make a sudden adjustment to having her daughter grow up and leave the nest when Heather is blessed with a new life. Have you experienced letting a

grown child become independent? How were your feelings similar and different from Jenna's?

8. Sometimes people of faith don't know what to say or what to do to comfort those who have lost a loved one. How does your faith help you help those who are grieving?

9. For Nora *One Perfect Day* ended in tragedy. For Jenna *One Perfect Day* ended in hope. How can that be? How can God's plan hold heartbreak for one family and hope for another?

10. Do you think Nora and Jenna should have met in person? How do you think such a meeting would have affected each woman?

Award-winning author Lauraine Snelling
weaves a heart-warming story of
love, loss, and second chances.

Just get by. Those words have gotten Maggie Roberts through ten long, hard years after a tragic accident sent her to prison. There, she's kept her heart walled up and her head down, so when a chance to work in a high-profile retired Thoroughbred racehorse program is offered to her, Maggie is reluctant.

Nevertheless, her love of horses makes the opportunity too tempting to resist. Maggie finds new purpose working with Breaking Free, an abused blood-bay gelding who lashes out at anyone who tries to help him. Maggie soon learns he'll be put down if he can't be controlled, and she is determined to save him. But when a local businessman sets his sights on adopting the horse, Maggie may have to let go of the one thing keeping her afloat.

BREAKING FREE

Available now wherever books are sold.